THE DEEPEST WATERS

Books by Dan Walsh

The Unfinished Gift
The Homecoming
The Deepest Waters

THE DEEPEST WATERS

A NOVEL

DAN WALSH

Revell

a division of Baker Publishing Group
Grand Rapids, Michigan

Published by Revell
a division of Baker Publishing Group
P.O. Box 6287, Grand Rapids, MI 49516-6287

Printed in the United States of America

ISBN 978-1-61129-518-4

This book is a work of fiction. Names, characters, places, and incidents are the products of the author's imagination or are used fictitiously.

To my sisters, Anne Dunlop and Mary Beth Cork,
whose constant love and support
are two gifts I treasure.

Set me as a seal upon your heart, as a seal upon your arm; for love is as strong as death. . . . Many waters cannot quench love, nor can the floods drown it. If a man would give for love all the wealth of his house, it would be utterly despised.

Song of Solomon 8:6–7

A Few Ship Terms for the Landlubber

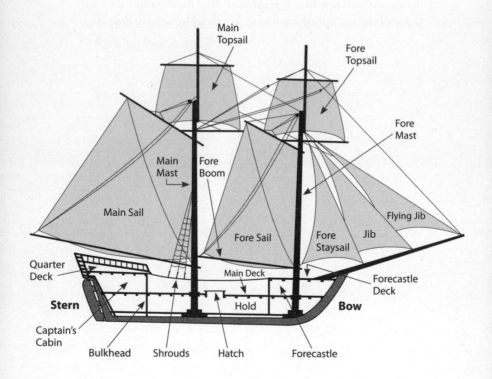

1

September, 1857

Yesterday, when it had become a certainty their ship would sink, Laura and John Foster held hands, as they had on their wedding day three weeks ago, and made a vow: when that moment finally came, they would leap into the sea together and slip beneath the waves. One quick inhale of water. It wouldn't be suicide. God had already determined it to be their last day on earth.

But that's not what happened.

Laura was still here, alive and alone. By now, John had most certainly perished along with the rest.

Her tears temporarily spent, Laura lifted her head and looked at the other women. Faces barely recognizable. Cold, wet, quietly weeping, or else staring at nothing, eyes locked in grief. All the men in their lives—husbands, brothers, fathers—were gone. The dim lantern light, shifting with the motion of the sea, moved them in and out of the shadows like phantoms.

The ship creaked and moaned with each rise and fall of the waves, as if sharing their pain. From the darkest side of the room, Laura heard a new sound. Heavy feet scuffing across the wooden deck. As the sound grew louder, she waited for someone to emerge.

"Pardon me, ladies. I surely don't mean to disturb you." The voice, aged and deep. "I can't see y'all at the moment, and I hope I don't step on nobody. I'll just make my way toward that lantern up ahead." She followed the sounds from right to left. "I brung something for ya. Those blankets we gave out gotta be damp by now. These ain't much, but I remembered we had some old sails in stow. Captain said it'd be all right if I cut 'em up and pass 'em out."

His voice was caring and kind. As he came into the light, Laura recognized the old Negro slave. He'd helped them when they first boarded a few hours ago. She knew he was a slave by the way the crew treated him. He set down a stack of folded cloth. "Can't see you ladies too good, but you hold up your hand, I'll give you one. If you got chillun, I give 'em one too. You in the shadows, just say Micah as I come by, and I'll get you one directly."

Several hands raised toward him. One by one, Micah handed out the cut sails. Laura's blanket was damp but not badly. She waited, to make sure there were enough for the elderly women and mothers with small children.

By his count, Micah ran short by twenty. "Don't you worry, got plenty more. I'll go cut me some and be right back." Laura didn't know how many had been rescued. She thought she'd heard just over a hundred. Maybe she should get up and help him. She wasn't injured. "Micah?" she called out.

"Yes'm?"

She stood up. "Can I help you?" She could barely see a path between them.

"That's kind, ma'am, but I'll be all right."

"I don't mind," she said.

"I know, but truth is, I'm not sure what the cap'n say. With the ship bobbin' up and down, and it bein' dark, I'd be afraid you bang your head or worse. Tell you what. When I get back, you can help me pass 'em out."

"Anything I can do. You've been so kind."

"Well, y'all been through so much, wish there was more I could do."

Just then the ship jolted upward. Laura almost fell.

"You all right, ma'am?"

"Yes."

"See," Micah said. "Just ain't safe walkin' around here in the dark. I'll be right back."

Laura reached out and found a wall near the doorway, then slid down in place. She could just barely trace the outline of a woman holding two children near, tucked back a few feet in the shadows.

"Mama," said one child, "how much longer till Father joins us?"

She heard the mother inhale deeply. "I'm not sure, son. Just try and sleep. We'll see what comes in the morning."

What comes in the morning.

Laura allowed the phrase to turn over once in her mind, but no more. She couldn't bear to think beyond the next hour.

2

At some point during the night, Laura fell asleep.

At some point after that, the sea calmed.

The ship now rolled gently through the waves, making the slightest creaking sound. The moaning was gone. But within moments of waking, the moaning inside Laura had grown worse. Her heart felt like a roof about to cave in. She had an urge to flee, if only to assuage these dark feelings momentarily.

Daylight poured through the hatch, allowing her to better see the hold where they'd spent the night. It was much larger than she'd imagined. Some ladies still slept, but the deck was covered with cut sails and wet blankets mingled together in piles. The ceiling wasn't tall enough for a person to stand upright, but almost. A woman wearing a blanket like a shawl climbed the stairway toward the sunlight. Laura joined her.

A warm wind blew from the southeast. The main deck was crowded with women and children. Most leaned on the railings and stared south toward the stern, looking back to where the two ships had parted last night. A handful of crew members busied themselves with the sails and rigging.

Laura was startled by the overall size of the ship; so small, a third the length of the SS *Vandervere*.

The *Vandervere*.

For almost a month the name had brought her instant joy, like a fairy tale. Sailing away on a steamship, a first-class cabin, pockets laden with gold, beautiful sunrises, breathtaking sunsets, traveling with the man she loved. Even more surprising, a man who loved her back. Before John, Laura had decided she was past the marrying age and must content herself with living alone.

Better that than a loveless marriage of duty and servitude.

Even toward that end, there had only ever been two prospects. None in her teen years or early twenties. But when she'd reached twenty-five a widower had come around looking for a woman to care for his children and clean house. Love and romance, out of the question. The second prospect had been an enormous, wealthy businessman. He'd built a brand new mansion in San Francisco. He'd taken her to a nice restaurant, then quickly by the house. As if to say, "Yes, but there is a house." She thought, "Yes, but you can't even make it up the stairs."

Nearly two years later, in a span of time when she'd banished any thoughts of love, John had bumped into her as she walked along South Park near Brannan Street, a book in hand. That should have been the end of it, a polite "excuse me." The book had fallen. They both bent to pick it up, and John caught her glance as they stood. Something in his eyes, something she'd never seen before. He handed her the book, then smiled. She thanked him and smiled back.

She walked to the nearest bench and sat down. She tried reading her book but had the strange sense that he had not moved, that his eyes were still upon her. She looked up, and it was so. And the smile had remained.

"I'm sorry," he'd said. "I don't . . . I want . . . oh bother," he said. "May I introduce myself?"

He did, and then he asked the most peculiar thing. "May I sit beside you?"

Before long, he'd asked if they could walk together. And then, would she join him for dinner. That night he walked her home and politely shook her hand by the porch, clasping just her fingers. "I am so glad to have bumped into you this afternoon," he said.

Laura didn't know what to say; she just smiled. He walked a few steps down the walk, turned, and looked at her. But it was the *way* he looked at her. She had never seen such a look in a man's eyes; it was something she had only cherished in books.

"May I call on you again?"

"Yes," she said, barely containing her joy.

"And when I do, may I call you . . . Laura?"

She nodded.

"I am working at the store all day tomorrow. May I call on you after dinner?"

"Yes."

"Yes . . . what?"

Laura was confused.

"May I hear you call me by name?"

"Yes . . . *John*," she said.

From that day on, they were Laura and John. And Laura had known a love more splendid than her best books dared promise, a happiness beyond even girlhood dreams.

"Mother, do you think any other ships came to the *Vandervere*'s aid last night, or maybe this morning?"

Laura turned toward the child's voice. A little girl, maybe seven or eight, a few steps away. Laura looked up at the mother and saw the tears in her eyes as she gazed out to sea. "Perhaps, my dear. That is my fervent prayer."

Laura thought back to the moment John had held out the

tickets for their voyage. "Look, Laura, I got them, for the day after we wed. No turning back now. We sail down the West Coast on the SS *Sonora*, hop a train across Panama, then take the SS *Vandervere* straight up to New York." His eyes had been wider than when a miner struck gold. He'd picked her up and swung her around.

But for Laura, heading back East was all and only about John.

His family lived there. Her family, what was left of it, was back in San Francisco. She'd never met John's parents, didn't even know what they looked like. She realized they'd be expecting to see *him* when the ship came in, the two of them, arm in arm, coming down the companionway. That's how they would know who Laura was: the one standing beside John.

But she wouldn't be standing beside him. She'd be standing there alone, just one of a hundred grieving women, strangers all. The sudden realization stole her strength away, and she slumped to the deck where she stood.

"Miss, miss, you okay?"

Her dark red hair fell about her face like a veil. She recognized the voice. It was Micah.

"Did you fall, miss? Can I help you up?"

"I'll be all right, Micah. Thank you. Just a little dizzy." She shifted her weight and wiped her tears on her sleeve. Out of nowhere a dog came from behind her and gently nudged her with its nose. She lifted her face to see it. It sat down and wagged its tail.

"Crabby, you leave her be," Micah scolded softly.

The dog was clearly a mutt, but it had the sweetest face. Muddy brown with a white stripe between its eyes that faded symmetrically on its forehead. Still sitting on deck, Laura reached up and petted its head. The dog shivered with joy at her touch. "He's all right," Laura said. "I love dogs."

"He be a she," Micah said, bending down to pet her.

"Did you say Crabby?"

"That's the name I give 'er. Most a' the crew just calls her dumb dog. And they kick her about. Weren't for the cap'n, I expect she'd be over the side. They all hate her, 'cept the cap'n and me."

"Why Crabby?" Laura asked. "She seems so sweet."

"She be more than sweet," Micah said. "Best friend I got on this earth. Sometimes . . ." He looked away. "Crabby the only thing on this ship remind me . . . God do love me."

Laura didn't know what to say. "She's beautiful, Micah."

"Yes'm," he said, looking back at her.

"But why Crabby?"

"She love to eat them crabs," he said. "Funniest sight to see, her run off with one of them things in her mouth, legs danglin' out the side."

Laura smiled and started getting up.

"Can I help you?" Micah asked.

"Thank you," she said.

Micah reached beneath her elbow and lifted her to her feet. "Deck's mighty slippery at this hour, but the sun come up a little more, and it'll dry out just fine."

He helped her until she regained her footing. "Thank you so much."

"You need Micah, just ask. Or tell Crabby, she always know where to find me."

She grabbed hold of the rail and looked out to the horizon. It really was a beautiful day, the air so fresh. No land in sight. She had no idea where they were. She heard yelling from the front, toward the bow, and turned. A large man stood on the forecastle deck, looking down. Several women were yelling up at him. "Why?" one screamed. "You don't know that!"

"Ladies, I won't argue the point with you. This isn't a democracy. You are guests aboard the *Cutlass*, and we'll treat you as such. But don't begin to imagine you can dictate to me or order me about."

The women fell silent.

"But I do see a need to set things straight." He cleared his throat. "Ladies," he shouted, "gather about, please. All of you. Men, gather the ladies by the stern. Micah, move those ropes to the side."

"Yessuh."

"All right, ladies," he yelled like a preacher. "My name is Captain Meade. Let me say how sorry I am for your loss. But you're learning what those who traverse the sea have always known. The Lord giveth and the Lord taketh away."

Instantly mothers drew their children close and covered their ears.

"There's no getting around that," Captain Meade continued. "But it does seem Providence has paid some attention to your fates, because here you are, and here we are. The sea is vast, and the storm blew us all miles off course. Your ship, as mighty as she was, lost power and was adrift. But God saw fit to have our paths cross, and so your lives were spared. This is where you must find comfort. We had no control of our first meeting and have no way to find the *Vandervere* again. One of my men had a word with your captain before the lifeboats parted. Your captain stated he didn't see how the *Vandervere* would last till midnight."

Gasps and cries spread throughout the deck. Laura felt nothing, emptiness.

"I'm sorry to say this, but it's the way things are, and you must accept it. There is no going back. The *Cutlass* has only eleven in its crew. We were on our way back home to Wilmington, low on provisions. But you ladies and your children are welcome to share them, such as they are. If the winds allow, we could be in New York harbor in three days."

A wave rolled the ship high. A few children fell; those by the rails took a firmer hold. Captain Meade remained steady.

"From now until then, I'll hear no more talk of turning back. By now the *Vandervere* is surely lost. You must accept this. The sooner you do, the better you'll be."

3

The SS *Vandervere* lasted through the night, but it was no use. Every man still conscious and onboard knew this. No one would say it. John Foster would not be the first.

His arms and shoulders ached, almost to the point of madness. Had he been in any other setting, he could not have restrained his cries. Another bucket passed up the line. He could barely grasp the handle. Surely the next one would fall to the deck.

But he took the next one—as he had for the last two days—from a Latin man in his midforties, an ambassador from Peru. He passed it up to an old miner, who'd spent his last nuggets buying passage back East. Beside the miner was a man who owned two banks—one in Oakland, another in Sacramento. John found this a matter of some wonder, how the storm had reduced men down to one social class: anyone who could hold a bucket.

He looked at the men in the line up ahead. Although the ship never stopped moving, the bow now pointed skyward, as if frozen upon some invisible wave. The men at the rear stood shin-deep in water that John was certain had just been passed up the line. The captain in his finest uniform had been shouting exhortations, over and over, insisting this was no fool's errand. It was buying them time. Until he gave orders that all was lost, they must continue. A second ship might still appear on the horizon and come to their aid.

They had known since the second day of the storm that the *Vandervere* had been dealt a mortal blow. A leak had sprung below the waterline, and they couldn't stop it. Then, this bucket brigade seemed to be doing some good. Now the ocean rose up the deck exponentially faster than a thousand, ten thousand buckets could withstand.

John looked out at the sea once more. The winds had slowed since yesterday, but he longed to see a placid, calming scene, if only for a moment. Still the waves rose and fell without ceasing, roving blue hills slamming into each other and into them. Every so often one great wave leapt above the rest and poured over the deck, knocking men down, sweeping some into the sea.

Those still able would find a bucket, stumble back into place, and begin bailing again.

So much water, coming at them from every side. John was certain that before long the ship must be swallowed whole.

Thirty minutes later, the *Vandervere* lurched violently, tossing men every which way. Dozens went over the rail. The rest slid down the deck toward the base of the ship, colliding so hard that some were knocked unconscious. Shouts and fearful cries to the Almighty rang through the air. John was still conscious but felt blows from several elbows and feet about his head and sides.

He wondered . . . was this it? Was it too late now to escape?

After bobbing up and down a few moments, the ship settled into a new position. Slowly, those on board untangled themselves and crawled up the deck. The *Vandervere* was now at a thirty-degree angle. It took every bit of a man's strength just to remain fixed in whatever foothold he could find.

John heard a door above them open and close. The captain emerged from the wheelhouse, the first officer by his side, both holding fiercely to the rails. "Men," he shouted, "I must release you from your task. You've fought the sea bravely, but she has won. No ship has appeared to save us. The *Vandervere* will soon fully give way to the sea. I'm giving the order to abandon ship. You have your life preservers, but they may not prove to be enough. Please, grab for yourselves anything that might float or assist you in the water. It has been my privilege to serve as your captain. I only wish I could have done more."

He and the first officer retreated from sight. John instantly remembered a conversation he and Laura had at the captain's table their first evening aboard. Someone had brought up the subject of shipwrecks and superstitions. The captain had said, "If that happens, I'll not survive. This ship goes down, I go down with her."

4

"I can't go overboard!" someone yelled. "I can't swim."

"Nor I," another said. "I don't want to die!"

John was an excellent swimmer, but it hardly mattered now. There was nowhere to go. Several crew members ripped hatches and shutters off their hinges. They waited for a wave to rise near the rail then jumped into the ocean. Passengers followed suit. But John could see that there weren't enough hatches and shutters for all the men on deck.

One older gentleman scolded a young officer. "You men should give those hatch doors to those who can't swim."

"You heard the captain," the man said. "It's every man for himself now."

John looked behind him at a group of men huddled in the corner. They weren't moving, their faces a mask of terror. Clearly they couldn't swim.

A junior officer yelled at them. "She's going under any minute. You men don't jump, you'll be sucked down with her."

John looked at a partially submerged stairway that headed below. He grabbed a sailor's arm as he hurried past. "Help me," he said. "I need to go down there."

"Sir, you don't want to do that."

"There's still a little time. We need to aid these men. I'll hold my breath and grab anything that will float. Just stand here as I come up and pass them out."

"I can't, sir. We've got to get off the ship. She's going down any second."

"Please," John said. "A few minutes."

The men stared at each other, John's eyes pleading. "Go," the sailor said.

"You'll be here?"

"Yes, go."

"What's your name?" John asked.

"Erik," the sailor said.

John pulled off his shoes, ran down the steps, and waded in. He took a deep breath and went under, feeling his way along. He opened his eyes. A few blurry shapes hovered above him. Chairs near the ceiling. He dragged them back toward the stairs.

He handed them to Erik, who tossed them to the men. "I didn't think you'd be here," John said.

"Me either," said Erik. "Hurry."

John dove back in the water, this time going the opposite direction. He found a small table. For the next several minutes, he went back and forth like this until he'd grabbed everything that floated, as far as his lungs would reach. There were still six men left in the corner who couldn't swim.

"I remember seeing bigger tables," John said, "in the dining saloon where we ate."

"They're bolted down," Erik said. "But just to keep them from sliding. A few good yanks should free them."

John took a deep breath and went back again, his strength nearly spent. In two trips, he freed up two tables.

When he brought them out, Erik said, "These should float two men each." They passed them out. Only two men left. Suddenly, the ship jolted, dropping deeper. Both men fell, then helped each other up. "We must go, sir."

"I just need two more," John said. "One for them and one for you and me."

"If we don't leave now, there won't be a you and me."

"Then come with me. It's not far."

Erik nodded, but John saw fear in his eyes. The water level now reached the top of the stairs. As John went under, he turned. Erik was following. He reached the first table and started to pull. Erik swam to the other side and pulled hard. The table quickly broke free. Erik swam away with it. John swam over to the last table.

He yanked and pulled until the first side broke free, but then he ran out of air. He turned and headed for the stairs. He grabbed a quick breath and started back. As he turned into the hall, he realized he hadn't seen Erik. He reached the table, broke the other side free, and towed it back. As he came out of the water, the ship moved violently to one side. Instinctively, John knew . . . *This is it*. He looked around. Erik was gone. He crawled toward the last two men, dragging the table behind him.

"That sailor," one of them said, "he took the last table and jumped over the rail with it."

"Here," John said. "Get up, we've got to go."

"Will it float us all?"

"I think so, but we don't have a choice." He led them to the rail. Both men were trembling. The sea looked so angry and alive. "See all the others." John pointed to over a hundred men spread out before them in the water, clinging to one thing or another. Some had drifted over a hundred yards away.

"If I go under, I'll sink," one of them said. "I won't come back up."

"That won't happen," said John. "Just take a breath, jump in, and hold it underwater. If you do, the air inside will force you back to the surface. All you have to do is kick your feet."

The man looked down. "I can't."

"Your name is Hansen, right?" John said.

"Yes, Robert."

"I remember," said John. "We had dinner together last week at the captain's table. You're heading home to visit your wife and children . . . in Boston, correct?"

"Yes."

"Robert, think of them . . . waiting at the dock to meet you. If you don't jump now, you'll never see them again."

"Are you sure I'll come back up?"

"Yes."

The sea decided for them. A rogue wave poured over the ship, sweeping all three into the water. Robert and the other man made it back to the surface. John found the table, brought it over, and helped the men take hold. But it was evident it wouldn't float them all.

"Where are you going?" Robert asked.

"I'll be okay," John said. "There's a life preserver right over there. Just start paddling away. We've got to get clear of the ship. They say it can suck you under if you're too close."

The men kicked hard and began to move away. John's arms were so tired. He put one through the life preserver and turned on his back to avoid swallowing seawater. Before they were fifty yards away, the ship began to move. It creaked and wailed like some dying sea monster; the volume was shocking. Everyone turned. John heard screams. He looked up and saw three men who'd climbed to the top of the masts; their feet dangled in the air. Suddenly, the bow of the *Vandervere* rose straight up, then dropped out of sight, taking the men down with her.

For a few seconds, huge bubbles floated up. Then nothing.

It was as if the *Vandervere* had never been.

All over the water, men screamed out, a furious blend of panic and fear. John listened, tried not to give in. But he thought, *these cries come with good reason*. They were now alone, adrift at sea, over one hundred miles from dry land. The waves tossed them up and down, a constant motion, forcing them to spend what little energy remained just to hold on. They had no food or fresh water. Nothing to protect them against the sun. Aboard the *Vandervere* they at least had the hope of being seen by another vessel. But now another ship peering out to the horizon would see nothing, would have no way of knowing they were there in the water.

John realized that all his efforts to help the men who couldn't swim had become as pointless as their bucket brigade had been. It had merely postponed the inevitable.

He thought of Laura, relieved she had been spared all this and was safely aboard the *Cutlass*. "Thank you, Lord. I couldn't bear it if she were here." Tears welled up in his eyes as he remembered how excited she'd been when they'd loaded all their wedding gifts into trunks to take with them. She had wanted to bring them back East to show his sister, Allison, whom Laura had never met.

I should have told her then. It was the perfect time. But he didn't. "God forgive me," he said quietly. "Don't make her pay for my mistake." He thought about the note he'd written. "Don't let her last memory of me add to her sorrow." These melancholic thoughts at least dampened the volume of the men shouting and pleading for their lives.

John thought back to a part of the vows he'd made three weeks ago at their wedding: "Till death do us part." Mere words then, formalities. He meant them sincerely but thought he at least had decades before they'd be called to account.

He thought once more about their wedding gifts lying in the *Vandervere*'s hull, now resting at the bottom of the sea. Certain that he, and all those floating out here with him, would soon join them.

5

The morning dragged on.

Time itself had slowed to where Laura could feel each minute pass. For the last several she'd watched a little girl try to gnaw the corner off of a biscuit. It made her grateful she'd lost her appetite.

"You don't have to eat that thing," Micah said to the girl, smiling.

"But I'm hungry."

This broke the mother's stare. She looked up from the deck at Micah. "I guess the cook isn't used to making biscuits for so many," she said. "Probably left them on too long."

"Wish that were so," said Micah. "They like that on purpose. Call it hardtack. I git the hard part, but not the tack part. Maybe 'cause it feel like tacks goin' down." He grinned, then leaned over and whispered, "Maybe one a' you ladies can ask Captain Meade to give that cook Smitty a hand. Else you'll be eatin' like this all the way to New York."

Laura smiled. It felt good to smile but somehow out of place.

"Just come to tell you ladies," Micah said, "coffee's 'bout ready, be a line right next to the one for biscuits." He started to walk away, then turned and whispered to Laura. "Wanted to tell you fust. I make the coffee, and if you like coffee, you'll like this."

"Thank you, Micah." Laura got up and followed him. The boat slid down a slight wave. She paused to steady her footing. Crabby emerged from somewhere and followed Micah, tail wagging.

Laura walked past a group of six men huddled off to the side, and fought a rush of resentment. They were the *Vandervere* men—the only *Vandervere* men—who'd survived. One looked at her, noticed her glaring, and quickly looked away. *You should look away.* She wished she had enough boldness to say what she really felt.

Why are you here . . . cowards, safe and sound, and my John is not?

She flashed back to an ugly scene that took place yesterday during the rescue. All day, small boats had rowed back and forth between the two ships, ferrying women and children to safety. The hurricane had passed, but the wind was still strong and the waves horrendous, mercilessly tossing the lifeboats about. Two hours on that lifeboat terrified her more than two days on the *Vandervere* battling the hurricane.

The wind and strong currents caused the ships to drift farther apart as each minute ticked by. By sunset, the gap between the ships had grown to four miles. Laura was the last woman to leave the *Vandervere*. She insisted she must stay with John. John and the captain pleaded with her.

John pulled her close. "Laura, you must go," he said. "The captain won't release the men until the last woman is safely away."

"I can't. What if they won't release you? There are hundreds of men left. What if—"

He gently put his finger to her lips. "Laura, it's in God's

hands. He brought us together. We must hope he'll bring us together again."

"Ma'am, there's no more time," yelled Lieutenant Ashcroft, a young officer on the lifeboat. "We must get underway."

"Mrs. Foster," the captain said gently. "Please."

She looked the captain straight in the face. "Will you promise John will be on the next boat over?"

"I will do my best," the captain said.

John and Laura hugged then kissed. A strong wave smashed against the ship, covering them in salt spray. The lifeboat rose and fell and banged against the side.

"Ma'am, please," Ashcroft yelled. "We must go."

She began to pull away. John handed her a black pouch. She knew what it was: all the gold they had saved for their trip. "Why are you giving me this?"

"Just take it, Laura. I'll feel better if it's with you."

He led her to the rail's edge. They quickly tied a rope around the bottom of her dress to keep it from blowing up as she lowered. Before taking her seat, the waves drenched her from top to bottom. She glanced at the others in the boat, about fifteen women and children. Three crew members manned the oars with the lieutenant. She sobbed uncontrollably as the little boat set off.

She turned back to watch John.

"I've written you a note, inside the pouch," he yelled. "Don't read it . . . unless you hear word that we—that we will not . . ." Tears poured down his cheeks. He looked away.

"John!" she screamed. "I must go back," she said to Ashcroft.

"Mrs. Foster, that's impossible."

"John," she shouted out again. "I love you." The words hung a moment in the air then fell to the sea, already overcome by the wind and waves. She continued to watch him growing smaller. She waved constantly until a great commotion interrupted her. The lifeboat rocked back and forth. She thought it might tip over. Two men appeared in the water, one on each side. They grabbed the edge and each flung a leg over, trying to climb in.

"Hold on, what's this?" a crew member yelled.

"You men get off," shouted Ashcroft. "You'll swamp the boat." He grabbed one of their legs and threw it back over the side.

The man on the other side got in, knocking a mother against her little girl. Laura recognized him, a gambler who rarely left the card table in the saloon deck.

"Let me in," the other man cried. "I can't go back, I'll drown."

A crewman was about to smash his fingers with a board. "Wait," said the lieutenant. "Bring him aboard. We're too far out. He can't make it back."

"With respect, sir. We're gonna reward him for jumping ship?"

"He just wants to live," Ashcroft said. "That's not a crime."

"But sir, the lottery."

"It's too late for that," said Ashcroft. Two crewmen helped him aboard.

"What does he mean about a lottery?" Laura asked.

"It's nothing," said Ashcroft.

"It's not nothing," said the gambler. "They spread word to the men of a lottery, to see who gets on the lifeboats after the women are off."

"Shut up, Simons," said Ashcroft.

"You do the odds, ladies. Four hundred men left, a rapidly sinking ship, twenty spots for each boat." He turned and looked at the three other crewmen. "You men aren't stupid. You know as well as I, this is the last boat going to the *Cutlass*."

They all looked at Lieutenant Ashcroft.

"Ignore him," he ordered. "Keep rowing or we'll never close the gap."

"That's right," the gambler said. "Keep rowing, men. But as you do, look at the sun. We might just get there before dark. I estimate two hours to close the distance. You think any more lifeboats will go out after dark? It would be suicide. I heard the captain say he didn't think the *Vandervere* would last past midnight."

The women all looked at Ashcroft. "Lieutenant," one of them said. "Tell us it's not true."

"Please, ladies. I have every intention of turning this boat around as soon as you are safely aboard the *Cutlass*."

"Ah . . . intentions," said the gambler. "A wonderful thing—"

Ashcroft struck him in the mouth, knocking Simons over. "I told you to shut up!"

After righting himself, Simons had rubbed his jaw and said, "Guess that proves my point."

Lieutenant Ashcroft had apologized for his outburst and kept assuring the women they would most certainly be going back for the men.

Laura held up her tin cup, and Micah filled it to the brim with hot coffee. Quickly a line of women formed behind her. She turned and walked past the gambler Simons, standing next to Lieutenant Ashcroft. It was odd seeing them together.

Last evening, when they finally had arrived at the *Cutlass*, things went exactly as the gambler had said. It was almost completely dark. The lieutenant had argued valiantly, pleading for the crewmen to return with him to the *Vandervere*. None would; they all just looked away. Several women had even offered to pay the men large sums of gold.

Finally, Captain Meade of the *Cutlass* intervened. "Lieu-tenant," he'd said. "Please climb aboard. All has been done that can be done. There's no hope of finding the *Vandervere* in conditions like these. You must see that. You've done your duty. It's in God's hands now."

Reluctantly, Ashcroft had conceded.

Laura set the cup of coffee down on a wooden barrel and reached for the black pouch John had given her, tied now to her belt.

His note was inside.

She desperately wanted to read it, if only to hear his words alive in her mind once more. But she dreaded what the words might say, what reading them now would mean. She wasn't ready. She reached for the metal cup instead.

Like a gull eyes a fish, the eyes of Ayden Maul fixed on a black pouch tied to a woman's belt. She was drinking a cup of coffee. He knew the pouch was full of gold.

Maul stood on a rope ladder halfway up the mainmast, with a keen view of all the ship's guests below. A pathetic-looking lot. One would never imagine the wealth they had brought aboard this ship. From what he'd seen, her pouch was just about average.

When the rescue operation began yesterday, no one knew who these people were or where they'd come from. Best he could tell, he was the only one that cared now. Bunch of stinking churchgoers and Bible readers on this *Cutlass* crew. This was Maul's first voyage among them, so of course they'd given him the worst jobs and dirtiest chores. Treated him barely better than that old Negro slave. When he'd been hired, Captain Meade gave him this talk about how he was giving him a chance to better himself. "Ayden," he'd said, "you show me you're worthy, and I'll consider a better wage for you our next time out."

Maul already had a better wage in mind for this time out.

He didn't see himself on this ship one day past New York harbor. He'd been small-talking these ladies a bit, pretending to care. They were all from San Francisco or thereabouts. The ones who'd struck it rich in the gold rush. He'd heard there was so much gold floating around up there they didn't even use paper money. Men bought shots of whiskey with a pinch of gold dust.

These ladies and their husbands were all on that steamship, heading back East to show off. That's not how they put it, but it's what he knew. All those men going down on that steamship yesterday would have given their women the last of their gold when they parted.

Like that little black pouch on that woman down there. Maul hadn't figured it out yet, but the right idea would come. Before they reached New York, he'd have enough gold so he'd never have to work again.

"Hey, Maul." He looked down. It was Maylor, the captain's first mate. "You ain't getting paid to stand there. Tie off that line and get down here. The decks need scrubbing."

"Aye, sir," he said.

It wouldn't be long now.

6

"You need to go right back down that hatch and change."

"Why?"

"You look absolutely ridiculous."

"It's only for today, until my clothes dry out. Captain Meade told the crew to let us borrow their extra clothes."

Laura looked over her shoulder at a young woman and her mother. She tried to remember their names but couldn't. The young girl did look ridiculous. She wore a tan shirt with puffy sleeves, several sizes too big.

"Those pants," the mother said. "You're wearing pants . . . oh, Sarah."

"I couldn't come out in just a shirt, Mother."

"What would your father—?"

The mother's expression froze as the realization sunk in. Her father wouldn't say anything. He was gone. The mother's eyes slowly dropped to the deck. Laura glanced at the daughter. She ran and fell at her mother's feet, crying. The mother put her arms around her shoulders.

Laura quickly walked away. But from scenes like this, there was no relief.

It was midday. The sun was shining high overhead. A cooling breeze blew across the deck. Bright clouds accented the brilliant blue sky and brought out the deep sapphire blues in the sea. Laura saw these things and knew they should affect her, but they did not. A collective heaviness cast a gray pall over every corner of the ship. It hung in the air like a thick fog from which no one could escape.

She walked toward the bow and found an open spot near the railing. The bottom half was solid and did a fair job of blocking the wind. She sat down, pulled her knees close, and slid her shawl up over her head. It was the closest thing to being alone.

"Lord," she whispered as quietly as she could. "I'm just . . . I'm so sad. I can't think, I can't feel. Now I have no one. I don't understand. Why did you give me John? I was already used to being alone."

She felt the ship move forward beneath her, heard the gentle splashes as the bow cut through the waves. She knew the *Cutlass* was on course for New York. Before Captain Meade went below, he had announced something about the winds being favorable today and how they were making good speed.

But even if the ship should double or triple its speed . . . it wasn't taking her anywhere she cared to go.

Laura was awakened by a sniffing sound. She didn't even remember falling asleep. She pulled the shawl off her head and looked into Crabby's smiling face. The dog took a few steps back and sat. She had something between her teeth. "What you got there, girl?" She reached out to pet her head.

"Something I made for her," Micah said from off to the side.

Laura looked up. He was rolling up a long stretch of rope. "It looks kind of like a crab," she said.

"What I was aimin' for. Made a' cloth and stuffin'. She wants you to throw it, and she'll fetch it back."

Laura reached for the toy. "Will she let go?"

"Not till you wrestle it a few minutes. She'll growl, but it's a happy one. You're the only lady on the ship she come to. I seen her sitting there right next to you, 'bout the last thirty minutes. Guess she got tired of waitin' on you to wake up."

Laura tossed the crab down to the lower part of the main deck. It didn't go far but slid a few feet more. Crabby took off. She lunged for it but slipped past it. Her body spun around and slid right into a bucket full of soapy water, knocking it over. A crewman had been sitting beside it, using it to scrub the deck. The water spilled all over his pants. He slammed his scrub brush down and stood up.

"Stupid dog," he yelled, loud enough to turn every head in his direction. "Had about enough of you and your stupid foolishness. Come here."

Crabby reacted to the man, cowering in fear.

The man reached over and with one hand grabbed her by the nape of her neck. He slung her back, ready to throw her over the side.

The next moment shocked everyone.

Laura had never seen a man move so fast. Just like that, and Micah was right beside him. He grabbed the crewman's arm, froze it in place, then swung his leg around in a motion that swept the crewman's feet out from under him. He crashed to the deck and let out a loud moan. Crabby ran off and hid behind Micah.

The man rolled over, looked up at Micah with eyes full of hate. "Why, you stinking black savage. I'll teach you to lay a hand on me."

Micah instantly retreated to the submissive posture Laura

had seen previously. "I's only tryin' to keep you from makin' a big mistake, suh," he said. "Can't be throwin' Crabby over the side like that. Cap'n wouldn't want that."

The crewman ignored him and reached for a leather strap hanging nearby on a nail. He swung it around and whipped Micah over and over. Laura screamed for him to stop. Women and children throughout the deck yelled at him to stop, but he kept beating him. Micah fell to the deck, covered his face with his hands. Crabby charged at the man, but he kicked her to the side, then whipped her too.

Laura hurried toward the scene, not sure what to do. Just then she saw a man lunge forward and grab hold of the crewman's hand, the one holding the strap. "Hit that man again, and I'll wrap this strap around your neck," he said.

As she got closer, she saw it was Lieutenant Ashcroft, from the *Vandervere*.

"Take your hand off me," the crewman shouted.

Instead, Ashcroft moved his face within a handsbreadth of the man. "I don't know if Captain Meade believes in flogging, but you say another word and I'll flog you myself to within an inch of your life."

The crewman's face broke, his anger suddenly dissolved. "I'm sorry, Lieutenant. Didn't recognize you without your uniform." He let the strap fall to the deck and stepped back.

"What's going on here?" Captain Meade yelled as he made his way to the main deck. Everyone backed away and made room. "Lieutenant? Maul? What's all this about?" He looked down at Micah, saw the welts on his face and arms. Micah got up.

Several women shouted their renditions, filling the deck with noise and confusion.

"Silence, ladies, if you please," the captain said over it all. They instantly obeyed.

"I was just teaching this slave here a lesson," said the crewman.

"You were beating him senseless," Ashcroft said.

"What did he do?" asked the captain. "One at a time, gentlemen. Starting with you, Lieutenant."

"Sir, I didn't actually see what the slave did, just saw your Mr. Maul here whipping him with that strap."

"Beg your pardon, Captain, but this slave here grabbed my arm and threw me to the deck."

"What?" Captain Meade asked. He looked at Micah, standing now. "I find that hard to believe."

Laura couldn't stand by any longer. "Captain, I beg your pardon, but I saw the whole thing."

"I'm not finished," Maul said.

Captain Meade looked at Micah. Laura saw something like compassion in his eyes. "Go on, miss . . ."

"My name is Laura, *Mrs*. Laura Foster." She explained in a few sentences what really happened.

The captain shook his head as he understood. "Maul, you had no cause to whip him like that. He's not your slave, and you are the lowest ranking man on the crew. And Micah, I can't have you striking the crew, no matter what. Do you understand? You could have asked one of the other men to intervene."

Micah nodded. "Cap'n, may I say somethin'?"

"What?"

"I meant no harm to Missuh Maul here. I truly didn't. But there weren't time. He had Crabby in his hand, another second he'd a' flung her over that rail. Rate we be movin,' she'd be a goner for sure."

Laura remembered what Micah had said about the captain liking Crabby too.

He turned to Maul, a stern look in his eyes. "Mr. Maul.

I'm only going to say this once. You are new on this crew so I'm going to give you the benefit of the doubt." He bent down and looked at Crabby hiding behind Micah's legs. He put his hand out, and she ran right to him, her tail wagging furiously. "Crabby here is under my protection."

"Yes, sir," said Maul.

"I don't care what she does that you don't like, don't you ever lay a hand on her or Micah again. Are we clear?"

Maul looked at Micah then down at Crabby, his hatred still present but subdued. "I understand, Captain. Won't happen again, sir."

"My apologies, ladies," the captain announced, standing to his feet. "A bit of misunderstanding here, is all. Sorry to have disturbed your peace. I've been informed that dinner will be served in about one hour. While I have your attention, I might as well inform you . . . we are running low on provisions. As I said, we will share with you whatever we have, but I had no way of knowing how much it would take to feed over a hundred mouths a day. Our cook tells me if we don't go to half rations, we'll run out a day or so before reaching New York. So . . ." He smiled ever so slightly. "I regret to say, not only will the food be terrible, but there will be less of it."

Everyone laughed. The comment seemed to sweep away the tension on deck.

For everyone, Laura observed, except Mr. Maul. He bent over and picked up his bucket. As he stood, he gave her a wicked hateful stare.

7

Up then down, up then down. The movement unending.

The heat scorched his neck and arms. And the thirst. *But don't drink. No matter how intense the thirst . . . don't drink.*

"I can't hold on, John. It's time."

"No," John said. "Robert, don't. Just a little more."

"Why? There's no point. I'm so tired."

"Can't you feel it, Robert? The waves are calming."

"Does it matter?"

"It will get easier to hold on. We can just float. Just a little longer, Robert. Think of Mary and your little ones. Hold on for them." John looked to his right. Robert's head faced away. He gave no reply. They had been sharing one of the wooden tables John had pulled from the dining saloon. "Robert?"

"A little longer then," Robert said.

For the last several hours John had watched as one man after another gave up and slipped beneath the water, like the man who'd shared this table with Robert. Some had announced their departures, calling out their names, a few last words to convey to loved ones should any out here survive. Others just silently disappeared. There were less than a hundred men floating in their group. All the rest were dead.

The big raft . . . there had been three men on it. Now there was only one. John quickly looked around, didn't see anyone swimming toward it. "Robert? Hey, Robert." John splashed him.

"What?"

"C'mon, the big raft."

"What?"

"There's room, enough for both of us."

"I don't have the strength to move."

"It's not far, maybe a hundred feet. If I can get us there, will you hold on?"

"I suppose."

The big raft . . . what he and Robert had named a pair of doors and hatches some men had tied together right after the ship sank. They had been eyeing it for hours. Well, John had; Robert had given up. It seemed big enough to hold four men, but John had only ever seen three. Two of them had been defending it savagely, kicking and punching anyone who came near. As the afternoon wore on and the sun had sapped everyone's energy, the battles had ceased. The two warriors on the raft had finally lost the will to fight.

Sometime in the last hour they had, apparently, lost the will to live.

"We're almost there," John said. "It's big enough for you to lay there a while and rest."

John felt Robert's legs start to kick beside him. He was still trying. John kept his focus on the prize as they closed the distance. It was too discouraging to lock eyes with anyone on his right or left as he went by. Such desperation and pleading on every face. But he couldn't help them, not anymore. He was spent.

The men were already in a state of exhaustion when they'd first entered the water, from days on the bucket brigade. Adding to that, for John, was the mental fatigue from constantly resisting terrifying thoughts that pounded relentlessly in his mind. Then the energy expended conjuring hopeful thoughts, which he didn't even believe.

For the moment, John's thoughts were few. The big raft alone consumed him. And how improved their situation would be if they could cling to it instead of this table.

After John pulled himself onto the raft, he reached back for Robert. He was gone. "No," he shouted, looking all around the table for him. "Robert," he shouted. He must have gone under.

John was just about to dive beneath the table when he heard, "I've got him, John."

He recognized the voice, the man's accent.

"Mr. Ambassador?"

"He's over here," the man said. "The other side of the raft. I've got his collar, but I'm too weak to pull him up by myself. And please don't call me that, John. After all we've been through."

"Yes, sir," John said. "Ramón . . . sir." Ramón Gutierrez, the Peruvian ambassador. The man who'd stood beside him on the bucket brigade. "I'm glad you're still here."

"As am I. For how long, who knows?"

John edged his way to the far side of the raft, and together they pulled Robert aboard. He didn't look well.

"I'm so thirsty, John," he said weakly. "I drank some seawater, I think."

"How much, Robert?"

"Just a little . . . but it didn't help."

"It won't help, Robert. And it will make you sick, or worse."

"He's right, Robert," said Ramón. "The man whose spot

you're taking on this raft tried quenching his thirst from the ocean."

Robert rolled over and threw up. Thankfully, just water. John quickly splashed it away. "That's good, Robert. You'll be fine."

Robert lay there on his side. "I'm so thirsty."

"We all are," John said, patting Robert on the shoulder.

John leaned over Robert and whispered to Ramón, "The other two men, before they disappeared, I saw them beating anyone who came near."

Ramón whispered back, "They had no wives aboard the *Vandervere*, so all their gold went down with the ship. I promised them each a thousand gold coins if they helped me survive." He smiled.

Instantly, John remembered the pouch of gold he'd given Laura. And the note. What was his beloved doing now, he wondered. Well on her way to New York and safety. He was glad of that but immediately stopped dwelling on what she might face once she arrived.

"Look," said Ramón. "To the west, a storm building on the horizon." Everyone within earshot turned and stared. "It appears to be coming this way."

No one said a word. Everyone was likely thinking the same thing—fresh water. If the storm was mild, that is. But then another thought . . . more deaths if it stirred up the wind and waves again. Even John doubted he could hold on through another round of that.

"You can see the end of it," someone said. "On both sides."

"Maybe it won't be so bad," said another. "I must have water."

They watched as it moved slowly toward them.

Suddenly a flash. "Was that . . . ?"

"Yes," said Ramón, "it was."

Lightning.

8

As Captain Meade had predicted, the winds had stayed firm all day, filling the sails of the *Cutlass* and drying out the dampness in Laura's clothes. Except for her undergarments, she felt completely dry. But the chafing on her skin caused her considerable pain. Walking was an especially painful task. She hadn't seen Micah since the terrible beating he'd received an hour ago. She went below deck to see how he fared.

She found him folding the cut sails he'd passed out the night before, facing away from her. Crabby sat dutifully by his side, admiring every move he made. Micah bent down to pick up another, patted her head, and said, "That's my girl." Her tail instantly responded.

"Micah," Laura said. "Are you all right?" Crabby turned and ran toward her. Laura bent down to greet her.

Micah turned also, much slower. Laura's heart fell as she saw the swelling on his face, especially around his eyes and mouth. She noticed him blinking back tears.

"Sorry, ma'am," he said, seeing she noticed.

"Don't be," Laura said. "I couldn't believe how that man treated you."

Micah gently shook his head. "That not be the reason for

these tears. I just been here thankin' the Lord, is all. How he been so good to me."

"I don't understand."

"I thought she be gone for sure." He looked at Crabby. "Didn't think I'd get to Missuh Maul in time. Then I'd be all alone. But the good Lord spare her, and me too."

"Aren't you upset? That man beat you so badly."

"I been beat worse, more times than I know, with nothin' to show for it. I'd take five more like it to save her, she been so good to me."

Laura couldn't believe what she heard. How does someone experience what he just did and within an hour find any good in it, let alone enough to shed tears of joy? She wanted to understand more about this unusual man. She had never spoken to a slave before.

"Well, I'm glad you're all right," she said. "And Crabby too." Quietly, she said, "You mind if I ask . . . has Captain Meade ever beaten you?"

"No, Cap'n been good to me. He do talk mean sometimes, but I 'spect he have to, keep order and such. But he's the best massah I ever have." He leaned forward and whispered, "Cap'n even read his Bible. Showed it to me once, all beat up and worn." He smiled. "Like me."

"I don't understand," she said. "He reads the Bible, but still . . . he *owns* you?"

An odd expression came over Micah's face, like he didn't understand the question.

"Hey, Micah," a voice boomed down from the hatch.

"Yessuh, Cap'n?"

"Smitty needs you, time to serve up chow for our guests."

"Yessuh, be right there."

Laura sat on the wooden steps connecting the main and forecastle decks and looked down at her bowl, half-filled with gray mush. She'd only eaten two spoonfuls and could hardly imagine downing a third. It put one in mind of oatmeal, less the cream and sugar, less the nutmeg, less the flavor. She'd heard someone call it gruel, which seemed entirely appropriate.

She forced another mouthful.

Dreadful.

Aboard the SS *Vandervere* there had been three distinct tiers of food and lodging: first class, second class, and steerage. Even in steerage the food appeared to be several classes above what the crew of the *Cutlass* ate.

The gruel did remind her of something pleasant: the most perfect oatmeal she'd ever tasted. But instead of dinner, it had been served at breakfast. What was it, two weeks before? She and John were aboard the SS *Sonora*, the *Vandervere*'s sister ship, which had taken them down the Pacific side of their journey. Every bite had overflowed with flavor.

They sat at this lovely round table, just the two of them. White linens, china bowls and cups, sterling silverware. The success of John's hardware store had enabled them to travel first class, something she had never done. It was midmorning. They had slept in. The waters were perfectly calm as far as the eye could see.

"John, isn't this moment amazing?" Laura said. "I have never been this happy. I didn't know a joy so complete was even possible."

He reached across the table and took her hand, sipping his coffee with the other. "I don't have words to say. I thought long and hard about where to go on our honeymoon. Narrowed it down to a half-dozen choices. I wrestled the hardest with this one. But now . . ."

"It's perfect, John. I love it." She squeezed his hand.

"Laura." He looked deep into her eyes when he said this. "For me, it's not the ship or that incredible view out there. Or even this very fine bowl of oatmeal." He smiled. "It is being here with you. Doing all this with you. Adding to our love, moments like last night, with you now as my wife. It's . . . I have no words."

She leaned forward and they kissed.

"See that man?" he whispered, pointing to a man standing alone against the rail looking out to sea. "That's who I was, what I'd be doing on this ship right now without you."

Just then someone began coughing loudly, jolting her from these pleasant thoughts. As she reentered the present, she saw it was a woman standing alone against the rail of the *Cutlass*, about the same distance as the man John had pointed to. Laura turned to her right, as if she might see John sitting across the table where he belonged.

Oh, John.

She quickly ate another spoonful of gruel. It was revolting, but it had the power to force her thoughts elsewhere. She looked around at the other women and children on deck. Everyone with a bowl wore the same disinterested expression. She knew she needed nourishment, and only that knowledge kept her eating until it was gone.

When she finished, she got up and walked the bowl back toward the table they'd set up to dish it out. It was obvious there were far more mouths to feed than bowls available. A number of passengers stood in line; their faces suggested they'd heard the early reviews about the gruel. Laura saw Micah had been reassigned and was now cleaning the bowls being turned in. Instead of handing hers in, she joined him and began to clean them too. He smiled and stepped aside.

"Ma'am, that's Micah's job."

She turned to face a gray-bearded man she assumed to be Smitty, the cook. "I'd like to help," she said.

"Well, I don't think the captain would approve." He slopped down another bowlful of gruel. "You heard him. Y'all are guests."

"We may be, Mr. Smitty. And we are very grateful to you, but how do you think we feel taking all your food and not even lifting a hand to help?"

Smitty's eyebrows raised. "I . . . well, I suppose it's okay then. But if the captain comes by, you will tell him you insisted?"

"I certainly will," she said. "The quicker we get these bowls clean, the faster people can eat, right?"

"I suppose."

No more was said. She continued helping Micah. A few minutes later, more ladies volunteered. In short order, everyone was fed, all the bowls and spoons cleaned, everything put away.

She decided to walk out to the bow and take in the sunset. It was hard not to acknowledge the wonder. Aboard the *Sonora* and *Vandervere*, almost every night, the Almighty had painted the most elaborate scenes across the sky, the brightest array of colors, each blending seamlessly into the other. Laura and John had never missed one, right up until the evening the storm had begun.

It amazed her, so many combinations of color, some she'd never imagined could share the same canvas. Then to see a mirror image of it all repainted on the face of the sea, especially on the Pacific side, where the sea had been calm every evening. Every ten minutes or so, the colors would shift and a new version would emerge, equally dazzling. She and John would stand there together, taking it in. Sometimes holding hands. When there was a breeze, he'd stand behind her and wrap his arms around her shoulders.

Tonight, it was as if the sky was on fire. Without a doubt, the most beautiful sunset thus far. How could the Lord, she wondered—*why* would the Lord—who could create such astounding images, why would he mar these same images by forcing her to view them alone?

She looked to her left. The rails along the western edge of the ship were lined with women, all captivated by the same humbling scene.

And like her, they too were alone.

Remembering.

9

"My, my, ain't that a sight to see."

Laura turned and saw Micah over her right shoulder, his face beaming, eyes wide and bright.

"Don't get to see many sunsets. Usually down in the galley cleaning up after supper. They all disappear 'fore I finish. Expect I have you to thank for that, ma'am."

"Me?"

"You started helpin', then the other ladies joined in. Next thing, we's all done and I got nothin' left to do. Figured with so many, I'd be cleaning till morning. Cap'n say I can come up here a spell."

"Well, I'm glad I could help. But you don't have to thank me, Micah. I was raised to help when there's work to be done, especially if I had a part in making the mess."

Micah smiled, still staring at the sky. "Be nice if more folks thought that way."

"Where's Crabby?"

"Well, she gonna sleep well tonight, her belly all full up. Lot a' ladies didn't finish their supper—can't say as I blame 'em—but Crabby, she ain't picky. She eat like a goat, so she a happy goat 'bout now." He pointed at the sunset and said, "Gonna be a nice mornin' for us."

"How do you know?"

"The sky say so. All red and lit up like that. Ever hear the sayin', red sky at night, sailor's delight; red sky at mornin', sailor take warnin'? Don't always turn out that way, but the three years I been out here, works most of the time."

"You've only been at sea three years? What did you do before that?"

"That . . . well it's a long story, most not worth tellin'."

His face grew serious. Laura felt bad for asking. She should have realized how hard his life had been compared to hers, or any free person for that matter.

"Tell you one thing, though," he said, smiling again. "I never eaten fancy food, but on land I sho' ate better than this gruel we get out here. Don't seem like the Lord meant people to eat such as that."

Laura smiled. "I don't know how you do it."

"Keep askin' myself the same thing, every spoonful. Then I say, Micah, man's gotta eat. And I remind myself, each day passes gets me closer to that banquet Jesus promises in the Bible. I 'spect I'll be eating mighty fine every day after that."

"Do you have a Bible?"

"No. Couldn't read it if I did. But my son Eli reads. Reads right well, like he been to a fine white school. Used to read me from the Bible every night back in Fredericksburg."

"Where is Eli now?"

"They come took him away."

"I'm so sorry."

He sighed heavily. "Readin's what did it. Got caught teachin' some black folk by a fire in the woods. Somebody in the big house saw flames through the trees, thought the woods was on fire. Lord knows where he is now."

She couldn't begin to fathom such a thing. "It is so wrong . . . what's happening to your people."

"Well, ma'am, kind a' you to say so."

Micah looked back at the sunset. So did she. Most of the flaming reds and yellows had shifted to subtler pinks and grays. The sun had dipped below the horizon. When she looked back at his face, he was smiling again.

How was that possible?

Ayden Maul was almost finished.

As soon as he'd seen the sunset and how all the ladies reacted to it, he instantly went below deck and seized his chance. By now, like ladies are apt to do, they'd all staked their claim to whatever little corner of the hold they'd slept in last night. He knew some had kept their gold in pouches tied to their waist, like that woman who got him in trouble with the captain today.

But not all.

He found dozens more pouches, carpetbags, and money belts, all sloppily buried under blankets and shawls. All filled with gold nuggets. Some of the carpetbags even contained little gold bricks. A staggering sight. He made mental notes of the largest caches. At the right moment, he would slip down here again and take a handful from each one.

Who'd know? No way to prove how many nuggets were in each lady's spot, or how many he'd have taken. He figured, added together, he'd leave this sorry ship with thousands of dollars.

He'd finally live the kind of life he'd always dreamed of. And it was all just sitting here, like ripe apples ready to pluck. Maul wasn't a praying man. But he might just ask the man upstairs for a few more marvelous sunsets like tonight.

Then another thought. Why wait till then?

He listened a moment. Nobody making their way down the hatch steps. He walked back to three of the biggest carpetbags and grabbed a handful of nuggets from each one. That's a better plan, he thought. Grab a little every chance he got.

Then he'd come back for the mother lode the night before they pulled into New York.

10

John looked down at the raincoat. It was a grim task, the most disturbing thing he had ever done.

"Are you all right?" Ramón asked.

"I'll be fine."

"I know it was hard," said Ramón. "But if we're careful and a worse storm doesn't come and overturn the raft, the water in this raincoat might just buy us another day."

The storm earlier that afternoon had terrified them as it passed by, but the lightning strikes never hit close enough to cause any real harm. Sadly, John had witnessed one man die from the sheer terror that it might. The storm had pelted them with a driving rain. The lightning had flashed and the thunder exploded all around them. But the winds were slight and, if anything, the rain seemed to calm the waves. Every man except one had his mouth wide open to drink in the fresh water.

On the outskirts of the group, one poor fellow started screaming, louder with each clap of thunder. After ten minutes, he let go of the door he'd been clinging to and swam away. Those nearby yelled for him to stop. John saw the whole thing. Where did the man think he was going? It was madness. He had swum about fifty yards when his arms began to move slowly. A few more strokes, and they stopped. Then they flailed wildly above his head, and he began to sink below the waterline.

John slipped off the raft.

"John," Robert yelled. "What are you doing? Come back."

John swam toward the man. The raindrops felt cool on his sunburned arms. He wished he could stop and drink them in. But he kept on.

When he finally reached the man, he understood why the man hadn't gotten far. John found him floating facedown, wearing a large raincoat. The sleeves and pockets must have instantly filled with water. John turned him over, but it was too late. His eyes stared straight up at nothing, his mouth wide open. John lifted his head above the water and shook him; he didn't know what else to do. Of course, the man didn't respond. His expression didn't change.

John swam back to the big raft, pulling the man behind him. At first, he didn't know why. Clearly the man was dead. No one paid him any attention along the way. They all looked straight up, mouths wide open, drinking in the rain.

"John," Robert said as he drew near. "What are you doing, is he alive?"

John didn't answer until he got within a few feet. "I was too late."

"Then why bring him here?"

Now John knew why, but he didn't want to say. He unbuttoned the man's raincoat then carefully pulled his arms free from the sleeves. "Robert, here . . . take this." He lifted up the coat.

"I see," said Ramón. "A wonderful idea. We'll form this into a large bowl."

By the time John climbed back on the raft, a half inch of

fresh water already covered the bottom of the coat. John was exhausted and allowed the other men to catch the rain. He laid back, opened his mouth wide, and drank it in. A part of him knew he should feel sorrow for the drowned man. At least a tinge of guilt for how quickly he'd removed his coat and cast him aside. He at least should have said a prayer, but he didn't have the strength. For the next fifteen minutes, he just lay there drinking in the rain.

Thirty minutes after that, the men stared at the most amazing sunset, formed by the remnants of the passing storm. John sat up and joined them, strengthened by the rainwater and the cool night air.

No one spoke.

The fiery sunset took him back to a similar scene in San Francisco: walking with Laura along the bay, just south of Rincon Hill. The colors spreading across the sky now were almost identical. But it wasn't the sky he remembered most about that evening. It was how nervous he was. He and Laura had been on numerous dates, but so far they had never held hands.

He had decided this would be the night.

He had held her hand in certain approved moments: as she stepped up or down from a carriage and, ever so briefly, when he said good night at the end of each evening. Even then, it was so hard for him not to linger when he did, to hold on a moment too long. But he had always let go, as a proper gentleman should. He didn't want to presume. Laura had never shown an ounce of flirtation so far. He was very glad of that.

The worry now was . . . if he did take her hand in his, what if she pulled back? If she felt he was being too forward at this stage? At times, she had been hard to read. He didn't blame her; it was the bane of their upbringing, the consequence of living under so many rules of etiquette and manners. A lady must be this way; a lady is never that way. A gentleman never does this; a gentleman must always do that.

Here they were, living in San Francisco, a new land, entirely free of such rigid boundaries, but they seemed chained by them still, as if sitting on a porch swing with their mothers peering through the curtains.

John remembered a strong wind had been blowing that evening. Laura had to hold her hat on with one hand. They'd been looking out at the bay as they walked. But the sunset quickly took center stage. John turned to face it.

Laura did too. "My word . . . would you look at that."

The rolling hills along the western sky had become dark silhouettes; the sky above them was on fire. They both stood and took it in a few moments. While Laura's eyes remained fixed on the scene, John kept stealing glances at her. Her free hand was just inches from his.

"Did we ever get sunsets like this back East?" she asked.

"Maybe," he said. "I never saw them if we did."

"Too many trees and buildings in the way," she said.

Just take her hand.

"That's one thing I miss," she said.

"What?"

"The trees back East. But I love how big the sky is out here and how far you can see in every direction."

"I do too," he said. "After dinner, are you still open to what we talked about earlier?"

She looked back at him. "You mean dancing at the Apollo ball?"

John nodded.

"I know I said yes before, but I've got to tell you . . . I'm getting more nervous about following through."

"We don't have to go," he said gently, though he wanted to badly.

"I've been to the Apollo once with my brother. But I just sat watching all the other young ladies, how well they dance—"

He reached for her hand; he didn't realize he'd done it until it was too late. "Laura, I'm only going there to dance with one young lady. Truth is, we'll probably both be terrible." She laughed but, more importantly, she didn't pull her hand away. Then he said, "I took dance lessons my mother forced on me in my youth. I've never even been to a real dance before."

She squeezed his hand. "Is that true?"

"Laura, if you dance with me at the Apollo tonight, it will be the first dance I've ever had with someone I have asked myself."

She smiled. And she'd given him a look that felt more like a wonderful prize. "Then I will dance with you tonight, Mr. Foster."

They'd continued to walk along the bay a bit farther from there, looking at the sunset, looking at each other. She'd held her hat with one hand and his hand with the other. But just as the sunset had faded then, it was fading now on the raft.

John closed his eyes, not wanting the memory to fade as well. He lay back on the raft, replaying the best parts over and over in his mind.

11

"Fear is such a peculiar thing."

When John opened his eyes, he saw stars. He must have drifted off. By the accent he knew it was Ramón. "What?" John asked.

"Think about it. We have this raincoat because a man died. And he died because of a fear that he *might* die. Can anything be more ironic?"

John sat up. Between the stars and the light of a half-moon he could see surprisingly well.

His stomach growled, but he felt stronger than he had all day. Amazing what a little rest and fresh water can do. The sticky saltwater feeling was also gone. He was surprised that he wasn't freezing and thought how much harder this ordeal might have been had it happened in October or November.

"If he had not been afraid," Ramón continued, "he would be alive right now, and it is we who might be dead tomorrow."

"I felt like I was dying today before the storm," Robert said. "Never drank rain before, but it was the most refreshing thing I ever tasted."

"You know this coat full of water will give us trouble tomorrow," said Ramón.

"Why is that?" asked John.

"Look around. All these men floating with us are fine now. They drank their fill of rain. But come midday tomorrow they're going to realize . . . we're the only ones with any water left."

"You're right," said Robert. "If we ration it between ourselves, it'll last all day tomorrow, maybe a few days."

"And if we share it with the others," said Ramón, "it will be gone in one sitting."

John looked out at the other men floating on the ocean. He couldn't see the outlying edges of the group, but it seemed they had lost a few more while he slept. "I think we should share it," he said. "Another storm could come."

"Or not," said Robert. "And we'll have nothing." He stared at the coat like it was full of gold nuggets. "I don't want to face another afternoon like today. I say anyone comes after this, and we fight. It's every man for himself now."

"Really," John said. "Where would you be right now if I'd thought like that yesterday?"

Robert glared at him.

"And what about this coat," said John. "I could have taken it off out there, grabbed hold of the door the man was clinging to, and kept all this water to myself."

Ramón smiled. "Has a point there, Robert."

"But you didn't," Robert said. "And the way you nodded off like that . . . I'd say if you did, you'd have fallen asleep and the water would have spilled out. And you'd have nothing. We were all tired, but we were the ones catching the rain so the coat could fill up."

"So, Robert, what do you suggest?" said John. "We start kicking anyone who comes near? Then just watch them die of thirst, one by one?"

"If we must."

"I can't do that. I won't do that."

"Then let's vote," said Robert.

"That seems fair," Ramón said.

"I don't think it is," John said. "Some matters are too big to entrust to majority opinion."

"Nonsense," said Robert.

"John, I'm surprised at you," Ramón said. "I thought all Americans believed in majority rule."

"We vote on a lot. But not whether a man lives or dies."

"That's ridiculous," Robert said. "What do you think juries do? Weren't you at that big hanging in San Francisco last year? Hung those two killers, Cora and Casey, right out there on Sacramento Street. Must have been ten thousand people watching. They got a trial, the jury voted, and the vote was all about whether they lived or died. And they died."

John remembered the hanging. And he remembered being curious enough to want to go see it. But Laura would've been mortified, so he pretended not to care.

"I think he's got you there, John," said Ramón.

"All right then," John said. "We'll vote."

"No, we won't," said Ramón. "I'm sorry, I've been toying with you men. Robert, as a delegate from Peru, I could never cast a vote that would bring harm to a citizen of your country. And you already know I'm not a fighting man. Though my preference is to keep the water for ourselves, I have to side with John on this."

Robert restrained his anger and looked away. A moment later, he turned back to face John and Ramón. "Well, then, we will all die out here together."

12

The night breeze calmed Laura's nerves.

She was still standing near the bow. About an hour ago, the first mate had called Micah away to some duty. She had no idea what time it was. But she felt relieved to have made it through her first full day without John. It didn't carry the weight of an achievement; she dreaded the thought of falling asleep, only to wake up and face another day. She tried remembering what it felt like when she was alone all the time, but it didn't help. That was a different kind of alone.

A picture came to mind: the large purple bougainvillea that grew just beyond her kitchen window in San Francisco. When in full bloom, it was almost shocking in its splendor. And it had bloomed just so throughout the summer. Everyone who saw it felt compelled to speak of its beauty. But just before the wedding, knowing she'd be gone a few months, she'd pruned it back. It broke her heart to see it after. Half its size, void of color. Its fullest branches lopped off and barren.

That was her now.

She noticed the sea had completely calmed. Maybe tonight she should just sleep out here on deck. She turned to find a suitable spot and noticed a young woman she had seen earlier today. She was about her age, the only woman on board who'd showed no signs of grieving. She was leaning on the rail at the same place as Laura, on the opposite side of the bow.

She turned and saw Laura looking at her and smiled. Laura nodded, and the woman walked toward her and extended her hand.

"I'm Melissa," she said. "Melissa Anders." She was pretty, a little shorter than Laura; her hair was a bit darker.

They shook hands. "I'm Laura Foster." She still cherished saying her last name.

Melissa walked past her and leaned on the railing where Laura had just stood. "I love this breeze," she said.

"It is nice." Laura came up beside her.

"I'm so glad the waves have stopped. I thought it would never get calm again."

Laura looked at her face, bright and focused. Not a hint of sorrow. "I remember seeing you on the ship."

"Which one?" asked Melissa.

"Both, I think."

"That's possible. I was on the *Sonora* and the *Vandervere*."

"I don't think I saw you but a handful of times, though," Laura said, then realized that, until the storm, she had been completely preoccupied with John.

"That was on purpose. I only came out when I had to, or when I knew the decks were mostly empty."

Laura wanted to ask why.

"I guess that might sound strange," Melissa said.

"You don't have to explain."

"I don't mind telling you. It was all those men. There must have been hundreds of them on board."

As soon as she'd said it, their eyes met, and Laura knew she'd regretted saying it. All but six of those men were now gone.

"I'm sorry," Melissa said.

"It's all right. Does that mean you are . . . spoken for?"

"Yes!" she said, her eyes as wide and smile as strong as any other woman in love. She made a face, as if apologizing for her zeal.

Laura understood: the love of her life was not on either boat. "It must be hard for you, being on this ship, with everyone else grieving their loss."

"It is, but I think I understand what you and the others are going through. I felt it the moment the hurricane took hold of the *Vandervere*. I've never been so frightened in all my life. The force of that devilish wind and the ship going up and down, never ceasing, sliding sideways then righting again. I was certain it would capsize any minute."

Laura felt a chill, remembering the horrors again.

"At some point, I knew I would die. And all the happiness inside me died. I thought I would never see my Tom again. We would never be married."

A few quiet moments passed.

"Well," said Melissa, "I'm sure you're tired. I know I am. I should probably go below and try to sleep."

"It was nice to meet you," Laura said.

"And you." Melissa turned toward the steps then turned back. "I haven't been able to talk with anyone since we boarded. I've so missed good conversation. May we speak again?"

Laura had enjoyed their brief chat but wasn't sure she was up to anything deeper. "That would be nice." Melissa disappeared into the shadows and Laura turned back to face the sea. She thought again of the phrase Melissa had just spoken: *my Tom*.

She remembered the moment she could say that about *her John*. How delightful it had been when she finally knew he was for real, when the fear that it was all too good to be true had dissolved. It came on the ride home from their fourth date, a night very much like this. The moon half full, with just about the same number of stars, even the same cooling breeze coming in off the bay.

The evening started back at her townhouse in South Park. On the first three dates, John had also picked her up there. He would knock then stand out by the sidewalk, waiting for her to come out. "To keep things proper," he'd said. "I wouldn't want your neighbors to ever have cause for gossip."

On the fourth date when he knocked, she opened the door slowly. It was already dark, the kerosene lamps flickering down the sidewalk. There stood John under the street lamp out front. So dashing, in a top hat and black frock coat, a golden silk vest, a white shirt and tie. Behind him, a two-seat, one-horse carriage with the most magnificent, shiny black horse. "What is this?"

"My dear, I did say tonight would be special."

"You did, but I thought . . . maybe a nice restaurant."

"You haven't liked the others?" He was smiling.

"No, they were very nice . . . but you said to dress up."

"And you did. You look wonderful."

It was the nicest dress she owned. "Where did you get this?" She pointed to the carriage.

"I bought it."

"You bought it? It must have cost a fortune."

"Well, I decided I want to take you to all the places I've been seeing on Shasta here." He patted the horse's neck. "They're much too far to reach by foot." He helped her into the carriage then stroked the horse gently on the nose. Shasta rested his head on John's shoulder a moment then lifted it high, as though at attention. John got in beside her and snapped the reins. "Let's go, boy."

They lurched forward, and she fell back against the seat.

"Sorry, Shasta's still getting used to this. And I'm afraid, so am I."

"How long have you had him?"

"I got him as soon as I moved out here. He's half Arabian. As soon as I saw him, I said 'You are mine.' We ride in the country together every Sunday after church. He can run like the wind."

"He's beautiful."

"He is." They turned down Third Avenue.

"Where are we going?"

"First to a very fine restaurant . . . not like those *other* places I've taken you."

"I didn't mean—"

"I'm just being playful. They *were* just nice. Tonight will be exquisite. After dinner, we're going for a ride. Have you ever been out to the Mission?"

"No." She'd wanted to, but it was way beyond the outskirts of town. She'd never feel safe taking a carriage there by herself.

"Well, the plank road out there is a bit bumpy. When we talk, it will sound like we're shivering. But they've turned the Mission into a wonderful place, especially at night."

Shasta had found his stride. That and the night wind made her cold. "I don't think we'll have to wait for the plank road to sound like we're shivering."

"I'm sorry. It takes a lot for me to feel the cold. Here, I brought a blanket for you." He reached under the seat and pulled it out. With the reins in one hand, he began to wrap it around her shoulders. She helped. He kept his arm around her shoulder a moment and drew her close. "I hope you don't mind. I don't want you catching a cold."

"I don't mind," she said, leaning in, trying to hide her smile.

Later, they had the most wonderful meal at the nicest restaurant she'd ever visited. Everyone dressed like they were going to the opera. It had chandeliers and rich burgundy curtains, china plates and white linen. She felt out of place at first, but John seemed perfectly at ease. The way he looked at her and the things he said soon put her at ease.

On the ride out to Mission Dolores, John told her about the places around San Francisco he wanted to take her in the coming weeks. Down the beach toward Black Point, then to Fort Point and the Golden Gate. The sand by the beach there, he'd said, was as hard and smooth as pavement. He rattled off a half dozen other spots, places she'd heard people talk about in town but she'd never been able to see. It thrilled her heart to hear it; not so much the thought of seeing all these sights, but the level of excitement in John's voice and the anticipation of going to all these places with him.

He had her back home by 10:30. The whole night, he was the perfect gentleman. But the whole night, she could tell . . . he was hers, *her John*. They were most definitely together now. All his language and mannerisms had said so. Why, he'd bought a carriage, just for them. After she'd closed the front door, she ran up the stairs so she could see him pull away.

She had done the very same thing on every one of their dates for the next year, right up to the night before their wedding. That night, his last words had been a delightful question: "Do you realize, my love, after tonight, we will never part again?"

She looked out at the sea now and tried but could not suppress the memory of a phrase from their wedding day: *till death do us part.*

Surely, God could not have intended them to part so soon. But here she was alone, with no reason to imagine she'd be anything but alone from now on.

13

Since he'd already slept a bit, John said he'd take first watch that night. The others were already asleep. He was responsible to make sure the bowl shape of the coat remained intact throughout the night. This meant all three men could barely move. If even one rolled over, a sidewall could collapse and the water would be lost.

John estimated an hour had passed. It was peaceful and quiet. The night sky amazed him, as it so often did at sea. But all he could think about was Laura. They had only been apart one full day. Already it felt like weeks. What was she doing now? What was she thinking? Maybe she was asleep. Or maybe . . . looking up at the same sky.

She must be so frightened.

Before the hurricane hit, they'd walk the *Vandervere*'s main deck every night, and they'd have the most wonderful conversations. He loved to hear Laura's outlook on life, on faith, on food . . . almost anything. On their first few dates she'd held back, unwilling to say anything until he'd almost have to insist. Then she'd say things he'd never heard before, unexpected things. She often made him laugh.

One lunch date in particular came to mind. They were

to meet at a small French restaurant on Montgomery Street in San Francisco, just off Broadway. What was its name? He couldn't recall. He'd invited her there thinking to impress her. The clothing shops and eateries along Montgomery rivaled the finest Paris had to offer.

He waited outside, then caught sight of her walking north down the sidewalk, mingled in a stream of passersby. She walked right past a dress shop, a haberdashery, a shoe store, and finally a jewelry store. She didn't stop and look at a single window display. Occasionally, she glanced up to catch the sign hanging above each store. Her only interest appeared to be finding the restaurant.

Noticing this, John stood right under the sign of their agreed-upon rendezvous. Wait, that was it . . . Le Rendez-vous Bistro. She saw the sign, looked down, and saw John standing there. He smiled and waved. Her head snapped back. He'd startled her. She smiled and waved back, then hurried her pace to meet him.

Once seated inside, her face was all smiles as she carefully placed a book next to her water glass. "I'm having such a wonderful time with this novel," she said.

Pleasure reading was a pastime he was glad to learn they shared. "What is it?"

"The latest book by Melville."

"The one who wrote *Moby Dick*," John said.

"That's him. It's called *The Confidence Man*." She picked it up, held it like a fine vase.

"May I get your drinks, monsieur . . . mademoiselle?"

John looked up at the waiter. "Coffee for me. Laura?"

"The same."

"Very good," the waiter said and walked away.

John smiled and thought about the appropriate pleasant-ries normally exchanged when people met, particularly a gentleman and a lady so early in their courtship. But Laura was different. She began their date bursting with excitement about a book.

John loved it. "So what do you like about it so far?"

Laura took a deep breath. "So many things! For one, it's so different than *Moby Dick*. It's still Melville but, I don't know, it's lighter and the characters—to me, anyway—are much more interesting. The story begins on April Fool's Day on a Mississippi steamboat heading to New Orleans."

"I think I remember reading a review of it back in April," John said. "When it first came out. It wasn't very kind. I think the review said the book would certainly sell, if only because Melville wrote it, but it wasn't up to his other works."

"John," she said, pretending to scold. "Since when do you care what some highbrowed reviewer thinks? Promise me you'll read it when I'm through."

"I'll give it five chapters."

"It starts a bit slow. You must give it at least ten before you decide."

"Ten then."

The waiter returned with their coffee, served in china cups with a floral print. "Are you ready to order, monsieur?"

They hadn't even looked at the menus yet. Laura quickly picked hers up. "Give us one minute," John said.

"Very well." He walked away.

Laura leaned toward him and said quietly, "I can't read a single word of this."

"That's not a problem. Do you like beef tips?"

"Yes."

"How about simmered and served in a French wine sauce with buttery potatoes and green beans?"

"That sounds wonderful."

John looked around and noticed their waiter standing off

to the side. John signaled him, and he quickly returned. John gave him their order in French. The man smiled as he wrote it all down and said, "Very good, monsieur," then walked away.

When John faced Laura, she seemed impressed. "You speak French too?"

"Actually, I don't. Just enough to order food. If I ever took you to Paris, we could only visit the restaurants."

Laura laughed. John realized something just then. How much he loved to hear her laugh. He wanted laughter to always be a part of their romance. "So tell me more about *The Confidence Man*."

"I'll say this," she said. "It really makes me want to travel on a steamboat someday. Or even better, on one of those huge paddle-wheel steamships that come into the bay every month or so."

"Where would you want to go?"

"I don't know yet. I just want to be on one. I think it would be a wonderful adventure."

John sat back in his chair and smiled.

"What?" she asked.

"Nothing," he said. "I just love talking with you."

John's previous conversations with women back in New York had always been so formal. Laughter never made an appearance. He remembered his younger sister Allison; she'd laughed often as a little girl. As she grew into her teen years, their mother had put an end to it. "We must form you into a proper young lady," she'd said. And that's what poor Allison had become: a younger version of his mother, just as proper, just as boring. There was nothing he could do to rescue her.

Laura was so different. It was refreshing to hear a woman so feminine and refined, yet one who'd thought so thoroughly about so many things. There had been no tension in their conversations, no fear of saying the wrong thing or forgetting to say the right thing. He had never imagined being in love could be so enjoyable.

Just then a small wave splashed hard against the raft, dousing him in saltwater. Dousing also these pleasant thoughts, replacing them with a more melancholic stream. He recalled what Laura had said back then, about wanting to take a voyage on a paddle-wheel steamship someday. She'd talked about it many more times as she read Melville's book. That's why he'd chosen this trip for their honeymoon.

But she wasn't on a steamship anymore. And neither was he.

He looked around. He was on a raft adrift at sea, protecting a coat full of rainwater in the middle of the night. His beloved was on an old wooden ship sailing farther away from him with every breath. By now Laura must have accepted the fact that the *Vandervere* was gone. She would believe that he was dead.

And if she believed that, she would have read his note.

He looked up at the half-moon lighting the sky. *Oh God, I don't know how or what to pray.* He heard someone moan, Robert perhaps. He must have been praying out loud. He looked, but the coat hadn't moved.

Please, Lord, ease her pain. Especially the pain I've caused. Go before her to New York and prepare the way.

14

Lexington Avenue
Two blocks north of Gramercy Park
New York City

Joel Foster stepped through the iron gate, up the curved granite stairs, and through the front door opened by Beryl, the family butler. Beryl held out his hand to receive Joel's silk hat. "The gate is squeaking again, Beryl. Get someone on it."

"Right away, sir."

The nicest of the family's three carriages remained out front; the driver had been instructed to wait.

"Your coat, sir?"

"I'm going to leave it on. I'm afraid Mother might be sending me out again in a moment. In fact, don't put my hat away just yet." He walked through the foyer toward the dining room.

"Is that you, Joel?" a woman called out. "Allison, you're slouching. Please sit up straight."

"Yes, Mother."

He walked in, and his mother lit up at the sight of him. She tilted her face to the side, allowing him to give her a peck on the cheek. He reached into a silver bowl for a warm biscuit.

"Joel, if you're going to eat, please sit down. I'll have the cook fix you an omelet."

"I've already had breakfast, Mother. Just got in from a sunrise meeting with some investors."

"Why so early?" she asked.

"The same thing I asked Father. Now he wants me back at the office by noon. Having a big catered lunch for some clients all the way in from France."

"Paris?" Allison asked.

"I have no idea, and I don't care," he said. "But I will be there by noon to eat those lobsters."

His mother glanced at the mantel clock, annoyed. "Didn't you tell him what I'd asked you to do?"

"I'm sorry, what was it you asked me to do again?"

Allison laughed.

"I'm not in the mood, Joel," Mother said. "And don't talk when you chew."

"I'm just toying with you, Mother. There was no need to tell Father." He was still chewing. "There's plenty of time to run your little errand and get back to the office for lunch. Why so tense?"

"You know why."

"The letter from the prodigal?" he asked. "Where is it?"

"There on the hutch, in the brown envelope."

He walked over and picked it up. A servant girl walked in. "Oh, Sally," Joel said, "the butter dish is empty. I must have another of those biscuits before I go."

"Yessuh, Missuh Foster." She grabbed the dish and quickly returned to the kitchen.

"Joel," his mother said, "you'll get smudges on the letter."

"It's not as if we're going to frame it." Joel unfolded the single page and read for a moment. "The SS *Vandervere*. He says it's supposed to arrive at three o'clock tomorrow. But you know these ships are never on time. Sometimes they don't even come on the correct day."

"That's why I want you to go down to the steamship company," she said. "It's close enough to the arrival time; they should be able to give us a better idea."

"I'll go, but I don't see how it will make any difference. Ships don't run on a rail, Mother. They arrive when they arrive."

"I've read these steamships are much more reliable. Just go, please, and see what they say." She released a deep sigh. "This whole thing is so unnerving. We haven't seen or heard from John in almost two years, and he sends us this? A single paragraph? I don't know if he plans to stay here, at a hotel, how long he plans to visit. Nothing."

Joel set the letter down, walked behind his mother, and rubbed her shoulders. As he did, she began to cry. "Why would he do this? Why does he treat us this way?"

"I don't think he meant to hurt you, Mother," Allison said. "I'm looking forward to seeing John again."

Her mother shot her an angry glare. "You don't understand the trouble he caused us when he left, the way he left. It was so . . . humiliating. I couldn't show my face for months."

"Don't you want to see him?" asked Allison.

"Of course I do," she snapped. "He's my son." She picked up a linen napkin and dabbed her eyes. "But he could have at least mailed us a few pages. Telling us how he's been, what his plans are. Now I don't know what to expect. My whole social calendar is up in the air." Her stern, in-control face had returned. "I simply must cancel that charity tea next week. We'll have to think of something, some excuse." She looked at Joel and Allison. "I don't want anyone to know about John coming home till we know what we're dealing with, is that clear? No one is to say a word."

"Mother," Joel said. "Please."

"I mean it, not a word."

"All right, but I think it's pretty obvious what's going on. John is broke and coming home in shame. Don't you think if he'd made a go of it, he'd have written more? There'd be two pages spouting off his achievements. He's broke and doesn't want to admit it. My advice? Have the staff make up his old room. He won't have money for a hotel, you can be sure of that."

"Then that's what I'll do," she said. "You go on now, to that steamship place. If you hear anything, you come tell me right after your lunch."

"I will," Joel said. "But if you don't see me until after work, I didn't find out anything more." He picked up the letter. "I'll bring this with me, to make sure of my facts."

"Take it," she said. "What good is it to me?"

15

"Robert, look what you've done! You may have just finished us."

John awoke to find Ramón yelling at Robert. Robert buried his face in his hands. He looked at John. "I've let all the water spill," he said. "Now we're dead." He was frantic.

John saw the coat. Most of the water was gone. Last night, he'd passed the watch to Robert. After a few hours, Robert was to pass it off to the ambassador.

Ramón put his hand on Robert's shoulder. "Calm yourself. Nothing can be done about it now."

"But we'll never get home now. We'll die out here."

John looked at the two men. He wanted to say something reassuring, but he felt no confidence for their future either. Their situation seemed bleak and would grow bleaker still as the cool morning gave way to another blistering afternoon.

Now one without water.

He had a thought, one that had been pestering him since they'd come on the big raft. He felt he had almost a duty to talk about God, maybe to share the gospel with these men, since it seemed clear that death was all but a certainty. He'd never explained it to anyone before. He'd just offered hints or alluded to it in a handful of conversations back in San Francisco. Laura would know exactly what to say. She had a way of introducing religious things that seemed as normal as conversations over tea.

John looked at the ambassador; his light, jovial demeanor had completely disappeared. He seemed as discouraged and anxious as Robert.

John didn't want to talk about this, but felt if he didn't say something now, he might not have the energy once the sun began to beat down. "Robert, Ramón . . . I agree, it doesn't look good. And you may be right, we may die out here . . . today, maybe tomorrow. I'm no preacher. But I've been listening to a good one for just over a year. I don't know where you gentlemen stand, what either of your religious backgrounds are . . ."

He paused. Neither man said anything. Robert was looking down. Ramón seemed lost in his thoughts.

"I thought this might be a good time to share something that happened to me last year. Well, actually, it happened after I understood something for the first time. One Sunday morning—"

"Please, John," Robert said. "I don't want to hear about church right now."

John looked at Ramón. He looked at John then turned away. He wore a look that said: *Do we have to do this?*

John stopped talking and looked out to sea.

For the next hour, hardly a word was spoken. John felt foolish. He kept replaying in his mind things he should have said, certain he had botched the whole matter terribly. But there was one encouraging note, something about himself he now knew to be absolutely true. And what he'd discovered surprised him.

He really wasn't afraid to die.

He wanted to survive, if at all possible, but he had no fear if this was indeed the end. With the water now gone, it seemed almost a certainty now.

The only heaviness he felt, and it bordered on unbearable, was the thought of never seeing Laura again. And the added care of knowing how afraid she must be of facing the future alone.

16

It was midmorning. Laura had awakened on deck a few hours ago to find Crabby lying next to her. She was still lying next to her. Laura had never spent this much time with a dog before. But she understood something of the joy this simple creature imparted to Micah each day. It seemed on every other level, and in every other part of her body, Laura felt either nothing or pain. Just looking into Crabby's happy face sparked something inside her, very close to feeling loved. Crabby also diverted her mind from deep thought and reflection, which itself was a gift.

Still on the bow, Laura looked down to the main deck. Only a few women and children remained in line, waiting for a cup of water and today a choice: half rations of gruel or hardtack. One of the children called them "rock biscuits." Micah had laughed when he'd heard it, said that's what he'd call them from now on.

Micah sat behind the wooden table, helping Smitty distribute the food. Laura looked down at Crabby; the dog's face looked as content as if she were sitting on the finest porch or the greenest lawn. Laura finally stood up, deciding she had no choice but to acknowledge the day had begun. Crabby also stood but stayed right beside her.

The seas were still calm, the water almost glassy. She could see the reflection of the clouds and sky all the way out to the horizon. The wind seemed half what it had been the night before. The sails were not taut and stretched as they'd been before.

Suddenly, Crabby started barking. Women behind Laura gasped and yelled. She turned to see a woman behind her climbing over the rail. Crabby ran to the woman and grabbed her dress in her teeth.

"Let me go," the woman shouted and pulled at her dress.

"What are you doing?" an older woman yelled. "Get back or you'll fall."

"Leave me alone," the woman said. Her dress ripped, and she went over the rail.

Everyone screamed at the sight. A large splash.

Laura looked over the rail as a dark blue shape passed by.

"She's gone over," someone shouted.

"Do something, save her!"

Children screamed.

A man's voice yelled from high overhead. "Man overboard." Laura looked up and saw Ayden Maul balancing on a rope, pointing down toward the woman splashing about, not ten feet from the side of the ship. She was already amidships. In a few moments, the ship would pass her by.

But no one did anything.

Laura hurried down the steps and ran along the rail, her eyes fixed on the woman, now near the back of the ship.

"Captain!" Micah yelled.

Laura turned to see Micah holding the end of a long coil of rope and standing a few feet from the captain.

"Go ahead, Micah," Captain Meade said. "But I fear you're too late."

Micah pulled off his shirt, revealing a startling sight. From his neck to his waistline, his skin was horribly discolored, his back a tangled mess of rippled scars. He tossed the shirt to the deck, wrapped the rope around his forearm, then dove overboard. Crabby ran to the spot, stood against the rail, and barked. Micah swam toward the woman now trailing behind the ship. Laura looked back at the coil of rope, unwinding as if on a spool.

All the women on deck ran toward the back of the ship to watch.

The woman in the water was already floating facedown. Micah was halfway there. The ship moved forward, forcing Micah to swim harder to close the distance. Laura looked back at the rope on deck. It was almost gone. He reached her just as the rope snapped tight.

"He's done it," a woman yelled. "He's got her." Everyone cheered and clapped. But Micah had only been able to grab her hand. Both were now being dragged behind the ship about fifty yards.

"You men," the captain said. "Haul them in."

Three crewmen pulled hard on the rope. When Laura looked back, Micah was on his back, one arm around the woman's shoulder, the other holding onto the rope.

"That's remarkable," a gray-haired woman standing next to her said. "He must be as old as I am. I didn't even know they could swim."

Thirty minutes later, the woman was resting on deck, a blanket around her shoulders. She appeared to be just over thirty. Some older women, thankfully the kinder ones, had gathered around her. Laura stood close enough to overhear. Melissa stood beside her.

Laura learned that she and her husband were poor. They'd spent all they had just to buy tickets back East on steerage. She had no gold pouch. With her husband gone, she was destitute. She knew the ship was merely a day or two from arriving in New York and couldn't bear to face what awaited her.

"Well, we'll help you, dearie," a sweet-faced woman said, patting her on the arm. "Won't we, ladies? Those of us that can, I mean."

"I will," said Laura. She stepped forward and reached for the pouch around her waist. "If each of us gave her a little gold, she could easily have a pouch like this one." She held hers up. Then she reached into it, took out a small handful of gold nuggets, and walked to the woman. "What's your name?"

"Sarah," the woman said. "Sarah Pullman."

"Here, Sarah." She dropped the gold in the palm of Sarah's hand.

Melissa followed her example and did the same. A few of the other women did and several more got up, saying they'd be right back, that their gold was down below. Within fifteen minutes Sarah Pullman had enough gold to fill a pouch as big as Laura's.

She was actually smiling.

Laura saw all the women around her were as well.

And so was she.

Someone else was smiling, watching the whole scene from above, standing behind the main topsail. Ayden Maul was delighted to see how easily these ladies parted with their gold. Handful after handful. No one counted a thing. It confirmed his previous notion that they had no idea how much gold they had. Which meant they wouldn't know how much they were missing.

Tonight, he decided, he'd go below and make his second withdrawal.

17

Joel Foster watched the city pass by outside his carriage window, as much as one could see down Broadway late on a weekday morning. The first half of the ride from Gramercy Park toward Lower Manhattan was at least pleasant. The shops, businesses, and hotels were all upscale, most just a few years old. Not too congested, not too noisy.

Things became increasingly crowded the closer one got to the Battery.

New York City was boiling over with industry and growth. Cotton, wheat, and corn exports had risen by almost 150 percent in the last few years. Iron factories had popped up all along the East River. The harbor did more business now than the seaports at Philadelphia, Boston, and Baltimore combined.

And all these ships and shipments, whether moving inland or across the sea, needed to be insured. Joel could hardly believe how their family's business had grown, tripling since John had left for San Francisco. The fool.

Most of their profits came from cotton. New York traders bought massive quantities from Southern plantations, sold and shipped it to England, then filled the empty hulls with European goods to sell when they arrived back home. And the Foster Insurance Company made a nice percentage of all this business, coming and going.

Joel rang the little brass bell to get his driver's attention. He felt the carriage slow. A little door slid over.

"Yes, Mr. Foster."

For a black man, his diction was amazing. Barely a hint of Southern accent, let alone the "yessuh" or "missuh" he normally heard from the hired help. "Turn left on Fulton. Head down to South Street. I'm not sure whether we head north or south from there. We're looking for the offices of the United States Mail Steamship Company. I'm guessing it's a big operation, should be easy to spot. Let me know when we arrive."

"Very good, Mr. Foster." The little door closed.

Very good, Mr. Foster.

Couldn't have said it better myself, Joel thought. Must be a story behind this. He didn't know much about the driver, supposedly a freedman, but he had his doubts. So many runaway slaves making their way north these days. One of his mother's projects. Everyone in their social circle was hiring Negroes, doing their part to offset all the inhumanity and injustice, or some other such thing.

Joel didn't care. If it helped her sleep at night or eased her sense of guilt for having so much of this world's goods, fine. Joel would take all he could get his hands on. His father had given him John's percentage after he'd left. With the exploding growth, he was nearly as wealthy as his father had been ten years ago.

But Joel wanted more.

His father had developed a chronic cough in the last few months. Joel wondered if it might not develop into something more serious. He wondered if his father had followed through on his threat to remove John's name from his will.

He wished there were some way to find out for sure.

The carriage stopped, the little door slid over.

"We're here, Mr. Foster. I'll get the door."

Joel stepped out into the sunlight.

"They won't allow me to park here, sir. But the office entrance is right over there. I'll keep an eye out for you."

"That'll be fine," Joel said. "Can't imagine I'll be more than fifteen minutes." He started walking then turned. "But we will need to leave as soon as I come out. Have a lunch date, and I absolutely cannot be late."

"I'll be here, Mr. Foster."

Before he went into the steamship office, Joel caught sight of a large ship looming like a cliff behind the brick building. He had seen these steamships out in the harbor but never up close. Must be well over two-hundred feet long, painted a shiny black with a bright red stripe running from stem to stern. It had three wooden masts and a single black smokestack rising from the center. He pulled his gold pocket watch from his vest. No time for gawking.

He walked through the door. A pretty dark-haired girl sat behind a deep mahogany desk. "How can I help you?"

"Where might I confirm the arrival of one of your ships?"

"Do you expect it today?"

"Tomorrow, I'm told."

"Right around the corner you'll see two long counters. Anyone behind them should be able to help you."

"Thank you." Joel followed her instructions and was soon walking on a shiny marble floor beneath crystal chandeliers. Not what he expected from a shipping office. Behind the counter a balding, round-faced man with thick, furry side-burns was writing something on a chalkboard. "Excuse me, my good man."

The man turned, eyed Joel's clothing, and instantly offered his undivided attention. "How can I help you, Mister . . ."

"Foster, Joel Foster. You have a steamship, the SS . . ." He held up John's letter. "The SS *Vandervere*."

"Ah yes, the *Vandervere*. One of the finest in our line."

"I see. Just wanting to verify, if at all possible, when you expect her into port."

"Very good, Mr. Foster." He turned and looked back at the chalkboard, eyes scanning the columns. "There she is. Tomorrow. Three o'clock."

"Same thing it says in this letter. No change then?"

"No, if there was, we'd know. And we'd post the change on this board."

"How would you know?" Joel asked.

"Well, the steamships are very reliable compared to the old sailing ships. They do have masts and sails, but they're rarely used. We're no longer at the mercy of the wind. That big paddle wheel keeps turning like clockwork, wind or waves, rain or shine. The *Vandervere* has already made this voyage from Panama forty-one times, so we have a pretty good idea when she'll arrive. She may be off a few hours, but I doubt it will be more than that."

"Really?" said Joel. "Glad to hear it. Thank you for your time."

"You're most welcome. Good day."

Joel tipped his hat and headed back toward the street. This little detour might prove advantageous. He decided to check back at the office and see what percentage of their business, if any, involved writing policies for these steamships. Whatever it was, he'd make sure they increased it . . . substantially.

Low risks, high profits.

His father had never even spoken of it. Perhaps he didn't know of its potential. Joel looked up, hearing the familiar sound of the family carriage coming down South Street from the north. Hardly a moment's delay. It pulled off in a loading area across the street. The driver climbed down as Joel crossed the street and opened the door facing the sidewalk.

"Where to next, Mr. Foster?"

Joel climbed in. He looked at his pocket watch. Just twenty minutes until his father's luncheon and those delicious lobsters. Should be plenty of time. "Back to the office. Have you been there yet?"

"No, sir."

"The Empire Building, at Broadway and Rector. Ever been down Wall Street before?"

"No, Mr. Foster."

"Right, well head down South Street and turn right at Wall. It's very busy, so keep sharp. You'll see Trinity Church at the end, can't miss it. That's Broadway. A quick left on Broadway and there it is, the Empire Building."

"Thank you, sir. I'm sure I'll find it."

"I'm sure you will. Say, I've forgotten your name."

"It's Eli, sir."

"Eli . . . right. Off you go then."

The driver climbed back up and took hold of the reins. Joel picked up his newspaper. He suspected this driver could read this newspaper he held in his hands. He had the unmistakable bearing of an educated man.

18

To John, this felt like everything he'd ever imagined the wrath of God to be.

The wind had died completely. The waves had stilled. It was a cloudless sky. The late afternoon sun, high overhead, burned incessantly. The thirst had become unbearable. His stomach growled and ached. There was no relief and no relief to come. And all day, no one had seen a single sail on the horizon.

"Here, John, it's your turn." Robert handed John the raincoat. The three men had decided they could derive at least some benefit from the coat, using it for shade. They rotated through shifts, approximately every thirty minutes.

John draped it over his head and shoulders. It actually seemed to yield some comfort. His eyes, now shielded from the sun's glare, could distinguish the horizon. He noticed, as he had many times aboard the *Vandervere*, how the horizon curved ever so gently from one end to the other. You could only catch this effect when you had a full view of it like this, when you could see a clear line between the ocean and sky.

"Isn't it absurd, John? That there was ever a time when men believed the world was flat?"

John heard Laura's voice in his head, almost audibly. He closed his eyes, wanting to see her face, to remember the moment when she'd blurted this out. It came back to him quickly. The sounds of the sea filled his ears then, as well. They were riding along in his carriage near the cliffs by Seal Rocks beach, west of San Francisco. They'd stopped to take in the Pacific view and give Shasta a rest. The carriage roof shielded their eyes from the midday sun, much the way the raincoat did for him just now.

"You can see the earth curving plain as day," Laura said, pointing to the horizon.

John looked to where she pointed then back to the look on her face, smiling.

"How could men who sailed out in the open sea for hundreds of years not notice that?"

"I don't know," he said.

"Have you ever seen those old drawings about what they thought would happen if they sailed out too far?"

John nodded. "Like the edge of a cliff, with the ocean dropping off like a waterfall."

"Yes, and they drew all these absurd-looking sea monsters swimming about." She sounded almost disgusted. "You men," she said, looking at him now. "You're always saying we're the irrational ones."

"I've never said that."

"You know what I mean."

"Do you hear that?" he said.

She stopped talking and listened. "Is that the seals?"

"That's the seals."

"Can we get out and see?"

"We have to get out to see." He stepped out of the carriage and walked to her side, helping her step down. "I love it out here," he said.

They started walking toward the edge, still holding hands. Laura instantly became aware of how high they were. "Oh John, let's not get too close." She squeezed his hand tight.

"We won't. But we've got to get close enough to see them. I've been out here dozens of times. I know a perfect place where we can sit and take it all in. You won't be afraid once you see. It's over here." He led her to his favorite spot.

"My, they are the noisiest things."

"They're even more humorous to look at. Especially the males. Big fat blubbery things."

Laura laughed.

They sat on a small section of flat rocks, with an almost unhindered view of the sea. Just beyond the beach a number of small boulders poked out from the water. Most of the noise came from there, between the waves crashing and the seals shouting out to each other. It was a bright sunny day, but near the edge the wind whipped about, instantly creating a chill.

Laura was starting to shiver. "Here," he said. He put his arm around her and pulled her close.

"Look at them all," she said. "There must be hundreds of them. And look at that big arch there. There's a hole right through the cliff." She let go of his hand to point these things out. Laura always pointed.

"I knew you'd like that."

"John, it's a lovely place. I can see why you come here."

"And why I wanted to share it with you," he said. He was staring at her. She kept looking at the water and the seals, but John could see her noticing him out of the corner of her eye.

Slowly, she turned and matched his gaze. He leaned forward and kissed her gently.

It was their first kiss.

He hadn't planned to kiss her today. He couldn't help himself. It was just . . . the perfect time.

Thankfully, she kissed him back.

They kissed once more then each pulled away, just a few inches, and looked in each other's eyes. "I love you, Laura."

Another first.

A tear formed in one eye. "I love you too, John."

He kissed her once more, then pulled out a handkerchief to catch the tear now sliding down her cheek.

Just then both of their heads snapped back in surprise, startled by the most grotesque sound. Then more sounds, even louder than the first. They turned to see two enormous males on the nearest rock island, banging their chests together and slapping their fins against the rocks.

They laughed hard at the sight.

"I think they're both in love," John said, "with that pretty one right there." He pointed to a smaller female fleeing the scene. She dove into the water. One of the males backed off and flopped into the water after her.

John and Laura sat together, taking it in for fifteen more minutes or so. John looked up at the sun, then down at the beach, trying to gauge the tide. "There's another place I'd like to show you on the way back to town."

"Where is it?"

He stood up and helped her to her feet. As they walked back to the carriage, he said, "It's down on the north side, a ways past the Golden Gate. If we leave now, we should get there close to low tide. The sand by the beach there is hard and smooth, easy to walk on. Sometimes there's hundreds of starfish lying all around." He helped her into her seat.

"I'd love to see that."

"After we walk along the beach a ways, we'll see an old shipwreck stuck in the sand, some old schooner. Don't know how long it's been there. But if the tide is low enough, we can walk right through the middle of it." He snapped the reins. "Let's go, boy."

John had felt the wind full in his face as Shasta circled back, heading east. In the next moment, his daydream clashed with reality, as a sudden wind whipped the raincoat right off his head.

Robert caught it just before it fell in the water. Both he and Ramón were sitting up, taking what comfort they could in the wealth of the breeze. John looked around, saddened that this moment with Laura had vanished so abruptly.

"By my guess, you've still got about ten minutes with the raincoat, John." It was Ramón.

"That's all right," he said. "You take a turn."

Robert handed it to the ambassador.

John closed his eyes again, trying to see Laura, but it was no use. He thought about what he'd said to her, the joy of walking along the beach together through a shipwreck. It didn't seem real then. A shipwreck. Not something to consider. Not something that actually happens to people.

He thought of the victims of that shipwreck near Black Point with something close to jealousy. Their ship had wrecked on the rocks near the shore. Most of them had probably survived. A simple matter of swimming a few dozen yards to the beach.

What he would give to see a shoreline again.

The next hour passed in silence. The earlier breeze had disappeared. The full heat of the sun once again took its toll. A growing weariness overwhelmed him, and he lay down to sleep. He wouldn't be at all surprised if he didn't awake again.

For the first time since boarding the *Cutlass*, Laura felt hot, even in the shade. During the afternoon, the sun had sapped what little energy she had left for the day. All the women were hot, but no one complained. The sails hung almost limp from the spars, only moving slightly for the occasional breeze. The *Cutlass* was barely moving. She knew this would likely delay their arrival in New York, but she was in no hurry.

There had been little activity on the ship that afternoon and barely any conversation. Except for Captain Meade occasionally yelling orders to his men. They appeared to be trying different experiments, anything to get the ship to move.

The one hope of relief was the setting sun. She stood up and got in line for dinner rations. The women coming away from the food line carried even less gruel in their bowls than they had at breakfast. The odd thing was, this concerned her. She really was hungry, enough to find herself longing for something nearly inedible.

As she drew close to the wooden table, Smitty dished things out. She had never seen him smile, and it wasn't his custom to engage the ladies in small talk. But his face now was almost a scowl, as if deep in thought or else harboring some significant offense. She glanced at Micah off to the side washing bowls, smiling as he customarily did. When he saw her, he widened his grin further still.

Laura turned and realized she was the last in line. She looked down into the big bowl and realized it was almost empty. Smitty scraped the sides just to come up with enough to form her serving.

"Ma'am," he said, nodding to her. He took the big bowl away and set it down beside Micah. He looked up at Captain Meade, who'd been standing on the deck above, looking over the rail at the proceedings. "A word with you, Captain, if I may," Smitty said.

The captain nodded then descended the wooden stairs.

Laura took her bowl and stood off to the side, far enough to give the appearance of distance, but she wanted to hear what the two men said.

"Captain," Smitty said, "I know you gave orders to feed the women first, and I been cutting their rations steadily throughout the day, but look. The bowl's empty. I don't have enough for the men."

"Just make some more," the captain said quietly. "Do it below. They can eat in my quarters. I'll eat when they're through."

"That's just it, sir. Based on what you said, I divided up what we had into bags, so we'd have enough to make it to New York. You said you thought we'd be getting there by tomorrow afternoon. Begging the captain's pardon, but I'm guessing with the wind dying down, that won't happen now. I've already used most of tomorrow's ration to finish out today."

"Smitty, just tell me . . . when will the food run out?"

"That's the point, sir. I have enough to scrape something up for the men tonight, then barely enough for breakfast tomorrow. After that, the cupboard's bare."

19

"I declare, two nights in a row. Gonna be mighty hard on ole Micah here after you ladies leave." He was staring at the sunset, happy as could be. Crabby was lying behind him, half asleep.

Laura didn't find the sky quite as amazing as last night, but it was hard not to stand in awe. The sea was the calmest she'd ever seen. They stood near the bow. She looked down the railing toward the stern, as last night, totally lined with women taking in the view. Small groups of children played some kind of game on the deck near the mainmast. "Did you hear about the food?" Laura whispered.

Micah looked at her, his expression unchanged. "Mean about it being gone?" he whispered back.

She nodded.

He looked back at the sunset.

"You're not concerned?"

"It'll be all right."

The food was awful and Laura was a bit perplexed at her own measure of alarm. But she'd never faced a time when . . . there wasn't any. Before she'd met John, she didn't always have money for new clothes or hats or books, but she'd never faced hunger.

"I gone hungry many a time. 'Afore it ever gets too far, though, the Lord always provide. Can't see him saving all you ladies and all them chillun, only to let y'all starve out here. Don't seem his way."

He said it with such certainty.

"You wait and see. Lord make the wind to pick up or bring some ship our way." He looked at her and smiled. "It'll be all right, you'll see."

"I wish I had your level of faith," she said. She felt a certain confidence just being with him.

"You doin' all right, you ask me. All you been through."

She had been through a lot. A picture of his scarred back flashed into her mind. She thought about what he'd said yesterday, how many times he'd been beaten. About watching his son being dragged away.

He'd been through a good deal more.

They stood in silence a few moments. He looked back at the sunset. She had many questions. "That was a brave thing you did today, saving that woman." He kept looking at the sky, but she saw his smile get bigger. "I have to say, I was shocked when you jumped into the water. How did you learn to swim like that?"

"Well," he said, turning to her. He scratched his chin.

"Actually, I am curious about that, but that wasn't what shocked me." She took a deep breath. "Don't answer this if it's inappropriate or it makes you feel uncomfortable."

He looked confused.

"It was your back," she whispered. "Before you jumped in the water, you took off your shirt. All those scars . . . I've never seen, I mean . . . how did you survive something like that?"

"It weren't just one whuppin'. Maybe four or five good ones

done that. Truth is, your first question about my swimmin' and how I got all them scars got the same answer."

Now she was confused.

"See, when I was younger, much younger, I didn't want to be no man's slave. All I could think about was running away."

"I can understand why."

"Well, the first time I's only fifteen. Got as far as the first river. That's when I knew I had to learn me to swim. Can't get far you can't swim rivers. They all over the place down South." He turned around to face her, his back against the railing. She sat on a wooden box nearby.

"Got my first whuppin' when the dogs traced me to the river's edge."

"Where was this?"

"Near a place called Beaufort, a ways south of Charleston. Where my second massah took me." He smiled. "Maybe I couldn't swim, but I sure could climb. Saw them dogs runnin' at me, yes'm, I sure could climb. But they got me down from that tree, those men pointin' they rifles at my face. They drag me toward this wagon, them dogs bitin' at me all the while. See here?" He turned his forearms over.

Laura saw maybe a dozen little pink specks on both.

"Still there after all these years. They tied me up, throwed me into the back of that wagon. Ride all the way back to Beaufort. Ain't had no food or water the whole time I been gone, and they wouldn't give me none when we got back."

"How many days?"

"Maybe three or four by then. But that was nothin' compared to what come next. My massah—when he see me—his eyes full of fire. Shoutin' about how good he been to me, and after all he done for me, this how I repay him. Had his men drag me into the back corner of the barn where they hang all the tobacco to dry. So dark in there. They tie me up so my feet be hangin' off the ground. Then he whup me with a strap, hard as he can, must be twenty, thirty times. I'm screamin' how sorry I am, how I never gonna do this again, but he don't hear me over all his yellin' about how he gonna teach me a lesson I never gonna forget. Finally, I just stop screamin' 'cause I be so weak and on account of the pain."

It was the most horrible story she had ever heard.

"Then they just leave me there, two full days, hanging like them leaves."

"No one looked after your wounds?"

"No, ma'am. Brung me no food or water neither." He looked up toward the sky. "I's just a boy, really. That first time I wasn't runnin' to be free. Just wanted to find my mama, be back home for a while." His eyes got watery, but he wiped them with his hand.

Laura got teary also. She couldn't fathom people treating each other this way. But she knew it must go on all the time in the South. Even now, young slaves were probably running away, getting caught, and being beaten just like Micah had been. She wondered how many were hanging right now in dark barns and cellars, their backs in shreds, hungry and afraid.

"Well," he said, turning back around to face the sunset. "Guess you could say I didn't learn my lesson."

"You ran away again?"

"Five mo' times in the next ten years. Each time I get a little farther. One time got all the way to Richmond. I's free almost four weeks in a row."

"And each time you got beaten like the first?"

"All but that last time I did. My massah didn't wanna pay to have me sent back, so he sold me right there in Richmond. My new massah brung me back to Fredericksburg. That's where I stayed. Where I had my wife and my three chillun.

That massah told me if I don't run, I could have me a family. But he don't tell me, when they get older, he gonna sell 'em off, one by one."

Laura stood up and walked to the spot on the railing next to Micah. She wanted to quickly change the subject for him. "So you stopped running away once you got to Fredericksburg."

"I did. I was gettin' too old and too tired to keep tryin.' Figured God must want me to be a slave for some reason. Why, even my own people helped me get caught. Twice it was other slaves turned me in. They hid me and fed me, said they'd help me. But then they give me up. One of my worst beatings was at the hand of another slave, a foreman this one massah put in charge of all the rest. For a white man's title, some better food, and a nicer roof over his head, he treat his own kind somethin' awful. So I decided to stay put. Take life as it comes. How I spent the next thirty years, right up until the cap'n bought me."

He looked over at her. "Pains me to tell it."

"I'm so sorry, Micah. I shouldn't have pried."

"No, I don't mind you hearing the worst part, long as I tell you the best part. The part why I *really* don't have to run away no more."

"I'd like to hear that."

"Somethin' Eli read me one of them times he was reading from the Bible. Gospel of John, I think. Somethin' Jesus say. Soon as I heard it, I knew I'd never fo'get it. Had Eli read it to me three times. Jesus say, 'Whoever committeth sin is a slave of sin, and a slave does not abideth in the house forever, but a son do. They'fore, if the Son maketh you free, you be free indeed.' All at once it come to me . . . no man is free when his heart ain't free. All them massahs I have, and all the bad things they done to me . . . they may be free the way man see it, but not the way Jesus see it. 'Cause they ain't free in here." He pointed to his heart. "But if Jesus can make my heart free, can't no man make a slave of me. Maybe they can on this earth, the way man judge a thing. But one day, God will set everythin' right. 'Tween then and now, Jesus set my heart free from all the hate and fear and sadness inside. And . . . if the Son maketh you free, you be free indeed."

His big, radiant smile returned.

Laura pondered again how this man who had lost everything dear to him in this world had come to possess such a profound faith in the world to come. It was so strong, it allowed him to soar, almost effortlessly, above all the hatred and fear and sadness. Things she still battled in her heart every day.

Lately, every minute of the day.

With all she had gained in this world and, even now, with all she had lost, her own faith seemed so shallow, so ineffective. She longed to know the freedom Micah enjoyed. Hearing his story did yield one immediate benefit: it allowed her to temporarily set her own losses aside. But she couldn't help but wonder what John would do if he had just heard this same story. He would find a way to help Micah.

Somehow.

She had no idea what she could possibly do, but she also knew somehow she must try.

20

"Micah, Captain needs you. Downstairs in his cabin." It was Maylor, the first mate.

"Yessuh, Missuh Maylor." Micah stood. "Been such a pleasure chattin' with you, Mrs. Foster."

"It's been my honor." She glanced at Maylor, who seemed totally bewildered by her remark.

As Micah climbed down the wooden stairway, Maylor said, "Captain needs you to clean up. The men ate in his quarters tonight. Shouldn't take you too long."

Laura said, "Can I help?"

"Sorry, ma'am. Captain said he just wanted Micah on this." He turned, and both men disappeared below.

Laura turned and looked back at the sunset, the brightest colors all drained away. But it was still something to see the sky mirrored so perfectly against the ocean. She realized that the serenity of this scene would be lost on Captain Meade and his men. For them, it meant just one thing: dead sails. She leaned over the railing and noticed the ship hardly moving at all. But at least her talk with Micah had dispelled any concerns of want and starvation.

"Don't tell me you're going over the rail now."

Laura stood up straight and turned to see Melissa smiling at her. "Can't say I haven't thought about it a time or two," she said.

"That was a nice thing you did for that woman today."

"I didn't do anything."

"Yes, you did," said Melissa. "It's one thing to talk about helping someone or feeling sympathy. You take action. You reached right into your gold pouch and helped everyone see what they could do for her. When it was over . . . well, it was the first time I've seen so many smiles on this ship."

"Thank you," Laura said. "Guess it must be nice not to have to hide your smiles so much."

"It really is. Although I don't see how this benevolent mood can last. Everyone's back to staring out to sea, with nothing but time on their hands."

"Well, if that happens, you keep your smile. You have no reason to feel guilty, just because you haven't suffered a loss. Where do you suppose he is now, your Tom?"

Melissa's face lit up. "He should be waiting for me in New York. Tomorrow is the day the *Vandervere* was supposed to arrive."

Laura had completely forgotten.

"Looks like we could be a few days late. Well, I think I'm going to head toward the bow, see if I can catch some kind of breeze." They exchanged smiles, and she walked away.

Laura stared out to sea. She stood there a number of minutes. For the moment her mind was as calm as the water. When she looked to her left, Melissa was standing beside her again.

"It's no better up there," she said. For a few moments, neither said a word. "I know we don't know each other, Laura, but I want you to know, I am sorry for your loss. What was your husband's name?"

Laura hated hearing John spoken of in the past tense.

"John," she said. She wanted to change the subject quickly. "So, what brought you out to San Francisco?"

"I needed to get away from Philadelphia. Tom and I were in love, at least I thought we were. But his family wanted him to marry a girl from another family—a better family, socially speaking. They pressured him and he finally gave in, and we broke it off."

"Were you engaged?"

"Not officially, but I was sure he was about to ask me any day. Instead, he wrote me a letter explaining how he did love me but that we could never be together."

"I'm sorry—what an awful thing to do."

"The worst day of my life. My brother invited me to come out West with him so I wouldn't have to face the pain every day. So, I left."

"I went out West with my brother too," Laura said. "Three years ago. His name is Michael. Our cousin went with us. They helped me get situated in San Francisco, then they headed north looking for gold."

It pained her to think of it now, but the hundreds, actually thousands, of men in San Francisco formed the strength of her brother's appeal for Laura to join them. Their parents had died the year before, and Michael had decided to use his part of the inheritance to join the gold rush. "Laura," he'd said, "there aren't any men left in the church or in the neighborhood to pursue you. They've all married or moved away. I've read in San Francisco there are at least five men for every woman. You're bound to find someone to marry you. Please come with us."

Michael could be kind, but he had no idea how much he'd hurt her talking this way. No matter the humiliation, it had worked. Remembering this now, though, only added to her sorrow. The truth was, no one had wanted her back East, and in San Francisco there had only been John. In her whole life there had only ever been John.

And now he was gone.

Pretending more interest than she felt, she turned her attention back to Melissa. "Obviously, your Tom had a change of heart," she said quickly.

"Yes! He did," said Melissa. "At the end of July he wrote me this wonderfully long letter begging my forgiveness and proposing marriage."

"What happened?" It was actually helping to hear all this.

"He said he knew he could never be happy with anyone but me, and finally persuaded his parents to change their minds. His mother was the main obstacle, but Tom said even she gave in. He said he wouldn't give her a moment's peace until she did."

"I'm happy for you," said Laura, glad to feel any measure of happiness inside.

Even if only for a few moments, even if only for someone else.

His pockets were full.

It amazed Ayden Maul, how heavy this stuff was. At the most, he'd only held a small nugget before, and that had belonged to someone else.

But this . . . was all his.

He folded over the last blanket from the last stash of gold he'd stolen from and slowly panned the room. The hold looked just as he'd found it. It was hard to pull himself away. Mustn't get greedy, he thought. Better to leave now before he got caught. Besides, with the winds dying down he had at least one more night to come back for a third dip.

He turned toward the stairs when he heard that stupid dog

scratching and sniffing at the hatch overhead. He'd closed it over before he went down, to give himself a little warning should anyone come. "Get out of here," he whispered angrily. "Stupid mutt."

But the dog ignored him.

21

"Whatcha got there, girl?" Micah asked.

Laura heard him and walked across the forecastle deck, sidestepping around two sleeping children. She stopped at a wooden rail that divided it from the main deck below. Micah walked across the main deck, carrying a stack of cut sails. Crabby was a few yards away, sniffing and pawing at the hatch that covered the hold where the ladies slept.

"You know you ain't allowed down there, girl. Come over here."

Crabby looked at him but instantly returned to her task. Maybe someone had left a bowl of gruel below, Laura thought. Hard to imagine it generating such interest, but Micah insisted she couldn't get enough to suit her. Micah set the sails down and walked over to her. He bent down and patted her on the head. Her tail wagged, but she kept pawing at the hatch.

Just then Micah's head cocked to the side, as if he'd heard a strange noise. He lifted the hatch lid. "Stay here, Crabby," he said and started to climb down.

Ayden Maul backed away from the stairs when he heard the hatch lid open. He picked up the small pile of damp blankets he'd brought down, to serve as his excuse should anyone catch him there. He watched as a pair of beat-up shoes came down the steps, followed by a pair of torn pants.

Shoot, he thought. Ain't nobody but that dumb old slave.

"Oh, it's you, Missuh Maul."

"Just me," Maul said. "Just thought I'd gather up these damp blankets down here. Some of the ladies must have left 'em. Ain't gonna dry down here overnight."

"Mighty kind of you, suh. But you ain't gotta be doin' that. That's Micah's job."

"I don't mind."

"Well, since you here, mind if I go back and get some of those cut sails I's fixin' to bring down? They done dried already."

Maul just wanted out of there quick. He felt the weight of the gold against his legs. "All right," he said, hiding his annoyance.

"Here, I'll take them wet things and bring 'em up. Then I'll hand down the dry ones. You don't gotta do nothin' but set 'em down somewhere. I'll pass 'em out."

Micah waited a moment.

"Okay, go." He handed Micah the blankets. Micah turned and went back upstairs. Maul followed him and waited by the opening.

"Here you go, Missuh Maul." Micah walked halfway down and handed him a stack. "Just one more stack and we done." A moment later, Micah returned. "Here you go."

Maul took the second stack, set them next to the first, then waited for Micah to come down the stairs.

"Thank you, suh," Micah said and stepped aside to let Maul climb up.

Maul stopped after a few steps and looked up. "Can you call your dog off?"

"She'll back away as you go up," Micah said.

"Even after yesterday . . . what I did to her?"

"Crabby? She already forgave you for that. You'll see."

Maul climbed a few more steps, but the dog didn't back off. In fact, she growled. "Let me by, you stupid dog," he yelled, then slapped his palm hard against the wood. When he did, his left foot slipped a stair. He almost fell but caught himself.

Then he watched as three gold nuggets fell out of his left pants pocket and skipped down the stairs. They slid across the deck like dice. Maul looked at Micah; he was staring at the nuggets. Quickly Maul grabbed the hatch and slammed it shut, then hurried down the stairs. Micah backed up, his eyes white with fear.

"Missuh Maul, what you doin' . . . you stealin' from these ladies?"

"Shut up," he said. He pushed Micah, hard. Micah fell back and tripped over a carpetbag.

Maul bent down and scooped up the three nuggets. He turned back toward the stairs.

"Missuh Maul, I can't let you do that. That's all them ladies got in the world."

Maul got up the first step. Micah ran toward him. Maul kicked him in the chest, and he fell back again. "You say a word about this, to anyone, and I'll kill you." But Micah got right back up and came at him. Maul couldn't believe it. The slave grabbed his leg and pulled. Maul kicked him again.

Just then Crabby started barking through the closed hatch. Maul knew someone would be coming any minute. He hurried down the stairs and tackled Micah. They fell to the deck. More gold nuggets spilled. Maul got behind him and dragged Micah up by his shoulders. Maul reached into his pocket, grabbed a large handful of nuggets, and slipped them into

Micah's pocket. He spun him around and punched him in the face. Micah staggered back against the wall.

The hatch door lifted.

Crabby was the first to come down. She ran right for Maul and attacked him, growling and biting him. Maul kicked her away. She howled in pain and limped over to Micah. Then Maylor, the first mate, came down, followed by Lieutenant Ashcroft.

Then that Foster woman.

"What's going on here?" Maylor yelled.

Maul reached over and grabbed Micah by his lapels. "Caught this slave down here stealing gold."

"I find that hard to believe," said Ashcroft.

"Let go of him," Maylor said to Maul. "Micah, is this true?"

"No, suh, I'd never steal from these ladies."

"I saw you," Maul shouted, raising his hand as if to strike him again.

"Put your hand down, Maul," yelled Ashcroft, taking a few steps toward him.

This is nonsense, thought Laura. Two older ladies came down the stairs, followed by Melissa. Laura made room for them.

"Mr. Maul," Maylor said. "I'm afraid we'll need more than your say-so to believe such accusations."

"You got more than my say-so," said Maul. "Check his pockets. He was shoving gold in them when I came down and caught him."

Maylor looked at Micah, gravely concerned.

"Suh, I ain't took no gold. See . . ." Micah reached his hand in one pocket and pulled it inside out. He reached his hand in the other, and his face instantly fell. He looked down, shook his head, but didn't move.

"Micah, let me see," Maylor said.

Laura was confused. She looked at Maul, noticed a slight grin.

"I didn't take these, Missuh Maylor. Honest, I didn't." Micah held out a palm full of gold nuggets.

The older ladies gasped.

"Micah," said Maylor, disgust in his tone.

Laura looked at each face. They were all buying this sham.

"Told you," said Maul. "Should I get the captain, sir?"

"Guess you better," said Maylor.

"But suh," Micah protested, "I's the one came down here and caught him stealin'. Honest, God is my witness."

"Save it for the captain," Maylor said.

Maul walked toward the stairs.

"Wait a minute," Laura said loudly. "This is absurd. Mr. Maylor, you know Micah didn't take that gold."

"Ma'am, this ain't your business," Maul said, walking past her.

"Mr. Maul is lying," she said. Everyone looked at her.

"What?" Maul said, as if deeply offended. "How dare you."

"Mrs. Foster," Maylor said. "How could you know that?" Maul continued up the steps. "Hold up, Maul."

"I saw Micah on deck just a few minutes ago," she said. "Didn't Mr. Maul say he caught Micah stealing when he came down here?"

"Yes," said Maylor.

"How could that be? That means Micah would have to be down here already." She looked around. "Isn't this hatch the only way in here?"

"It is."

"Then Mr. Maul has to be lying," she said. "I was on the

forecastle deck. The hatch lid was closed. Crabby was sniffing and scratching at it. I saw Micah go over to her. I saw him come down here. Mr. Maul was nowhere in sight. I kept watching right up until you and Lieutenant Ashcroft came down. That can only mean Mr. Maul was already down here, before Micah came."

"That's the truth, Missuh Maylor. What she's saying. I come down 'cause Crabby makin' such a fuss, and Missuh Maul already here."

"You're lying," Maul shouted. "Both of you."

"Come down here, Maul," Maylor said. "Lieutenant Ashcroft, will you please get the captain?"

"Gladly."

"Sir, you know these two are friends," Maul said. "Look at the way they ganged up on me yesterday. She'd say anything to protect him. How do you explain the gold in his pockets?"

"Mrs. Foster, we did catch Micah with the gold."

"*He* musta put them there," said Micah, pointing at Maul, "when he was fightin' me."

"Why don't you check Mr. Maul's pockets?" Laura asked, playing a hunch.

Everyone looked at Maul.

"What, you gonna listen to her now?" Maul asked.

"Show me your pockets," said Maylor.

"I will not. This is ridiculous."

"I wasn't asking, Maul."

Maul stalled a moment. He looked toward the top of the hatch. Laura had the impression he thought of running but realized he had nowhere to go. His shoulders slumped, and he obeyed. One pocket held a small handful of gold, the other was filled with it. The room was thick with tension. Laura looked at the women, their faces in shock.

Lieutenant Ashcroft came down the stairs, followed by

Captain Meade. "What's going on here?" the captain said. "Lieutenant Aschroft tells me we have a thief on board. Mr. Maylor, have you sorted this out?"

"I'm afraid I have, sir." He spent a few minutes briefing the captain on the events that had just occurred.

When he finished, Captain Meade turned to Maul. "To me, Maul, you are the lowest of the low. It's one thing for a man to steal bread when he's hungry. But to steal the last savings from a group of widows in distress is despicable. I can't imagine how a man could stoop to such a thing. Mr. Maylor?"

"Yes, sir."

"Check Maul here from head to toe. Make sure you get every last nugget of gold. Then take two men and bring him to my quarters for a dozen lashes. He cries out, he gets a dozen more."

"Yes, sir."

"Then I want this thief confined to quarters for the remainder of our voyage. By confined, I mean he is to be tied there. He doesn't move anywhere on this ship without escort. Maul, the moment we anchor in New York I want you off my ship."

Maylor walked over and grabbed Maul's shirt and pushed him toward the stairs. Laura looked away as they climbed out of sight.

"Captain," Laura said, "seems we owe Micah our gratitude. Apart from his actions, Mr. Maul might have gotten away with his theft."

"Well done, Micah," the captain said.

"Hear, hear," said Lieutenant Ashcroft.

Melissa and the other women offered their thanks.

Micah picked up Crabby and patted her head. "Y'all been through so much," he said. "But Captain, I think you better have someone check around Missuh Maul's bunk for more gold. I's up on deck last night, saw him coming out of here about this same time."

An hour later, Maul sat alone in his bunk. His back stung with the smallest motion. It was dark, his wrists were tied, his gold . . . it was gone, all gone. Instead of leaving this ship a rich man, he would leave it penniless as before. And humiliated.

He swore to himself, someone would pay dearly for this. That Foster woman. As soon as she got clear of the ship in New York . . . he would exact his revenge.

22

The sun had set long ago. It was a moonless night. But the stars were out, allowing the men on the raft to see each other fairly well. No one moved. No one had moved for hours. John sat with his knees pulled to his chest, his arms crossed, his head resting on them like a pillow.

It had been a difficult day.

John wasn't sure how many more men had given up and drowned. Just before dark, he'd glanced across the group floating together and saw a number of empty tables and hatch doors drifting away. He had little fight left in him. The hunger pangs had subsided, but the thirst was still so strong. A slow torture, draining his life away.

"Are you awake, John?" It was the ambassador.

Talking was like a task. It took work to move his lips. "Barely."

"I don't think I can face the sun again tomorrow," said Ramón. "I've never felt so weak."

"I don't even want to think about tomorrow," John said.

"I suppose we really aren't going to survive this. I truly hoped we might. Are you awake, Robert?" Ramón asked.

Robert didn't respond. John realized that was what Ramón was hoping for.

"I really do appreciate what you tried to say earlier," Ramón said quietly. "I may have pretended not to care, but at this moment, I think . . . I think I might want to hear what you were trying to say."

John assumed he was talking about his feeble attempt at sharing the change God had made in his life.

"When you were asleep, Robert and I actually talked about it a little, exchanging our pathetic tales. Turns out our stories are similar."

John looked over at Robert, sound asleep. Even in the starlight, John could see blisters on his lips.

"I don't think I've thought about God since my childhood," Ramón said.

"I didn't either," John said, "until I moved to San Francisco. I even skipped attending church the first few Sundays. Figured who'd know. But guilt got the better of me. I picked one close to my house and hid in the back row. But for the first time, I heard a man explain things plainly." John glanced at Ramón.

Over the next few minutes, John did his best to communicate the thing that had made the biggest difference for him when listening to that pastor. It was the difference between faith and good deeds, of trusting in what Christ did on the cross for him instead of trying to earn his way to heaven. As he finished, he hit an invisible wall of fatigue. "I'm sorry," he said. "I'm probably not making any sense."

"I think I understand, John. And I hope you're right. Or there's no hope for me. At this moment, I'm quite certain my good deeds are lagging far behind. I see no chance of ever catching up."

John smiled, then winced at the pain it caused.

Ramón turned away, looked out over the water. "I wish

I'd spent more time with my family," he said. "Especially my children."

"How old are they?" John asked.

"I have two boys, thirteen and ten, and my little girl, Adriana. She's eight." He smiled as he said her name. "They loved me, at least I think they did. I was hardly home but a few months a year."

John wondered if he knew he talked about himself in the past tense. "How about your wife?"

"Regina, a good woman. But we were not that close. Our families were both wealthy. An arranged marriage. I was eighteen, she was fifteen. What did I know of being married? I was a boy. We cared for each other . . . in our own way. Perhaps we even loved each other. But all this talk . . . I am suddenly so tired. What about you, John? Do you have any energy left to tell me of your bride? I can tell . . . you married for love."

John smiled. His lips were cracked, his cheeks were chafed and burned, but he didn't care. "I certainly did." A gentle breeze started to blow.

"Do you feel that, John?"

"I do." It felt wonderful. "Her name is Laura."

"Laura . . . is a nice name. Tell me of Laura."

So John did.

He talked about how they met in South Park. The surprising depths of their conversations. The places his horse Shasta had taken them. Breakfast at Sans Souci, dances at the Apollo Hall. Reading books together by the bay on rare moments when the wind didn't blow. He talked for ten minutes, maybe more. He talked slowly, restraining most of the words that rushed through his heart.

In the middle of telling how he'd proposed to Laura, his strength ran out. He laid his head back on his arms. For a few moments, neither man spoke. "Give me a few minutes," John said. "And I'll finish."

"It's all right, John. It's obvious . . . she said yes."

He smiled, too weak to lift his head.

"Now I understand why you fight so hard to live," said Ramón. "With such a woman by your side, you have much to live for."

For a few moments, there was only the sound of a growing wind and gentle waves lapping over the raft's edge.

"Could it be that simple?" Ramón asked quietly, as if thinking aloud.

John knew what he meant. "It is," John said. "Just pray, Ramón. He will save you, even now, even out here."

Ramón smiled. John smiled back. His mouth felt like it was tearing at the edges.

"I must sleep now, John. But thank you for your words."

John laid his head down on his arms. Weariness and fatigue enveloped him. His breathing slowed to an almost dormant rhythm. He knew sleep must come but feared, should he give in, what would keep him from falling into the water? And if he did, how would he ever make it back to the raft? Even if he made it through till morning, if he was this weak at night, how could he endure another day in the blistering sun?

Until now, he'd held out hope that his survival thus far might be a sign that God would return him to his beloved.

But that hope had faded.

23

Laura stepped out on deck, instantly shielding her eyes from the morning sun. The wind was blowing again. The crew climbed up and down the rope ladders, releasing the sails to take full advantage. Captain Meade shouted out orders, using terms she didn't understand. She leaned over the rail; the ship was definitely moving.

About half the women and children stood along the rails or walked about the deck. She noticed the wooden table was in place, the one used to serve breakfast, but Smitty was nowhere in sight. Micah scrubbed a section of deck just beside the table. Crabby lay beside him. A little girl sat next to Crabby, petting her back. The little girl said something that made Micah laugh. Crabby wagged her tail and appeared to be smiling.

Just then Smitty appeared from the galley doorway, carrying the now familiar bowl of gruel. He didn't set it down on the table. Instead, he called up to the captain, who turned and peered over the rail. Captain Meade shook his head. Smitty said something and the captain nodded. Smitty said something else to Micah, then set the bowl on the table.

"Ladies," Captain Meade called out. "Excuse me, ladies . . . would you all gather around?"

In a few moments, those on deck formed a half circle around the captain. Several more hurried up the steps from below. Laura saw Micah quickly trying to dry the deck area he'd just cleaned. He picked up his bucket and hurried below.

"Thank you, ladies," said Captain Meade. "I have some difficult things to discuss with you." He paused and took a deep breath. "This being a small ship, I felt it best to speak freely rather than let even worse rumors spread. First, I'm sure most of you are aware of the incident last night. Don't know what you've heard, but I'm sad to report one of my men—the newest man—has turned out to be a thief. But thanks to the quick action of my man Micah and Mrs. Foster's sharp mind, he was caught in the act and we recovered everything he stole."

Many of the ladies turned to face Laura, their faces a mixture of confusion and thanks. An awkward applause followed.

"Can I see a show of hands," the captain said, "for those who brought gold aboard, how many know exactly how much gold you should have?" He looked around, but no hands raised. "So none of you know how much might have been stolen?"

"We all left the *Vandervere* so quickly," one lady replied. "There was no time to count anything."

"I understand," said the captain. "Then the only fair way I can think of to repay you is . . . after breakfast, I'll be in my quarters. Mr. Maylor here, my first mate, will take a seat at this table. All you ladies who kept your gold below, bring it to him. He won't take it, just get a head count. He'll tell me how many, and I'll divide the gold that was stolen in equal parts. Then you come, one by one, to my cabin, and I'll give the gold back to you."

To Laura, the clamor of voices expressed mostly approval of the plan. But one elderly woman yelled, "How are we going to know this won't happen again? I don't mean any disrespect, Captain, but that gold is all I have left to live on. Will we have to take turns guarding it ourselves?"

"I understand, ma'am," said Captain Meade. "I'm sorry to put you all through this. But trust me, the thief is confined to his quarters. He will not bother you again. And I've instructed my crew, no one else is allowed into the hold until you leave this ship. Except Micah, that is."

"How do we know we can trust him?" someone yelled out.

"Ladies . . . if it weren't for Micah, we wouldn't even know the gold had been stolen, let alone have it all back, ready to return to its rightful owners. I'd trust Micah with my life."

That silenced any remaining concerns.

Laura looked around for Micah but didn't see him anywhere. A pity he didn't hear what the captain just said. But it did give her an idea, a way to finally do something to help.

"Ladies, there's more," said Captain Meade. "I'm sure you're aware breakfast is being served a little late this morning. The wind has picked up a bit, but yesterday we lost an entire day, and we were already low on provisions. To put it plainly, we are almost out of food. In fact, there is only enough to feed the children this morning."

Laura expected this announcement. The mood instantly became somber.

"How long until we reach New York?" someone asked.

"If this wind stays steady, we could be there late tomorrow," said Captain Meade.

"So we have nothing to eat until then?"

"That's . . . about the size of it. But I have another option. Wanted to let you ladies be a part of this decision, since it involves you and especially your children. I could change course slightly, still head north but shift to the east a bit. I planned to bring you all the way to New York. In fact, someone told me today is the day your steamship is expected there. But the sea isn't obliged to follow our plans. Been at this most of my life and, believe me, this is normal. Anyway, we may yet see another ship on this new course that might share some provisions with us. That would allow us to keep going north till we reach New York. But if we don't, I can have us into Norfolk, Virginia, by nightfall."

"Virginia?" a young mother cried. "All my family will be waiting in New York. How will we get there from Virginia?"

"Ma'am . . . that's the thing, see. You'll have to fend for yourselves from that point. I suppose some of you can book another ship to New York. Some can take a train. Or . . . I can keep us going straight north until we all get to New York. You won't eat for two days, and neither will your children after breakfast, but my men have gone without food much longer than that, so they'll be fine with either decision."

"Will we have water?" someone asked.

"Plenty of water, either way," he said.

"Captain," another woman yelled, "I'm sure I speak for all the ladies. We want to thank you and all your crew. First for rescuing us. And now, for sharing your food with us. Clearly, you'd have plenty if it were just your men on board." This seemed to instantly reset the mood, and the women erupted in strong applause.

"Thank you, ladies." The captain's mood seemed to lighten again. "I'm going to head down to my cabin a spell. Those of you with children can get them fed. Then you all talk about which of the two places you want to go. Let me know what you decide." He stepped away from the rail, and the crowd began to disperse.

Laura hoped the captain's good mood might continue long enough until she could meet with him and explain her idea, the one she came up with to help Micah.

24

An hour later, the children had all been fed, and a head count had been taken for those whose gold had been stolen. After a spirited debate, the majority had decided Norfolk would be best, for the sake of the children.

Laura didn't care either way.

A new line had formed, leading to Captain Meade's cabin. Because she'd kept her gold with her, she didn't have any gold coming. But she couldn't think of a better opportunity to speak privately to the captain. She'd tried to get at the end of the line, but a number of older women came in behind her.

She stood by the captain's door. Everyone else had gone in and come out in just a few minutes. The door opened. It was Melissa.

"Such a nice man," she said, smiling as she walked past.

"Come in, Mrs. Foster." Captain Meade was smiling, sitting behind a thick oak desk.

She was terribly nervous. She walked in and sat down. The room was spacious compared to anywhere else on this ship, but no bigger than her small spare bedroom back in San Francisco. She looked briefly out the three windows along the back wall, eyeing the wake of the ship as it cut a path through the emerald sea.

"Nice to be seeing a wake again," said the captain.

"Yes," she said. To the right was his bunk, built into the port side. Above it, three shelves of books. There it was, the one book she had wanted to see.

His Bible.

"You've got your pouch of gold, I see," said the captain, obviously trying to move things along. On the desk beside his left arm were four small piles of gold nuggets. He slid one off by itself. "If you'll hand it to me, I'll put these right in there."

"Actually, Captain, I'm not here for gold. I've kept mine tied to my waist the whole time. But I thought this might give me a chance to talk with you briefly. There's something I'd like to ask you to consider."

The captain leaned back. "Well, Mrs. Foster, ask away. If I can oblige, I most certainly will. You've been quite an asset ever since you've come aboard. Especially last night, helping clear up who the real thief was. Even the other day, when Maul was beating on poor old Micah."

"Well, actually . . . it's poor old Micah I wanted to talk to you about."

"Oh?"

"He's your slave, correct?"

"Yes." He sat up. "Paid eight hundred dollars for him three years ago."

It sounded so unbelievably wrong, but he said it without a thought. "I don't know exactly how to say this." She glanced over at his Bible. "I've had a few conversations with Micah. He's told me you are a Christian, and you even read your Bible on a regular basis. I see it, right over there."

His expression became serious. "I am . . . and I do. But I

don't see how that should concern you. Have I acted in an un-Christianly manner somehow?"

"No, sir. You have been a remarkable demonstration of Christian care and service to us the entire time."

He exhaled a relieved sigh.

"It's . . . well, it's Micah. I . . . I don't understand how you can keep him here, on this ship, as your slave."

"Mrs. Foster, keeping slaves is not un-Christian. In fact, the Bible teaches it is perfectly fine, long as you treat them with respect."

"You think the Bible says it's fine for one man to enslave another?"

"Enslave? I haven't enslaved anyone. Micah was born a slave. Slavery's been going on in this country for hundreds of years. You ask Micah, he'll tell you I've been the best master he's ever had."

"That is what he said."

"Did he ask you to talk to me about this?"

"No, and I don't think he ever would."

"Then I think we need to bring this conversation to a close. There are a number of ladies waiting outside."

"I know. Can I speak with you about this some other time, later this afternoon, perhaps?"

"No, I don't think so. I don't think there's anything else to say."

"But Captain, how can you as a Christian keep another man—also a Christian—as your slave? How can that be something God would ever approve of?"

"Come now, Mrs. Foster, you can't be serious. Clearly you are an abolitionist. Millions of people up North are."

"I'm from the North, but now I live out West in San Francisco."

"They don't have slaves out West?"

"Not in San Francisco."

"Well, they do in the South where I come from. By the millions. I know of pastors who have slaves, and I've heard many a sermon—from my own pastor—about what the Bible says on this. I'm not doing anything wrong."

"How can you say that, sir? Do you know what slave masters from the South have done to him? Have you seen his back?"

"I'd never do that to Micah."

"And slave masters from the South have torn his family apart, one by one. He doesn't even know where his children are. How can that be something God approves of?"

The captain stood up. "I'm sorry, ma'am. But we really must end this. I don't know all the Bible verses. I couldn't quote them one by one. But they are right there in the Good Book." He pointed to his Bible. "They even had slaves in Jesus's time. He never tried to stop it, never said a word against it. I know Saint Paul talked to slaves who were Christians, told them how they ought to treat their masters. Never told them to rebel or run away, or talked about how wrong it was that they were slaves."

Laura shook her head. This was hopeless. "Captain, I beg your pardon. I didn't come here to make you angry."

Captain Meade took a deep breath, rested his large palms on the back of his chair. "I understand, Mrs. Foster. We just have a difference of opinion, is all. The whole country's divided on this. Don't see you and me solving the issue of slavery here in my cabin."

"No, you're right. I apologize for taking so much of your time."

She stood up and turned toward the door.

As she put her hand on the knob, the captain said, "Mrs. Foster, I really do appreciate all you've done on this ship. Hope there'll be no hard feelings between us."

"No, Captain. And thanks for your kind words."

Laura stepped into the dark hall. A gray-haired woman in a bonnet walked past her, glaring as she stepped through the doorway. Laura walked by the three remaining women, trying not to make eye contact. She paused in the shadows. There across the deck, framed by the doorway, was Micah on his hands and knees, scrubbing.

Crabby lay next to him, wagging her tail at something he'd just said.

25

Captain Janus Houtman was pleased.

He had been trying to get the *Angeline* back on course for the last two days. The voyage had begun back in Holland almost four weeks ago. After a stop in Southampton, he and his twelve-man crew had crossed the Atlantic uneventfully but then ran into the outer bands of a terrible hurricane. They tried to sail around it, but the storm was massive. Even on the outskirts, the wind and waves had their way with his little ship. But she'd held up well.

And now, borne on the strength of a prevailing east wind, the *Angeline* was finally making good time, plying a south-westerly course toward Charleston. A sufficient speed, it seemed, to keep the English ambassador, Giles, from offering any more ridiculous sailing suggestions.

Mr. Giles was his only passenger. The money was signifi-cant, the Englishman's fare equal to half the cargo in his hold. But Captain Houtman still regretted taking him on. Houtman stood next to the wheel, manned by his first mate, Conklin.

"He's doing it again, sir," said Conklin.

"Where?"

Conklin's eyes pointed forward. Houtman glanced toward the bow, saddened to see Mr. Giles . . . at it again.

Over the last two days, he'd asked Giles several times to stop engaging his crew in mindless chatter about politics and culture. The man appeared to have no useful skills except conversation, something entirely useless aboard his ship.

Houtman had talked to the men, to make sure; not a one cared for anything Giles had to say. They felt trapped in his net, so to speak. He'd ask questions as a pretense for dialogue, but it was a ruse. He'd quickly shift into a monologue, roaming through any number of pointless topics. Then talk until he'd wrung out every last drop that could be said on the subject. Before they could politely excuse themselves, he'd plunge into the next one.

Presently, he had young Pieter cornered by the bow.

"Steady as she goes, Mr. Conklin."

"Aye, sir."

Houtman made his way forward to rescue the lad.

As he climbed the stairs to the forecastle deck, to keep his composure in check, he reminded himself that Giles was not a part of his crew. Once again, Giles had blatantly disregarded what Houtman had told him to do. But he was not insubordinate; he didn't appear to be *able* to stop talking. Besides, Houtman reminded himself, it would all be over soon. If the winds remained steady, he'd be free of Giles this evening, tomorrow morning at the latest.

"The Dred Scott decision is fascinating. Really, Pieter, you've never heard of it?"

"No, Mr. Giles," said Pieter. "This is my first trip to the States. Mostly I'm trying to learn English words." Pieter looked over Giles's shoulder and saw Houtman. His face reflected instant relief.

"Well, Dred Scott is a Negro slave. Back in—"

"Excuse me, Mr. Giles."

"Oh, Captain. A beautiful day, don't you think?"

"A fine day. Pieter, I believe your break is over."

"Yes, sir, Captain."

"Been a pleasure chatting with you, Pieter. We'll catch up later then."

Pieter walked quickly toward the stairs.

"Uh . . . no, you won't, Mr. Giles. Are you forgetting what we talked about not two hours ago, when you were *chatting* with my cook, Willem?"

"But Captain—"

"But nothing, Mr. Giles. I assume you still hope we'll reach Charleston by nightfall."

"You assume incorrectly, sir. We must absolutely reach Charleston by nightfall. My meeting with the Southern senators is tomorrow afternoon."

"Then you must absolutely stop having these conversations with my crew. The crew of a ship works together in a certain rhythm. Your conversations disrupt that rhythm. How many times—"

"Whoa!" Pieter shouted from the main deck. "What is that? Do you see it?"

Captain Houtman and Giles both turned toward Pieter.

Several crew members, manning the ratlines on the various masts, also began to shout.

"I see it."

"There it is."

"How is that possible?"

"It's a bird," Pieter said. "See it? A big one."

Houtman tried to focus where they pointed but was no longer in possession of youthful eyes.

"It's over this side now," said Pieter.

Houtman turned, right into a pair of flapping wings. Then

feathers. A screeching sound. Something big smacked into his head. He raised his arms to fend off the attack.

Mr. Giles fell to the deck, screaming like a woman.

Houtman grabbed the bird, first by its talons, then by its beak. The bird bit his hand over and over again. Finally, Pieter rushed in. He grabbed the bird by its wings and flung it to the deck, then stomped on its neck, killing it instantly.

For a moment, there was silence.

Giles screamed out, "What was that? What is going on here?"

"Quiet, Giles," said Houtman. "Show some restraint." He looked down at his hand. It was trembling. Blood began to flow from cuts caused by the bird's beak.

Giles sat up.

"Captain, your neck is bleeding also," said Pieter.

Houtman could feel the sting now. He pulled a handkerchief from his pocket, dabbed the area, looked at the blood, then held it to his neck. Several crew members rushed to the forecastle deck to see what happened.

"Gentlemen, I'm fine. It was just a stupid bird."

"But Captain . . ." Pieter said.

"I'm fine, men. Everyone back to your posts. Just a few cuts."

The men turned and headed back, except Pieter and Willem the cook. "Would you like me to dress it up, Captain?" Willem asked. "Looks big enough to feed us all."

Giles rose to his feet. "The most bizarre thing I've ever seen."

"For me, as well," said Houtman. "I don't know, Willem. Perhaps it has some disease. Why else would it attack me like that?"

"Maybe it was just tired and looking for someplace to rest," said Pieter. "We must be seventy miles out from land."

"Still," said Houtman, "not worth the whole crew getting sick over. Pieter, toss it over the side. Let it feed the fishes."

Pieter picked it up by the tip of its wing. "What kind of bird is it?"

"Some kind of large gull," said Giles. "Not sure of the exact name, but it's a gull, I'm sure. Gulls are a fascinating species—"

"I don't want to hear about gulls, Mr. Giles," Houtman said.

"Right."

"I'm going to my quarters to dress these wounds."

"May I help?" asked Pieter.

"Yes, it will go quicker with assistance." Houtman climbed down to the main deck. As he headed for the doorway that led to his cabin, he shouted to Conklin at the wheel. "Steady as she goes, Mr. Conklin. Stay the course."

"Aye, Captain."

Just then, the strangest feeling came over him. He stopped walking. He had been at sea since he'd been a boy. He had read of birds flying out this far from land, but he'd never seen one before. And he'd certainly never been attacked by a bird aboard a ship. In fact, he had never known of anyone who had experienced what he just did.

It's just not normal, he thought. There must be a reason, some purpose. The bird attacked him as if fighting for its life. He stepped back and shouted out to the crew. "Did anyone see from which direction the bird flew?"

"I did," answered Pieter, standing right behind him. "It flew from the northeast."

"Are you certain?" Houtman asked. "You're saying the bird flew toward us from farther out at sea."

"Yes, Captain. I'm certain of it. It was the oddest thing I ever saw."

"Yes . . . yes, it was," he said. This made even less sense. It could not be a coincidence. Just then, he had the distinct impression this was a sign from God.

He took a few more steps back until he could see Conklin at the wheel. "Mr. Conklin?"

"Yes, Captain."

"We are changing course. I want to take the *Angeline* on a direct northeasterly course."

"Beg your pardon, Captain. We're heading back out to sea?"

"You heard me right, Mr. Conklin. Northeast, as quickly as you please. Inform the crew. I'm going below to dress these wounds."

"Aye, aye, Captain."

Houtman looked behind him at Pieter smiling widely. Houtman could tell the lad loved an adventure. And so did he. He hadn't done anything this outlandish since he was Pieter's age. But it had to be done. He dreaded Mr. Giles's reaction but feared ignoring a sign from God far more.

As he walked through the doorway, he heard a distinctly British voice shouting behind him. "Captain? Captain Houtman. The ship is turning. What is the meaning of this?"

26

The carriage slowed to a stop outside the Foster mansion in Gramercy Park. Joel looked out the side window. He heard the driver climb down. A moment later the driver opened the carriage door.

"Will you be staying awhile, sir?" he asked, as he stepped out of the way.

Joel got out. "I think not." He looked at his pocket watch. "From here, we'll be heading to that steamship dock we went to yesterday. I'm just checking to see if Mother wants to join me. Shouldn't be but a few minutes."

"Very good, sir."

Beryl must have heard the carriage; he opened the front door just as Joel reached the top step. Joel handed him his hat. "Don't put that away yet, Beryl. I may be coming right back out."

"I'll wait right here, Mr. Foster."

"Mother," he called. No answer. He walked into the dining room. No one there. "Mother, are you here?" He walked through to the library, then out to the glass patio. "Oh, Allison, there you are."

His sister sat by herself at the white iron table, a cup of tea in one hand, a book in the other. The veranda spilled over with flowers and ferns. Something must be in bloom, he thought. It smelled wonderful.

"Mother is upstairs," she said as she looked up from her book. "Be nice to her, Joel," she whispered. "She's beside herself about John."

"That's why I'm here. Last night she said she might like to go with me to pick him up. The ship is due in thirty minutes."

"She's been in her room all morning. But honestly, Joel, please don't tease her today. You'll set her off, then I'm the one left to face it after you're gone."

Joel didn't appreciate being instructed by his little sister and didn't dignify her suggestion with a reply. He turned and walked back through the library, then the dining room, almost bumping into Sally coming out of the kitchen.

"Sorry, Missuh Foster. I didn't see you."

"It's all right, Sally. Have you seen my mother?"

"She probably still in her room. I brung her breakfast, but she didn't eat a thing. Then I brung her lunch, same thing. Don't think I see her come out all day."

He walked through the living room, then ascended the grand staircase. "Mother," he yelled toward her closed door at the far end of a balcony that overlooked the living room.

The door didn't open. He knocked then walked in. She was dressed and ready to go, sitting by her vanity. "There you are, Mother." She stared at herself in the mirror, but then he realized, she wasn't seeing anything. She still hadn't heard him. He walked up and rested his hands on her shoulders. She jumped as if he'd snuck up on her.

"Joel," she cried. "It's you."

"Of course it's me, Mother. Are you coming?"

"What?"

"I'm heading to the dock, to pick up your long-lost son. Last night you hinted that you might like to come."

"I thought I did. Last night. I don't know."

"What's the matter?"

She didn't say anything for a few moments. "It was so hard after John left," she said, now looking at her hairbrush. "But then life became normal again, and it's been normal for so long now. I don't want all this disruption. I don't like not knowing who John is anymore, what he may have become. What people will say about his return." She looked up at Joel through the mirror. "You know, no one talks about him anymore. They haven't for over a year."

"Mother, you are a strong woman. John is nothing. He shouldn't cause you so much grief. He never cared for our society, our standing in the community, the life you and Father have built. He has never cared for anyone but himself. When he comes, I won't allow him to cause you any trouble. I promise."

"But he's my son."

"Yes, but he is also a man, and he must take responsibility for himself. I'll tell you what. I'll go pick him up and take a measurement of things. You stay here. If I sense he will cause you any discomfort, I'll just bring him to a hotel and pay for it myself."

"No, you can't do that. He might wander about, start meeting our friends here and there. Who knows what he might say?"

"Then I'll bring him back here and tie him up in the attic."

She laughed. Joel always knew how to divert her attention with levity.

She sat back on her chair and patted his hand. "You go without me, but bring him back here. I do want to see him." She looked up at Joel, smiling.

As the carriage approached the dock area, the streets were packed. Hundreds, if not thousands, of people milled about. Yesterday afternoon, Joel had begun to investigate the steamship industry, to evaluate it for their insurance firm. One thing he'd read explained the crowds. Many of these new ships carried upwards of four to five hundred passengers. The SS *Vandervere*, John's ship, was as big as they come.

The carriage stopped. The little door slid over. "I'm not sure I can get much closer than this, Mr. Foster. I see an area designated for carriages, but it's completely filled, and the distance between is overrun with people."

Joel was still not used to such vocabulary from the mouth of a Negro. *Designated. Overrun with people.* "Then I shall have to exit here," Joel said.

"But how will I find you, sir? After you've picked up your brother?"

"Open the door. I want to look around."

The driver opened the carriage door. Joel stood on the step. The steamship office was just a half block away. He looked behind them. "See the corner behind us? The crowd thins out before it reaches there. That's where we'll rendezvous."

"Would you have a time in mind, Mr. Foster? I can keep circling until I see you."

Joel looked back at the dock. One thing was painfully obvious. The *Vandervere* was nowhere in sight. He looked at his timepiece; it was due in five minutes. He seriously doubted it would suddenly appear. "The problem, as I see it, is we have no ship at dock. No ship, no brother to pick up. I'll make my way through the crowd and wait until we either see the ship arrive or learn when they expect it to. Check back at that corner every twenty minutes."

"That's a great distance for you to have to carry any trunks or other baggage your brother may have with him."

"Good point. When he arrives, I'll have him stay by the baggage and I'll come meet you. Then we'll bring the carriage to him. I expect shortly after the ship arrives, these crowds will thin out considerably."

"Very good, sir."

Joel left the carriage and weaved through the throng. When he neared the steamship office, he noticed along South Street a line of heavily guarded black wagons covered in armor. He recognized them instantly. They were used to transport large sums of money between businesses and banks. Then he remembered, the *Vandervere* was said to be carrying over twenty tons of solid gold: bricks, bars, and coins freshly minted in San Francisco, taken from the rivers and mines in northern California. Hard to believe the gold rush still pumped out such wealth eight years since it began.

Closer to the water, Joel noticed a shaded pavilion designated for those waiting for first-class passengers. He seriously doubted John was traveling in anything but steerage. But that didn't matter. Joel was first class, and he dressed as such. No one would dare question his right to wait among them in the shade.

An hour later, still no ship.

A nervous spokesman for the steamship company finally came out and took a position on a wooden deck above the crowd. He began yelling through a bullhorn. Very quickly the clamoring crowd fell silent and listened.

"The US Mail Steamship Company regrets the delay of our ship, the SS *Vandervere*. It is very unusual for it to be this late, and we are sorry for your inconvenience. We have learned there was a major hurricane in the seas off the Carolina coast a few days ago. We received a wire from a sister ship that just docked in Charleston. The captain of that ship reported significant delays as a result of the storm. We're certain this is the cause of the *Vandervere*'s delay."

A groundswell of murmuring began.

"But have no fear," the man shouted, regaining the crowd's attention. "Our ship in Charleston is much older and smaller than the *Vandervere*, and she made it through the storm just fine. We are convinced we shall see the *Vandervere* sailing into New York harbor any minute. But we are sorry we cannot give you more specific information at this time. We have watchers posted at the entrance to the harbor who will wire us the moment she appears. We'll come back and tell you the moment we have any news." With that he walked back into the building.

The murmuring returned, even louder.

Joel had been right: ships could not be relied upon to arrive on a set schedule. Paddle-wheel steamship or otherwise. He decided to step into one of the nicer bars that had sprung up along South Street to accommodate the ships' passengers, and have a whiskey or two.

What a bother this whole thing had become.

The official from the US Mail Steamship Company walked across the deck, down a flight of stairs, and back into the main office, taking no questions, making eye contact with no one. As soon as he closed the door, someone else locked it behind him and pulled down the shade.

"How did it go?" the steamship vice president asked, pacing in front of his desk.

"I said what you told me to say. Tried to sound convincing."

The vice president walked over to a window, lifted the shade an inch or two, and peeked outside. "They seem relatively quiet."

"I expect they will, sir," said the other man. "But for how long?"

The vice president walked back to his desk and looked down at the wire they'd received from their sister ship in Charleston. She had made it through the hurricane, but referring to her as "just fine" was a serious exaggeration. Two of her three masts had snapped. Six crewmen had been swept overboard. The pilothouse had literally blown off the deck. And she carried almost four feet of seawater in her hull.

And no one had seen or heard a word about the SS *Vandervere*.

27

It was late in the afternoon. Laura felt so weak.

But she wasn't alone. Every face on deck sagged from heat and hunger. Even the men shuffled their feet as they went about their tasks. This late in the day there was but a little shade to be had, and far too many seeking its few degrees of comfort. At least there was a steady wind. She wondered how many more hours they must travel before they reached Norfolk.

"Sail ho!" a loud voice rang out overhead.

Laura looked up to the crow's nest, as did everyone on deck.

"Sail ho!"

The sailor pointed toward the northeast. Everyone ran across the deck to the port side, eyes scanning the horizon, hoping to catch a glimpse of whatever he'd seen. Laura was amidships, but she didn't see a thing. It was clear no one else did, either. Soon Captain Meade and Maylor were at the bow. The captain extended his telescope in the direction the sailor had pointed.

Laura watched him. After a few moments, he nodded his head. Then handed it off to Maylor.

The captain walked over to the rail dividing the two decks and shouted up to the crow's nest. "Mr. Tompkins, if you please. She's too far out for me to tell. Any sign of her direction?"

Laura looked up. Tompkins also had a telescope. "Aye, sir, I think . . . yes! She's turning, sir. I do believe she's seen our flag. She has, she's turning in our direction."

A big smile came over the captain's face.

Everyone cheered and applauded.

Laura looked to the northeast again but still couldn't see anything. A moment later Crabby jumped up beside her and looked over the rail. Laura patted her on the head. She heard footsteps and turned to see Micah coming up from the hold. Sweat poured off his face, but he wore his ever-present smile.

"I hear we seen a ship?" he asked.

"Yes," she said. "I haven't seen it yet, but the captain has, and the sailor up there."

"Then it's for real. Take a while to see things down here. But you can be sure it's for real."

"That sailor said the ship was turning, coming our way."

"Thank you, Lord," he said. "I been down there prayin' up a storm someone come. Just couldn't see the Lord not feeding all these chillun, and you ladies been through so much." He walked over next to Crabby and looked out.

A few minutes later, Melissa cried out from the bow, "I see it, I see it!" Soon, a number of others joined in. A few minutes more, Laura and Micah saw it too. Just a dot of white on the horizon.

But it was there.

Fifteen more minutes, and everyone could plainly see its sails.

It took just over an hour for the ships to draw near enough for the captains to communicate. The ship that had come to their aid was named the *Goodspeed*. It was instantly clear to Laura it was both larger and newer than the *Cutlass*. She counted fifteen crewmen on deck and in the rigging.

"A pretty ship, that one," said Micah.

"It is," said Laura. "What are they doing with that rowboat?" she asked.

"That not be a rowboat," he said. "That be Cap'n Meade's yawl. He sendin' some men over to talk to the other captain 'bout our situation. See maybe he can buy some supplies. I heard Cap'n Meade say to Missuh Maylor, he really hope to get to New York instead of Norfolk. Partly to get you ladies where you 'specting to go, partly so that steamship company repay him for all he's lost helping y'all."

That seemed fair to Laura. If they could at least eat something, she didn't care if she spent another day on this ship. She didn't know anyone in Norfolk or New York.

She watched as the captain's yawl, led by Maylor, reached the *Goodspeed*. Maylor stood and had a brief exchange with the other captain. The *Goodspeed*'s captain turned and said something to his crew. The men on deck burst into action. Soon, crates and barrels were handed down to Maylor's crew. The crew and passengers onboard the *Cutlass* cheered and applauded, and the crew of the *Goodspeed* responded by waving back.

Captain Meade's yawl sat low in the water with all the added cargo. Maylor waved off the next round of supplies. He reached up and shook hands with the other captain, who bent over the rail for the exchange. Something else was said, and Maylor's crew began rowing back to the *Cutlass*.

Laura wondered what might be in those barrels and crates. She was surprised how hungry she was, and the hunger seemed to intensify with the hope of being fed.

"Would you look at that," said Micah.

They both watched as another small boat lowered from the *Goodspeed*. Once it sat flat on the water, several crew members climbed down. Then the captain himself climbed aboard. More crates and barrels were lowered to the second boat until it, too, was full. The captain waved off the last crate, and his men started rowing toward the *Cutlass*.

"He bringin' us more," said Micah. "Just like Jesus, doin' more than we can ask or think."

Maylor's boat reached the side of the *Cutlass*. "I best be helpin' them with all that food," Micah said.

As the food from Maylor's boat was lifted aboard the *Cutlass*, Captain Meade stood nearby awaiting the arrival of the second boat. After the crew handed up the food, he helped the *Goodspeed*'s captain up and to his feet. Women and children crowded around. Laura was close enough to hear what they said.

"Captain Meade, my name is Captain Benton of the *Goodspeed*." They shook hands.

"It is my honor, sir," said Meade, "to welcome you aboard my ship. I hardly have words to say to express my gratitude and that of my crew and passengers."

Captain Benton smiled and looked at all present. He was shorter and of smaller frame than Meade but about the same age. "After your Mr. Maylor explained the nature of your distress, it is I who am honored to play a small part in your efforts to rescue these women and children."

Captain Meade turned and faced the crowd. "Ladies, gentlemen . . . you've seen us loading these stores of food, more than we'll need to reach New York by tomorrow. But Captain Benton didn't just give us the necessities we asked for." He pointed to the mound of crates and barrels. "In these are hams and chickens and potatoes and flour. Captain Benton will have us feasting for our remaining meals at sea."

The response was immediate and loud. Laura clapped as well.

After the applause subsided, Captain Meade spoke again. "Captain Benton has refused to accept any repayment."

Another round of applause and cheers.

Captain Benton held up his hands. "Please, please, this is a small thing. God has been good to me. You all have been through so much and have suffered such great loss. I only wish I could do more to assist you. Please know, my crew and I will be praying for your safe journey home. And that God would comfort you in the days ahead."

Half the people watched as Captain Benton and his crew rowed back to their ship; half gathered around the crates and barrels of food, talking about what they hoped to eat for dinner. Laura walked to the opposite side of the ship, alone, and stared out at yet another sun beginning to set. Captain Benton's comforting words had the opposite effect on her; they simply reminded her of the greatness of her loss.

A moment ago she was clapping for chicken and the taste of a cooked potato.

She'd happily eat gruel and hardtack for the balance of her life just to have John back again.

28

After an hour sipping drinks at the bar, Joel went outside and crossed South Street toward the steamship company's dock. It was obvious the ship hadn't arrived; the same-sized crowd still filled the area, spilling out into the street. Armored wagons still lined the curb.

He looked at his pocket watch. The *Vandervere* was over two hours late. By his estimate, his driver would have already made six passes by their agreed-upon rendezvous point. Joel had, perhaps, fifteen more minutes before he'd come around again. Enough time to investigate the current status of things.

He found a walkway along the back side of the steamship office that led down a narrow alley behind the building. It came out on the water side of the property. Just up ahead Joel saw the first-class passengers' pavilion. Workers from the steamship office were passing out drinks and small sandwiches. He instantly regretted the money he'd just spent at the bar until he realized they were only serving iced tea.

He found a table next to a finely dressed man with a well-trimmed beard and spectacles. He appeared to be working through an entire plate of sandwiches. "Excuse me, my good man. Any news on the *Vandervere*?"

The man looked at him, finished chewing, and said, "No, and we are not pleased. We've been here for hours, and they think serving us sandwiches somehow makes up for it."

"No one has come out with any news?"

He shook his head no and picked up another sandwich. "The wife has this huge dinner planned. Relatives coming from all over the city, welcoming home our son. Dinner is supposed to be served in thirty minutes. I dread coming home empty-handed."

Joel felt almost the same way. His mother must be frantic now. She wasn't a patient woman. Joel stood up. "Thanks for the information."

The man nodded and kept chewing. Joel decided it was time to make something happen. He couldn't wait here all night. He'd walked by several doors in the alleyway a few moments ago. Perhaps entrances for office staff. He went back and banged on the first one. No one answered. He walked to the second door. A sign beside the door read "Employee Entrance Only." This time he banged until someone opened the door.

A young man dressed like a clerk opened it a crack. "I'm sorry, sir. This is for employees only."

Joel shoved his boot in the opening just before the door shut. "Young man, open this door."

"Please, sir. I'm not allowed to—"

"You will open this door or else get someone with the authority to open it. I am Joel Foster, vice president of the Foster Insurance firm. I'm not accustomed to being treated this way."

"But sir . . ."

"If someone doesn't open this door and speak with me this instant, I will walk around this building and tell that multitude out there that the *Vandervere* has sunk."

There was a brief pause. "I will get someone. Please don't do that."

The door closed. Less than a minute later, it was opened by the same gentleman who'd spoken to the crowd an hour ago. "Mr. Foster, please come in, follow me. I'll bring you to Mr. Holden's office. He's our vice president."

Joel followed the man through a maze of paneled hallways toward a finely trimmed mahogany door. He stepped into a smoke-filled room. There was a large desk at one end, surrounded by bookshelves. The other end resembled a living room with rich leather furniture. Three men, about his age, sat on the chairs and sofa smoking cigars, studying a map spread across a coffee table. A tall, older man paced in front of the desk.

The man turned as Joel walked in. "Mr. Foster, correct?" the older man asked, extending his hand. "I'm Arthur Holden. How can I help you?"

Joel noticed something he'd recognized in the face of many a businessman over the years—panic, covered by a fake smile and bright eyes. They were definitely hiding something. "You can tell me what's going on, the real story, not the fabrication your man here told us an hour ago."

Holden acted surprised. "I don't know what you mean, Mr. Foster."

"What are those men doing over there with those maps?"

Holden looked at them. "They're trying to estimate the *Vandervere*'s whereabouts based on the information provided by our sister ship in Charleston."

"And if they figure it out, will you be sending your man out to the crowd with an update?"

Holden hesitated. "We're not sure."

"Mr. Holden, people have been waiting for over two hours."

"With respect, Mr. Foster, what benefit is there in telling them something we can't possibly be sure of?"

"You may not be certain, but you must know something, some general idea of when the ship will arrive. How far off course could it be? I've heard the *Vandervere* has made this trip over forty times. Yesterday, one of your men boasted of how accurate these steamships are. How they're no longer dependent on the wind."

"They are very reliable."

"So . . . what are we talking about? Two more hours of waiting? Two more days?"

Holden walked behind his desk but didn't sit down.

"You really don't know, do you?" Joel said. "Well, here's what I know . . . I am a busy man who cannot afford to wait around for hours for a ship to arrive."

"We are sorry, Mr. Foster. We—"

"I'm not finished." Joel walked over to Holden's desk. He pulled a business card out of his coat pocket and wrote on the back. He handed it to Holden. "My card. The address of our family home is on the back. You send a courier to that address the minute the ship arrives or when you know it will."

"I think we can arrange that," Holden said.

"Yes, I think you can."

Joel walked two blocks to the rendezvous point. He didn't have to wait five minutes before the carriage arrived. Sweat poured off the young driver's face.

The driver held the carriage door open.

"To my parents' house, Eli," said Joel.

"Your brother's ship did not arrive, sir?"

"No, and they don't know when it will, either." He stepped in. "They'll send someone when it does," he said through the window. "After you drop me off to explain things to my mother, I'll need you to take me around to my house. Then stay on call in case that courier arrives."

"I understand, sir."

Fifteen minutes later, the carriage pulled up to the family home. "I won't be long," said Joel.

"I'll be here, Mr. Foster." He stepped down and opened the door.

Joel walked slowly up the granite steps, trying to think of what to say. Beryl opened the door and received his hat.

"Will you be staying, sir?"

"Once again no, Beryl. Mother still upstairs?"

"Actually, no, Mr. Foster. I believe she's in the dining room."

That's good, Joel thought. At least she's finally eating.

"Is that you, Joel?" she called out.

"It is, Mother," he yelled back, "but only me."

Allison ran out of the dining room. "What's wrong? Where's John?"

"Nothing's wrong," he said, unsure if he believed it. "His ship is just late." Allison followed him into the dining room. His mother sat at the head of the table, at her end. She was looking down, rubbing her temples. His father wasn't present, but that wasn't unusual. He missed dinner most evenings.

"I can't believe this," she said. "I've been on pins and needles all afternoon, my heart feels like it's going to burst. And after all this, no John?" She looked up at Joel and Allison. "Is that what you're telling me?"

Allison took her seat.

Joel remained standing. "Mother, you're the one who thought these new ships are always on time. I'm the one who said there's no such thing."

"So what now?" she asked. "Aren't you going to eat? Have a seat, we'll fix you a plate. Roast beef, corn, potatoes . . . and what's that Southern pie Sally made?"

"Sweet potato pie," Allison said.

"Stop, Mother. I can't stay." He wanted to, desperately. They had the best cook in Gramercy Park and, since Sally came, the best desserts as well. "You know Evelyn expects me to eat at home every now and then."

"So when will John's ship come?" asked Allison.

"They don't know," said Joel. "Not exactly. Some storm off the Carolina coast got all the ships off schedule."

"A storm?" his mother asked.

"Not to worry," said Joel. "It just slowed everything down. When the ship does arrive, the steamship company will send a courier right to your door."

"And then what?" she asked.

"Then you'll call for the driver to come get me, and I'll go pick John up."

"Can I go with you?" asked Allison.

"No."

"Why not? It's a big carriage. I won't be any trouble."

He looked at his mother for support.

"I think it would be good for your sister to go. It's been too long since all my children shared the same carriage."

Joel sighed. "Well, I've got to be going."

The things he had to put up with to stay on her good side.

29

Laura stood by the railing and looked down at Crabby lying at her feet. She had such a contented look as she gnawed on a ham bone. She held it in her front paws, turned it from side to side. Occasionally it would slip and fall to the deck. She'd grab it then freeze, see if anyone might challenge her for this prize. Then she'd be lost again in the glory of the moment. Enjoy it, girl, Laura thought. After eating so well, she had to admit, good food could make one happy.

For the moment.

Earlier, as the women sat about the deck, devouring the rich fare Smitty had prepared, they no longer seemed to be sailing a ship of sorrow. Women who hadn't said a word in days chatted casually and freely, exchanging memories of past meals enjoyed with family and friends in better times. Many had shared recipes, ways they would have prepared the meal differently. Several had offered Smitty suggestions. He nodded here and there, feigning interest. This went on for over an hour. Combined with the heat that faded with the setting sun and the strong, steady breeze . . . Laura had actually felt something very close to joy herself.

For the moment.

Now the dishes were all clean. The sun had dropped below the horizon. Night was coming fast. Their last night at sea.

Laura hoped it would be her last for a long time to come. She was ready to be back on solid ground. Earlier while cleaning up, Captain Meade had announced that if the winds stayed steady all night they should arrive in New York harbor by early morning.

Laura still had no idea what to expect when she met John's family, even *how* she would meet them. Whenever she had asked him about them, John would give vague answers and often change the subject. They seemed to have caused him a good deal of pain, which only added to her apprehension now.

She thought about John's note. Maybe he'd written instructions about meeting them. The moment she considered it, a scene rushed into her mind. She saw the sea rising and falling. The wind howling. She was back in the lifeboat. John was on the *Vandervere*, standing beside the captain. Huge waves slapped against the side. "I've written you a note, inside the pouch," he yelled. "Don't read it . . . unless you hear word that we—that we will not . . ." Tears poured down his cheeks, then he'd looked away.

The image was so strong. She reached out her hand for him, was about to call out.

"Mrs. Foster?"

John disappeared.

"Are you all right?"

She pulled her hand down, grabbed hold of the rail. She looked to her right. "I'm fine, Melissa." She must change the subject. "Are you looking forward to tomorrow?"

"I can barely contain my happiness," Melissa said. "I let some out while we ate. The ladies were in such a jovial mood."

"It was wonderful to eat real food again."

"It was. But already I can tell the old mood is returning."

Melissa said this as if she didn't realize Laura was among those struggling.

"But I can understand why, since this is the last night before we reach New York. I'm so glad I don't have to be that way with you."

Laura sighed. She wished Melissa would be that way, at this very moment. She wasn't up to hearing her release all her anticipated joys.

"But if we're to be in the harbor early in the morning, I better head down and get some sleep. All this excitement has made me very tired. Don't want Tom to see me with puffy eyes."

"Well, good night then," Laura said.

"Good night." Melissa turned toward the hold.

Puffy eyes, thought Laura. What must it be like to have that as your great concern? How about . . . meeting a strange family you've never met, in a strange place you've never been? How about . . . becoming a widow on your honeymoon? Losing perhaps the only man who ever loved you or will ever love you for the rest of your life?

30

Maybe he was losing his sanity.

Captain Janus Houtman did not consider himself a superstitious man. Many who made their living at sea were; perhaps most were. He'd always prided himself on being rational and levelheaded. What he was doing now could be considered neither of those. For the last half of the day, and now into the night, he was sailing back out to sea, away from his destination, because a bird had hit him in the head.

His crew had not uttered a word of concern, let alone defiance. But he saw suspicion on their faces, the way they turned away when he looked at them. The nervous chatter that ended as he drew near.

At the moment, Houtman stood at the tip of the bow and looked out across the sea. What was he expecting? What did he hope to find by following this new direction? Earlier he had an argument with Mr. Giles that had almost come to blows. Houtman had no logical defense to offer. But he had a certainty in his heart that he must pursue this course; it was as strong as if an angel had appeared and handed him a scroll.

He heard footsteps behind him. He turned and saw Giles

emerging from the shadows into the lantern light, heading in his direction.

Not again.

"Captain, you must reconsider," Giles said, climbing the stairs to the forecastle deck. "Do you see the time?"

"I know what time it is, Mr. Giles."

"Based on what you said this morning, we should be pulling into Charleston harbor this very moment." He stood beside him. "I should be seeing the lights of the city growing bigger by the minute. Instead, what do I see? A dark sky and an even darker sea. You have us sailing into oblivion, Captain."

"Mr. Giles, please. We've been through this already."

"Have we? And what did we conclude? That some deranged gull flew into your head and, for you, it is a message from God. And where is God taking us? Back out to sea? Do you suppose we are to sail all the way back to England? I looked at a map a little while ago. Did you know that's where this course is taking us?"

"We're not going back to England."

"Then where are we going, Captain?"

"I . . . I don't know, not yet."

"You don't know. Then let me ask you this: I'm supposed to be in Charleston for my meeting tomorrow afternoon. It's the very reason I made this voyage. If we turned around this instant, would we be in Charleston in time for my meeting?"

Houtman wanted no part of this conversation. "It's possible. But I have no control over the winds."

"Then I insist you turn this ship around this instant!"

"You insist?" Houtman yelled back. "You don't insist."

"Captain, you were paid to bring me to Charleston in a set amount of time."

"Is that so? I don't recall signing any contract to that effect. In fact, when I was asked how long this voyage would be, I recall giving an estimate only, then emphasizing what I have always believed . . . the sea does as she pleases."

"But this delay is not the sea doing as she pleases, Captain. It is *you*," he shouted. "Doing as you please!"

Houtman needed to end this. How could he argue from reason when he had no reason to give? "Mr. Giles, I will make this concession . . . if valid justification for my decision does not present itself by morning, we will turn around and head back to Charleston."

Giles paused to consider. "Will we still make it in time for my meeting with the senators?"

Houtman sighed. "No, we will not."

"Then I reject your offer!" He was shouting again.

Houtman could not have a passenger yelling at him in front of the men. "You reject my offer, do you?" Houtman yelled even louder. "It was *not* an offer, Mr. Giles, and you have no leverage to bargain with. You have the authority of a box or a crate. Or like this barrel here, and no more. You will go where the ship goes, and the ship goes where I say it goes."

"You hear that?" Robert asked.

"I hear something," said Ramón. He nudged John. "John, did you hear that?"

"I think John's asleep," Robert said.

John heard something also, but he felt too weak to jump into the conversation.

"Sounds like people yelling," said Robert. "Coming from that direction." He pointed off in the darkness.

"Could just be one of the men on the fringe," said the ambassador, still lying down, "yelling at some hallucination. Probably drank seawater."

"No," said Robert. "There it is again, and look . . . isn't that a light?"

"Where?" said Ramón.

Robert pointed, now on his knees. "Look, it is . . . some kind of light."

"Gentlemen," said the ambassador. "I think that is a light. Much too low to be a star."

Now John's eyes opened. It *did* sound like an argument, well off in the distance. He hadn't heard a sound all day but the wind and splashing of waves. This was quite different. John sat up and looked where Robert had pointed. There was a light, two lights, actually. "Men," he yelled to all the men floating on tables and hatches nearby, "scream out for all you're worth. That is a ship out there."

They instantly began to yell and shout.

"Jesus," he said quietly, "are we saved?" He felt the urge to cry but had no tears. He joined in yelling, "Here we are!" with all the strength he could find.

"Captain, Mr. Giles . . . with all respect, sirs, would you men stop talking a moment?"

Houtman and Giles instantly stopped. They looked at young Pieter, astonished to hear him address them this way.

"Listen," he said, his face beaming in the lantern light. "I hear something, getting louder, there off the starboard bow."

Houtman heard it now also. He rushed to the nearest rail. "Do you hear that, Mr. Conklin?" he yelled toward the stern.

"I do indeed, Captain. I am turning her in that direction."

"Very well," said Houtman. It was the voice of men crying out in distress. He was certain. He wanted to jump, to cheer. But he could not, so he looked at Giles. "I believe that sound, Mr. Giles, may very well be the reason that deranged gull struck me in the head."

Giles just looked back out to sea toward the growing sound, on his face a look of utter amazement.

31

"The lights are getting bigger," Robert yelled. "Do you see them?"

No one answered. They just kept shouting. But it was obvious to John. The lights *were* getting bigger.

The ambassador sat back and buried his head into his knees. His shoulders moved up and down. He was sobbing. So were many others. Tears of joy. Shouts to God. Parts of Bible verses. Phrases from memorized prayers. John heard them all, mixed in with their cries.

Robert looked back at him. "We are spared, John. God didn't abandon us."

John continued to watch as the ship moved closer. There was no moon to aid them, and the starlight was hindered by scattered clouds. He tried but couldn't see all the men in the larger group. He wondered how many were still alive. How would they know if they'd rescued them all?

Twenty minutes later, John saw parts of the ship lit up by a half dozen lanterns. Finally words came from the ship, someone yelling. John asked everyone to be quiet. No one heard him. Robert did and shouted for the rest to be still. Everyone stopped, listened.

"We don't see you," the voice said with some kind of accent. "How many are you?"

John whispered to Robert, who shouted, "Fifty, maybe a few more."

"Are you in a ship or a boat?"

"No," Robert yelled. "We're shipwrecked, floating at sea."

"For how long?"

"Several days," Robert yelled back. "Can you help us?"

A long pause.

"Yes, we have room for all of you. Plenty of food and water."

The sky erupted with shouts and cheers and praise. John collapsed on the raft, overwhelmed and exhausted.

He had just one thought . . . *Laura*. He would see his love again.

Though he hadn't had a drop to drink in days, from some reservoir within, tears finally came.

"Captain," said Mr. Giles, "this is the most remarkable thing I have witnessed in the entirety of my life. I offer my most humble apology."

Houtman looked at Giles. His hat was off, his head bowed. It was the oddest scene. "Apology accepted, Mr. Giles." He had felt like such a fool just minutes ago. Tears filled his eyes as he looked back toward the voices. This *was* amazing. He had no words. It was a story he would tell his children and his grandchildren. And they would tell theirs.

"Keep talking to them, Pieter, until we draw close enough to begin the rescue."

"Yes, Captain."

He looked back at Pieter, then the rest of his men spread throughout the deck, so proud of their teamwork. Without instructions, they had already reset the sails to slow the ship's speed. Four of them were at work preparing the small boat.

Within twenty minutes, the ship had reached the main body of men. Houtman leaned over the rail. It was hard to see anything a few feet beyond the lanterns. The rescue boat was quickly lowered. A moment later, he heard a loud splash. One of his crewmen yelled, "Stop or you'll swamp us."

"But I can't swim."

"Then let us pull you aboard."

More splashing. "I can't swim."

"We've got you, sir. Calm down."

Houtman needed to do something. "You men on the water," he called out. "This is Janus Houtman, captain of the *Angeline*. Please don't panic or rush the rescue boat. We can only take a few at a time. But you have my word, we will stay all night if we have to, until each of you is safely aboard."

This calmed things considerably. Houtman heard a new noise on the opposite side of the ship. More men were calling out for help from that side, slapping the side of the hull. Three crew members rushed to help and tossed ropes over the side. "Wrap these ropes around you. We'll pull you up."

In ten minutes, between the rescue boat and the ropes, fifteen men were on board. Not a single one could stand. But they had all asked for the same thing: water. His men were ready to give them all they desired.

Houtman stepped in. "Careful," he said. "Start with sips only."

"But we haven't had anything to drink in days," one of them said.

"Which is why you must sip the water now. We have plenty, but you'll be sick if you drink your fill. Trust me."

The men reluctantly obeyed.

His crew lifted another small group of men from the rescue

boat. Houtman bent down and asked one of them, "What ship are you from?"

"The SS *Vandervere*," came the quiet reply.

"The *Vandervere*," said Giles, standing beside Houtman. "I know of this ship, part of the steamship mail line. I thought someone said there were only fifty in your group?"

"I don't know about that," the man said, looking down.

"This can't be all," said Giles. "The *Vandervere* carries over five hundred souls. Where are all the others?"

A pause.

"Gone," someone else said. "A ship came just before we sank, rescued the women and children."

"How many?"

"Just over a hundred, I think."

"Thank God for that," said Houtman. "That means over three hundred men are lost?"

"I think more than that," said the man. "Closer to four hundred I'd say."

"How awful," said Giles. "What of your captain and his officers?"

"All gone," he said. "None of the crew survived, except a few of lower rank, the ones that rowed the women in the lifeboats. Could I have another sip?"

"Certainly," said Houtman, standing up. The extent of the tragedy began to settle in. A massive loss of life. He'd never heard of such numbers from a single shipwreck. To have played a role in this miraculous deliverance for these fifty men was still a thing of wonder, but . . .

Four hundred souls. Gone.

32

"We need to paddle faster," Robert said. "Look how many have already boarded."

John didn't have the strength to keep up with Robert.

Robert noticed. "John, can't you go any faster?"

"Robert, what difference does it make if we get there a few minutes faster? You heard the captain, they're staying until everyone is onboard."

Robert turned around, paddling just as hard, but Ramón slowed to John's pace. "An amazing thing," he said. "We haven't seen a single ship since the *Vandervere* sank, and God brings one right to us on the darkest night yet." He smiled. "Robert, I say let's savor this moment."

For the next few minutes, no one spoke as they paddled. They just watched the rescue unfold. John didn't see or hear any stragglers behind or beside them. He kept calling out, just to be sure. He wished he had a lantern. The three men stopped paddling as they drew near the ship. The raft floated right into it, bumping it gently. A few yards away, three other survivors were being lifted from the small boat to the ship. A crewman held a lantern over the rail in their direction. "How many more are there?" he asked.

"I think we're the last," John said.

"Are you sure?"

"How many are already aboard?"

The man asked someone. "With these three, there are fifty. How many on your raft?"

"Three."

"Does fifty-three sound right?"

"I can't be sure," said John. "I lost count. But that seems close."

"Well, let's start getting you men up here. Who goes first?"

"John should go," said the ambassador.

"I agree," said Robert.

John felt honored. He crawled to the front of the raft, stood up carefully. A crewman dropped a rope formed into a large loop. John stepped into it and two men lifted him aboard. As soon as his feet touched down, he crumpled to the deck. He quietly patted it with his hands as small puddles formed from the water in his sleeves. The deck felt rock hard, like land.

"Who's next?" John heard the crewman say. "You go, Ambassador," he heard Robert say. He heard them groan as they pulled Ramón up. John turned to watch when suddenly several men yelled all at once.

A splash, then another.

"The raft flipped over," a crewman shouted.

"I can't swim." It sounded like Robert. The next phrase, garbled.

John stood up and rushed to the rail. "Robert," he said. Robert didn't answer. A crewman dove in. John dove in behind him. He splashed around in the darkness, grabbing for anything. He felt an arm and pulled.

"Let go." It was the crewman.

John wiped the water out of his eyes. "Robert, say something." Still no reply, but he heard splashing and coughing in the darkness beyond the raft. He swam toward it, but when he got there, it stopped. "Robert."

"You men," the captain yelled. "Jump in and help him. You others, bring your lanterns here."

Treading water, John took a deep breath and descended into pitch blackness. His arms reaching every which way. He didn't feel a thing. He went back up for another breath, heard voices calling out Robert's name, then went under again a few yards away. This time he went deeper. He was almost out of breath and ready to return when his fingers brushed something.

He grabbed at it, a collar.

Robert.

He grabbed it with both hands and kicked upward. And kicked. Where was the surface? He had energy for one last kick, then he must let go.

He kicked again but still didn't break through. Strong hands grabbed his shirt and pulled. He gasped as fresh air rushed in. "Help me, I've got Robert."

"You head back," one of the crewmen said. "I got him."

John swam toward the lantern light, but he just couldn't make it. His arms suddenly became too heavy. Instinctively, he rolled over on his back and tried to float, tried to catch his breath. He felt so sleepy. He started drifting off.

"Where's John?" he heard Ramón shout. He sounded far away.

"There he is," someone shouted. "Pull him here."

33

The doorbell rang at Joel Foster's brownstone on East 22nd Street in Gramercy Park. He and his wife, Evelyn, had only three house servants, hand-me-downs from his parents' staff. Lounging in his library in his favorite chair, puffing on a fine cigar, he awaited the coming interruption. He was actually surprised it hadn't come hours ago.

"It's the new driver, sir, sent from your mother."

Joel pretended not to hear a moment, then set his book on the table. "Let me guess, Edward. He's here to pick me up."

"It would appear so, sir."

"Right. He didn't hand you a message?"

"No, Mr. Foster. As before . . . your mother says to come right away."

He stood up and followed Edward to the foyer. Edward moved so slow these days. Out of respect, he didn't pass him.

"Your hat and coat, sir."

"Thank you, Edward. I believe my wife is upstairs with the nanny. Tell her not to wait up for me. I have no idea what to expect."

"Very good, sir."

Joel hurried down the steps. The driver already had the

carriage door open. As he ducked his head getting in, he said, "Any news?"

The driver closed the door. "The courier from the steamship company still hasn't come, sir. It's why Mrs. Foster sent me. She's quite upset and insisted something must be wrong."

Why couldn't she believe him? He'd told her you couldn't rely on ship schedules.

"Mr. Foster, begging your pardon, sir." The driver's eyes pointed to something lying on the seat across from Joel. "Took the liberty of picking that up on the way here. A newsboy was selling it on a corner. Looks like this newspaper agrees with your mother."

Joel held the newspaper up to the window, letting it catch the light from a street lamp. The *Herald*, late evening edition. The headline read:

SS *VANDERVERE* MISSING?

Beneath it, a smaller line said:

Ship Carrying Over 500 Passengers, 20 Tons of Gold Fails to Arrive.

"Great . . . just great." Joel tossed the paper down.

"I do something wrong, sir?" the driver asked through the carriage window.

"No, Eli. I'm glad you caught this. My parents have the morning edition delivered. I need you to make sure my mother doesn't see it, unless that ship arrives overnight. If it doesn't, they'll be saying worse things than this by tomorrow. Let's get over there now."

"Yes, sir." The driver climbed into his seat, and the carriage took off.

Joel picked the paper back up. He longed to keep reading,

but the light was too dim. The press was so irresponsible; they had no regard for the consequences of their wild speculations. He knew they couldn't have gotten any new information from the steamship line. They'd never say anything to the newspapers. Now the families of hundreds of passengers, not to mention the unstable financial markets, were given all this fuel to pour on the fire of their fears. He must keep his mother from seeing or hearing anything about this, until the ship came into port.

Just then, an image flashed into his mind—the panicked look on the vice president's face earlier that evening. The sense Joel had that he *was* holding something back. Joel wondered what it was. And how much longer he'd have to wait before he found out.

34

"Land ho!"

Laura almost dropped her plate of ham. Everyone rushed to the port side to look. She set it on a barrel and joined them. The sailor in the crow's nest proclaimed the news again.

At first she didn't see it. A dozen hands pointed in the same direction. She followed their lead and finally saw it. Just a thin brown ribbon stretched over a small fraction of the horizon. But it was there. It had been just over a week since they'd boarded the *Vandervere*, but it felt like a month or more.

Land.

She wanted to be excited, and a part of her was. These emotions warred against more dominant, melancholic themes. This sighting meant they were closing in on New York, maybe the entrance to the harbor itself. This thought became the first domino in a string of dreadful thoughts and images, each seeking to take a turn to torment her.

She looked at the faces of the other women, those she knew had also lost husbands. They were still smiling and pointing. How did the sight of land change anything? Was she alone in this struggle? Or were they all just putting up a good front as she was?

She looked but didn't see Micah or Crabby anywhere on deck. She hoped to spend at least a few minutes with him before they docked. Somehow, being around him could pull her away from these dark feelings. She thought she knew why. Every day of his life was, and would always be, so much more difficult than hers, even now without John.

Lord, let me learn what you've taught him, how to find joy even if . . .

She didn't finish her prayer, didn't want to say the words. She looked at the doorway leading down to the galley and crew quarters. The women weren't allowed there without special permission. Micah must be doing chores for Smitty. All the food they received yesterday had also created more work for him.

But it was so delicious.

She walked back to finish her ham and fresh bread, savoring every bite. The captain had announced they could eat as much as they liked this morning. He expected this breakfast to be their last meal onboard. When she finished eating, she walked back to the rail. Already the land filled more of the horizon than before, another section appearing to the north.

"That's New York, I'm sure of it," an older woman said. She looked up at the sails. "With the winds like this, we'll be there in no time."

Laura didn't get it. She had heard this same woman talking two days ago about losing her husband of forty years on the *Vandervere*. Now she sounded excited.

Just then she heard a dog bark. She turned in time to watch Crabby slide across the main deck and snatch the toy crab in her mouth. She ran it back to Micah, who'd thrown it from the bow. He noticed her watching, nodded, and smiled. Crabby scrambled up the stairs and dropped the crab in Micah's hand. He threw it again. Laura walked over and climbed the same stairs as soon as Crabby ran past.

"Good morning, Micah."

"Mornin', Miz Foster."

"Didn't think I'd see you for a while, with all that extra food to deal with."

"Me neither," he said. "A number of ladies came in, insisting they clean everything up. Cap'n said okay."

"I should go help them."

"No, you stay put, ma'am. These ladies say they the ones that couldn't help before. Every time they try, too many others volunteered. You helped plenty already. Ever been to New York City?"

"No."

He walked to the port side and looked toward the land. Laura walked up and stood beside him. She felt something land on her feet. It was Crabby's crab. She was about to pick it up when Micah said, "Enough for now, Crabby. Come sit." She picked up her crab, walked behind them, and sat beside Micah. "I never been, neither. Furthest north I ever been be Baltimore."

"When I left for San Francisco with my brother, we sailed from Philadelphia."

No one said anything for a few moments. "You got kin to meet you?"

"Oh, Micah, I don't even know what they look like." Tears filled her eyes. "And they don't know me. I was supposed to meet them standing next to John."

"Well," he said, "I have a feeling things will be all right. You'll find each other somehow. But you cry if it helps. 'Spect all you been through, you have it comin'."

She wiped her eyes and looked at him. "But that's just it, Micah. I don't want to cry anymore. All I do is cry, and I think it's all I'm ever going to do. I don't think I will ever be happy again." She wiped her remaining tears. "How do you do it?"

"Ma'am?"

"How do you . . . keep happy or get happy again so quickly after something goes wrong? Your life is so much harder than mine, even with all I've been through. But whenever I see you, you are joyful. I've never met anyone like you."

He smiled. "So you want to know my secret?"

Laura smiled back. "Yes, very much."

"Nobody ever ask me this before."

"Well, I'm asking."

"I guess it be this . . . live in the day, 'cause that's all we been given, trust God fo' the rest."

"Live in the day," she repeated.

"And trust God fo' the rest. Yes'm."

"That's it?"

"That's it." He looked out over the water. "See . . . we got no control over things that happen in life. Not just slaves, white folk got no control neither. Even rich and powerful ones got no control. Nobody got control. Only God. Rich folks got they money and power, make them think they do. But all they do is worry and fret over what might happen next . . . tomorrow, next week, next year. Got no joy in what God do for them today. Don't even see it. Don't thank him for it. Just run right by it, trying to stop all these things they afraid might happen, things that can't be stopped. And it gets them no place. No place but angry and sad."

Laura realized she never lived in the day, never kept her thoughts anchored in the day at hand.

He looked at her, smiled, and said, "See, it's all them heavy thoughts steal our joy, the one's we ain't meant to carry."

It sounded so simple to hear him say it, but these weren't just words for him. Micah was describing how he lived. "I wish I could make myself do what you're saying. But I've been this way . . . maybe all my life."

"Well, you don't have to grab hold of it all at once," he said. "Just one day at a time."

He bent down, reached his hand out. Crabby dropped her crab in it. He tossed it down to the main deck, and off she went, tail wagging. "Or you could do like Crabby. A day's way too long for her. She live moment by moment, and she got way more joy than me."

35

"Look at all the ships," a little girl yelled. "And all the build-ings. We're really here, Mother. See?"

"Almost," her mother said.

To Laura, the little girl's glee seemed close to Christmas cheer.

Over the last two hours, those little ribbons of land had grown to fill Laura's view on all sides. But someone had said they were still south of New York harbor. Laura's eyes traced what the little girl saw, trying to understand the fascination. She envied how children could simply will away unpleasant thoughts, give themselves fully to whatever the day presented.

Then it dawned on her: this is what Micah did, what he was trying to explain. Live in the day, don't worry about things beyond your control. The outlook of a child. She looked out over the water again. There *were* a lot of ships in the water and a lot of buildings along the low-lying hills.

It was diverting to think about, but it didn't make her happy. But the diversion itself kept her mind off unhappy things. And that was something. So she thought some more.

The scene put her in mind of San Francisco Bay. It had nearly as many ships as she saw here. Once, when they were standing inland on one of the hills west of town, John had said that San Francisco harbor looked almost like a forest of dead trees, referring to the hundreds of masts rising in the air. The difference here was that the ships were moving, in every direction, and they came in every shape and size. There were even miniature steamships, some half, some a third the size of the *Vandervere*. None of the ships, of course, paid them any mind. The *Cutlass* was just one more ship making its small contribution to the crowded scene.

They sailed next through an area where the waterway narrowed, almost to the width of a wide river. It was much calmer, but the winds kept the ship moving steadily forward. Laura stood a few women away from the old woman from New York, who had now become the unofficial touring guide.

"This land on the left," she said, "that's Staten Island. It doesn't look like an island, but it is. Over here," she said, walking across the deck, "this is Brooklyn. My word, look at how much it's grown. I'd hardly recognize it. There must be a hundred more buildings than when I was here last."

To Laura, Brooklyn by itself seemed as densely populated as all of San Francisco. Docks and wharfs occupied every lineal foot of the waterfront. It seemed to go on forever.

"We're so close now," the woman said. "Right around that curve, things will open right up and we'll be in the harbor."

Everyone stopped talking and just stared ahead, waiting for the next spectacle to come. Laura walked toward the bow, looking for any open spots along the rail. She saw one, just right of the centerline. As she climbed the steps to the forecastle deck, the ship slid to the right, almost causing her to fall. But she shifted her weight just right and held fast. Ironic, she thought, here on the last day at sea she was finally getting her sea legs.

The breeze was stronger here and quite pleasant. As the

ship turned, just like the old woman had said, they came into a wide section of open water. Up ahead she saw a large island, with a rounded fort on the left side and a bigger fort in the center. They seemed to be headed straight for it. She wondered what it was. Manhattan was supposed to be an island, but this seemed much too small. She missed hearing the old woman's narration, so she headed back to the main deck.

As she came down the stairs, she noticed a flatboat on the port side. She stopped a moment to watch. It seemed to be aiming right for them. It had a small pilothouse and a single stack belching a trail of black smoke. Three uniformed men were onboard. Not dressed like police, more like naval officers.

Captain Meade must have seen it. He shouted out some orders, and his men instantly began adjusting the sails. The ship soon responded and began to slow down. The captain said something to Mr. Maylor at the wheel, then walked to the side, nearest the approaching vessel.

"Ahoy there," called the man in the center. "May I speak with the captain of this ship?"

"I am he. Meade's the name. This is my ship, the *Cutlass*." The spot now became center stage.

"We're with the US Barge Office. My name is Officer Gentry. Where are you coming from, Captain?"

"Originally from Wilmington, sir. But coming here wasn't our plan."

"So you don't have a berth arranged anywhere in the harbor?"

"No sir, but we—"

"May we come aboard, Captain? Our job is to do a brief inspection, verify the contents of your ship for customs."

"Mr. Gentry . . . the contents of my ship are all on deck." The *Cutlass* had now slowed to a crawl. The flatboat was almost beside her.

"I don't understand, Captain."

"Sir, these women and children are from the SS *Vandervere*."

"What?"

"It's a steamship, a very large one. It—"

"I know of the *Vandervere*, Captain. It's been in all the newspapers, last night and this morning. It's been missing since yesterday afternoon. Are you saying—"

"These women and children are from the *Vandervere*, yes. She . . ." He looked up and down the rails. "We rescued these women and children four nights ago, as she floundered off the Carolina coast."

The three customs agents looked stunned. The one on the right sat back on a crate. The one named Gentry looked at all the passengers, including Laura. "I am so sorry, ladies. I had no idea."

"Can you help us, Mr. Gentry?" the captain asked. "We don't know where to go from here."

"Are there any other ships . . . coming?" Gentry asked.

Captain Meade shook his head no. It was clear; he didn't want to continue speaking plainly, for the children's sake.

"No . . . no other ships?"

"Where would you have us go, sir?" the captain asked. "I was thinking we might berth where the *Vandervere* planned to go, at the steamship company's dock."

"I don't have the authority to approve that," said Gentry. "But I agree with your idea. The island straight ahead is called Governor's Island. I've read the steamship company has stationed a telegraph operator there, on the western tip at Castle Williams. He was supposed to alert them the minute the *Vandervere* arrived. I believe you should go there. If you'd like, you could come aboard and we could take you there now. You could direct your men to steer your ship nearby. I'm sure once the steamship officials understand the situation, they will give you permission to dock at their berth."

"Very well, sir. I accept your kind offer." The captain walked to the center of the deck. Everyone was already looking at him. "Ladies, I know these last few steps will be difficult ones to make. But God has spared you all and brought us safely to port. I trust he will keep you once you leave my care. I will see you once more, after I communicate with the steamship company. But I suspect after that, things will get very hectic and busy. So let me say, on behalf of my crew . . . though I wish we had not met under these circumstances, it has been an honor and a privilege to serve as your captain. We will . . ."—he looked to be choking back tears—"never forget you."

The customs agents escorted Captain Meade to the dock by Castle Williams. He had never been on a steamboat before and was surprised by its speed. Also by the noise and smell. The senior agent got off the boat and helped him find the telegraph operator. They shook hands, and Gentry said as he departed, "Our prayers are with you, sir."

Captain Meade turned and began to explain what happened to the young telegraph man. As he did, the young man's face turned white. Before Captain Meade finished, he politely interrupted him. "Sir, it would take twenty minutes to transmit all of that to the main office. What would you have me say to them in as few words as possible?"

Meade thought a few moments. "Say this: 'SS *Vandervere* sunk off Carolina coast 4 nights ago. My ship, the *Cutlass*, rescued 109 survivors. All the women and children are safe, 6 men. No other survivors. Request permission to berth at your dock immediately.' Then sign it, 'Captain Meade.' Will that work?"

After finishing the message on his notepad, the telegraph operator nodded, then turned and began tapping the device.

At the US Mail Steamship Company's main office on Manhattan, the atmosphere was all darkness and dread. Two of the women on staff had fainted when they heard the news. All speculation had ceased. That which they'd feared most had come upon them. A massive loss of life and over twenty tons of gold.

Gone.

"We can wait no longer, gentlemen," said Holden, the vice president. "I've just given permission for the harbor master to steer the *Cutlass* to our dock. It could be here within the hour. There will most certainly be an investigation into such a calamity. I don't want them to have any basis for accusing us of concealing the truth."

He called out the names of three men and handed them each a sheet of paper. "These documents say the same thing," said Holden, "our statement regarding the sinking of the SS *Vandervere*, what we can affirm as of this moment." He directed one of the men to read his to the press gathered out front, one to read his to the families still waiting in the first-class receiving area, and one to read his to a group of couriers. "It is only one paragraph," he said. "Make sure the couriers copy down what is said word for word, and then have them leave immediately. I don't want the families to hear this news from the street corner before they've heard it from us."

36

The doorbell rang.

Joel waited a moment to let Beryl answer it, but he'd instructed him to give any messages to him, not his mother or sister. Earlier that morning, his father had sent the driver to pick him up, then asked him to stay with his mother and sister, and to "take care of this matter until it was resolved." He, on the other hand, "simply must get to the office." Joel supposed there *was* something to do at the office; there was always something to do. But he knew the real reason: his father hated family drama, wanted no part of it.

The door closed. Beryl walked over, message in hand.

"It was the courier we've been expecting, sir."

Allison ran out from the dining room and stopped in the doorway. "Is that him? Is John home?"

"No, Allison. Just the courier from the steamship line."

"Joel? Who was that?" His mother's voice called from the balcony above.

He looked up. The door was open, but she was still in her room. "Just the courier, Mother," he shouted back. He unfolded the paper and began to read.

US Mail Steamship Company

From the desk of the vice president:

We have just received confirmation of the worst possible news. The SS Vandervere sank somewhere off the Carolina coast four days ago. A ship named the Cutlass was able to rescue 109 passengers, which represents all the women and children aboard, but only 6 men. The captain tells us there are no other survivors. We have no names as of yet. His ship should be arriving at our dock with the survivors within the hour.

We will provide more information as soon as possible.

"What, Joel?" said Allison. "What does it say?"

Joel walked backward until his legs bumped into a chair, then he sat.

"Joel, what's the matter?"

He looked up. Beryl was staring at him. He looked away. Joel searched and found Allison's face. He didn't know what to say. "The ship . . . John's ship. It's gone."

"What?"

"The *Vandervere* has sunk . . . four days ago."

"No . . . no! It can't be."

They stared at each other a moment. Allison ran back to the dining room, sobbing.

Joel wanted to run after her, but he knew first he must

find the courage to go upstairs. He read it again. He didn't know why. It still said the same thing; it would always say the same thing.

His brother was dead.

But only 6 men.

Joel knew John could not be among them. They would have to be the men who'd rowed the lifeboats; that was the only conclusion that made sense. John died four days ago, along with several hundred other men when his ship went down.

Joel didn't even like John. He wasn't sure if he ever had. They were different in every respect. He'd actually been glad when John had left for San Francisco. Everything in Joel's life had instantly improved with his parting.

But then, it was his brother. His brother was dead. Why couldn't these words attach themselves to at least one emotion? He was aware only of the dread inside about breaking the news to his mother. But what arrangement of words could take this note and build hope in any direction? He started slowly up the stairs, rehearsing the first line he'd say as he walked into her room. Before he got far, she came rushing out.

"I can't wait any longer. What did the courier say, Joel? When will John's ship arrive?" As soon as she looked into his eyes . . . "What's wrong? Tell me what's wrong."

"Let's go back in your room."

She reached for the note. He pulled it back.

"Please, Mother, do as I ask. I will tell you, but not here." He gently spun her around, and she walked into her bedroom. He passed her and pulled her vanity chair next to the upholstered bench at the foot of her bed. "Have a seat." Tears streamed down her face as she sat.

He sat on the bench. She grabbed the note from his hand. He didn't stop her.

She read.

"No, no, no, no . . ." Quietly at first, then louder. "No, no, not John, not like this . . ." The words poured out until she was almost shouting, then she dissolved into sobs. The note fell to the floor. She reached for it, but her hand just dabbed at the carpet; she was crying too heavily to see.

Joel put his hand on her shoulder. She reached up for him with both arms, so he just held her as she cried. He felt a lump in his throat, and his face became hot. He'd never seen her like this. He didn't know what to do or say.

Suddenly, she sat up and wailed loudly, shaking her head back and forth. She bent forward again, holding her head in her hands. "No, no, no, no . . ."

"Mother, it will be all right." It was a pathetic thing to say. "We'll get through this." Another empty cliché. What should he say? He heard footsteps behind him. He turned. It was Allison standing in the doorway. Her eyes all puffy, tears streaming from them. She ran and put her arms around their mother and released a fresh barrage of tears.

Tears formed in his eyes. Feelings surfaced, not thoughts. Confusion. Desperation. He got up and closed the door. The staff mustn't hear this. He turned. Allison was sitting at Mother's feet now, grasping her hands.

His mother raised her head slightly, looking at Allison. "I am a terrible mother."

"No, you're not," said Allison.

"I am. I'm a terrible mother."

"Stop it, you're not."

"All I cared about, all I ever cared about was how John embarrassed me. What my friends would say behind my back, what they'd think. Even now, I wasn't looking forward to him coming back."

She lowered her head and began to sob again. "Now he's never coming back."

37

As soon as Captain Meade had returned to the *Cutlass*, the atmosphere quickly returned to the dark, depressing place it had once been. No one said a word. The tour guide had stopped pointing out sights. Laura sat on a crate, her shawl wrapped around her shoulders, staring down at the deck. Even the children had lost their glee. Most huddled close to their mothers, their faces buried in their laps.

No one cared to see New York any longer.

What the captain had said to the customs agent, and the agent's reaction to those words, forced them to remember who they really were. Widows and orphans about to face the reality of sudden loss, a future filled with emptiness and uncertainty.

The sky had turned overcast, as if cooperating with the shifting mood. Laura heard a new sound. A crowd, not cheering, but making considerable noise. She looked up. Docked on either side of the *Cutlass* were dozens of sailing ships and smaller steamers. Every few seconds she heard a loud bumping sound. She walked to the far side of the ship and saw a tugboat pushing the *Cutlass* into the docking bay, gently banging it sideways.

She leaned over the rail and saw the steamship company's dock about fifty yards ahead. It was triple the size allotted to the ships on either side. That's when she saw the crowd, hundreds of people. The clamor had brought most of the women to their feet. They began to line the sides of the ship and peer into the crowds.

Probably hunting for a familiar face, she thought. She wondered . . . was John's family out there? They must be. Captain Meade had sent word through the telegraph operator. If they *were* out there in the crowd, then they already knew.

John was gone.

The word involuntarily repeated in her mind. She forced it to stop and looked back at the faces of the crowd. Those she could see looked either sad or worried. She turned to face the women and children lining the ship's rails. Most were crying quietly.

Except one.

Melissa, standing by the bow, leaned forward on the rail. She also scanned the crowds. Undoubtedly looking for "her Tom." Her heart must be bursting with joy, longing to give full expression to all that her good manners and upbringing had kept properly bottled up inside. Laura wanted to be happy for her, but she had no happiness to spare.

Her John was gone. It was time to accept it.

Joel knew it was a pointless task.

"As long as there is a shred of hope, Joel . . . please," his mother begged.

They were all still in her room a full hour after they'd received the news. She had rotated through every horrific emotion the human soul can bear. Joel had stopped trying to console her with words. Allison's words seemed to have some effect, but just as she'd pull his mother out of the pit, she'd fall back into it herself. "All right, I'll go," he said. "Will you be all right if I leave you?"

"Of course I won't be all right. I'm never going to be all right again." This unleashed a fresh outpouring of sobs.

He walked over and kissed her on the forehead. "I'll be back as soon as I can." He started for the door. Allison followed. He opened it and whispered, "Keep her up here until I come back."

She nodded.

"Just make sure. She'd hate herself later if she made a scene in front of the staff. See if you can get her to drink some tea."

"I will. Do you think there's a chance John could be among the six men who survived?"

Joel shook his head. "I don't see how that's possible."

New tears slipped down Allison's cheeks. Joel squeezed her hand and left. As he walked downstairs, he called out to Beryl, who was already standing by the door with Joel's frock coat and hat. "Is the carriage still out front?"

"Ready to go, sir."

He walked briskly by and hurried out the door. The driver knew the way. Within ten minutes they arrived at the same corner that served as their rendezvous point before. The crowd was just as big.

The little door slid over. "I can't get any farther, Mr. Foster."

"This is fine," Joel said. "We'll do the same thing as yesterday. Check back every twenty minutes."

"Yes, sir."

The carriage door opened. They were startled by a newsboy shouting behind them. "Papers, get your papers here! *Vandervere* sinks, hundreds lost."

He repeated it over and over in staccato fashion. Joel wanted to slap him. He walked toward the crowd, turned, and said to the driver, "This won't be a repeat of yesterday. I shouldn't be here very long."

He crossed the street, walking along the outskirts of the throng. Every few steps, he heard someone wailing and crying like his mother. The long line of armored wagons was gone. Of course, he thought. Their shipment of gold is no longer coming. He looked down the street and noticed the corner of the office building and remembered the alley he'd discovered last night.

He came out of the alley just in front of the first-class families' pavilion. It was half-filled; all who were there wept and wiped their eyes with handkerchiefs. Next to them stood a new crowd—the press. They hovered around the back office door like little birds waiting to be fed.

Just then he saw the ship, an old two-masted bark. Must be the *Cutlass*. It had apparently just arrived; men were still tying it up. It could be any one of a hundred old ships crowding the harbor, Joel thought. He decided to stand near the group of reporters. They'd likely be given any news as soon as the steamship management was ready to part with it.

Even still, he knew this was a pointless task.

38

"Mr. Holden, may I make a suggestion?"

Holden lifted his head from his desk, the vice president's desk. But for how much longer? He looked at Parker, a mid-level executive. His likely replacement.

"I think I've found a way to instantly thin out the crowds," Parker said. The other men looked at him. No expression on their faces. No one had slept a wink all night.

"What is it?" Holden asked.

One of the men peeked out the back window. "The *Cutlass* has fully docked, sir."

"What's your plan, Parker?"

"We know all the women and children survived but only six men. I'm sure the majority out there are waiting to see if their particular loved one is among the six male survivors. If we could get the captain to release them first, everyone else would know there's no reason to wait any longer."

It was an excellent idea, Holden thought. Said with the characteristic lack of empathy for others a large corporation expects from its top executives. But he saw a problem. "The captain will never go for it, Parker. You don't release men before the women and children, not in a situation like this."

Parker thought a moment. "Then perhaps he'll just give us their names. We can read it aloud before we release the women and children. We'll achieve the same result. We can fashion our appeal to the captain, saying how much harder it would be on the ladies, especially the children, to have to pass through so many people when they disembark."

"Do it," said Holden.

The crew of the *Cutlass* lowered the gangway. It was such a rickety thing. Laura couldn't imagine any of the women, especially the mothers, feeling comfortable using it. Maylor called down to some of the men on the dock, asking their help to secure it.

Just then a finely dressed man came out of the steamship office, catching everyone's attention. Reporters shouted at him as he passed by. Their cries were echoed by the crowd standing nearest the building. He ignored them. "Are you the captain?" he asked Maylor as he reached the gangway.

"I'll get him," said Maylor.

"First," said the man, "we're not going to use this." He pointed to the gangway. "Please have your men pull it back. We'll use ours. Much sturdier, with rails on both sides."

"Fine," said Maylor. He went below to get the captain. The men on the dock exchanged the gangways. A few moments later, Captain Meade appeared.

"Permission to come aboard, Captain? The name's Parker. I'm with the steamship line. Just need a word with you, if I may."

The captain nodded, and Laura watched as the two men walked toward the rear of the ship, then up a ladder all the way to the stern. Captain Meade nodded several times. The man got out a sheet of paper and wrote some things down.

They shook hands and headed back toward the gangway. Parker walked down to the dock, turned, and said, "We'll make this announcement right away, Captain. As soon as the crowd thins out, feel free to begin releasing the women and children at your discretion."

"Very well," said Meade. "As soon as my passengers exit the ship, I would like a word with those in charge."

"That will not be a problem," said Parker. "They're expecting to meet with you. And again, may I extend our deepest gratitude for your heroic care and hospitality of our passengers. We are in your debt, sir."

The captain nodded. He turned to face the ladies. "It won't be long now, ladies. If you haven't already done so, it's time to gather your things."

What things, Laura thought.

Joel watched as a man he recognized from the office last night—one of the men reading maps—came out the back door. He obviously wasn't there to bring news, because he walked right past them toward the ship. Less than ten minutes later he came back. The reporters shouted their questions again. He paused a moment and said, "We'll be making a major announcement momentarily."

He headed back into the steamship office, every eye now fixed on that door.

A few minutes later, the man who spoke to the crowd last night came out carrying a paper in his hand. He walked up the stairs to the deck overlooking the crowd.

The crowd grew silent.

"Ladies and gentlemen," he shouted from the bullhorn. "I have some news to report. As you can see, the *Cutlass*, the ship that rescued surviving passengers from the *Vandervere*, has arrived. Those of you waiting to reunite with the women and children aboard the *Vandervere*, please stay where you are. They will be released from the *Cutlass* very soon. But we are very sorry to also report that those of you waiting for any of the men . . ." He stopped for a moment. He seemed to be choking back tears.

"The papers reported correctly that 6 men have been rescued. There were 568 passengers aboard the ship, 103 were women and children. We are so very sad to say that . . . 459 men aboard the *Vandervere* have perished. I could read the 6 names of the men who survived, but all 6 have indicated to us they have no friends or family in New York City."

The news washed over the crowd like a tidal wave of grief. Cries and wailing broke out across the wharf.

The man turned to walk away. Instantly reporters shouted questions. Most seemed to be asking the same thing. He stopped and pulled the bullhorn back to his lips. "I'm being asked if we're certain there are no other ships coming with more survivors. What we are certain of is this . . . the SS *Vandervere* sank four nights ago. Since then we've had no telegraph reports of any other ship rescuing survivors from any port anywhere along the East Coast. And we've learned that the captain of the *Vandervere* sent word to Captain Meade of the *Cutlass*—four nights ago—that he didn't expect his ship to last the night. This seems fairly conclusive."

As expected, Joel thought, coming here had been a pointless task.

39

Laura's head dropped. Her legs suddenly felt as if they might give way. She gripped the rail. She didn't know why hearing this steamship man should make any difference, but it did. He had just officially announced something she'd known to be true since the first night she boarded this ship. But it hit her now with the force of finality. There was no reason to pretend anymore. It was time to face a fact she could no longer ignore.

She looked up as hundreds of mournful cries suddenly unleashed through the air. Dozens of women fainted and fell to the ground. Men shouted and shook their fists toward the steamship office door. But no one came out. Why would they? There was nothing left to say.

She realized just then that she was standing at the very place she was supposed to be. The place where the long voyage from San Francisco to New York was supposed to end. But nothing else—not a single thing she and John had talked about—had gone according to plan. She was completely alone.

She remembered John's words, the last words he'd spoken to her when they parted.

The note.

It was time.

She reached for the pouch. But a great commotion caught her eye. She looked up and noticed most of the crowd dispersing. She must hurry. John's family was out there. And now they knew he hadn't survived. Without him beside her, how would she find them? John meant for her to read the note when she was sure he had not survived. Perhaps he'd written something more about them, something that would help them find each other when she arrived.

Her hands trembled as she loosened the pouch from her belt. She sat on a crate and tried to untie the knot around the pouch, but it wouldn't give. It had gotten wet. She couldn't pull it free.

She looked up again. Half the crowd was gone. *Please, Lord. Help me get this free.*

Finally, it came loose. She pulled the string, and the pouch opened, like the petals of a black flower. John's note rested on top of the gold nuggets. She pulled it out and held it in both hands.

These were his last words to her.

She unfolded the paper. Tears fell on the page. She quickly looked away. *The ink will smear.* She took a deep breath and tried to regain her composure.

The tears finally cleared enough to read.

My beloved Laura,

If you are reading this, then you are now convinced that death has parted us. I fully expected to grow old with you, my love; to live out days, weeks, months, and years together. The thought of it has provided me the greatest joy. But if we are parting so soon, there are some things you absolutely must know.

First . . . my life, before discovering your love, was like a harsh journey up a steep incline, only to reach a landing and find myself staring out at the most magnificent view. Your love has been breathtaking. I hadn't lived before you came, merely existed.

Second . . . and sadly, there is some news to tell you. I hate that you are finding out this way; I have only myself to blame. My parents don't know that we are married, only that I am coming home. I intended our arrival as a married couple to be a surprise. But I could not be certain they'd find it a happy one. I have only hinted to you about the degree of estrangement which exists between me and my family, hoping that when you finally met them in New York, they would fully accept you (and me). I held out some hope that we might have a pleasant visit, a new beginning. But I also knew the possibility existed that they would reject us both, for reasons too complicated to explain here.

Please forgive me for any

hardship I've caused you by withholding this information. Adding to your grief is the last thing I want to do. Laura, you must know this, and cling to this for all the years you remain on this earth . . . my last thoughts will be of you, and only you. I will think of your face, your smile, the love I have cherished in your eyes, our precious conversations.

If it must be so, that I am to sink into the deepest waters below, you are and will always remain my only love.

John

Laura fell to the deck.
The note fell from her hand.

40

Joel couldn't believe it. He was actually crying.

The tears just came; it didn't make sense. He didn't think of John anymore, hadn't given him a moment's energy in two years, until his mother had asked him to check the ship's schedule two days ago. He must compose himself; the carriage was just one block from the Foster home.

Perhaps he should have the driver turn left up ahead, not right. Head for the Foster Insurance office downtown. By rights, his father should be told. He should be the one to break the news to his wife. It was his responsibility, not Joel's.

The carriage came to the last intersection. Joel let the moment slip away.

His father would have accepted the task, but all the while he'd have despised Joel for forcing it upon him. He would know Joel had allowed a moment of weakness to overtake him and come running to Daddy. And we couldn't have that, could we? The Foster family empire had been built on firm resolve and steel will. No place for weakness or sentiment. Such was the sad lot of women and the infirm. And weak men . . . like John.

Why couldn't the old man have been the one who died instead of John?

The carriage stopped. He heard the driver climb down. The carriage door opened. Joel exited, his eyes fixed on the large mahogany door. It opened before he reached the knob.

He handed Beryl his top hat and coat but couldn't look him in the eye. A memory flashed into his mind. Beryl with a full head of hair, bouncing John on his knee in the parlor, then both of them being scolded by his father as he left for work. "Not what I pay you for, Beryl," his father had said.

Beryl had loved John dearly.

Allison rushed out from her room upstairs. She looked over the balcony, and her eyes instantly locked onto his.

Joel shook his head . . . no.

Allison fell to the floor, sobbing. The tears continued as Joel walked slowly up the stairs. Another image. John and Allison playing hide-and-seek in the backyard garden. Joel, the big brother, sent to put an end to their destruction of the begonia beds. As a child, he had never played with his siblings, with either one of them.

He turned left at the head of the stairs and bent over her, patting her gently on the back. She didn't respond. He stood up and looked at the closed door leading to his mother's room.

Foster men are strong.

But he didn't feel strong. Still, he walked straight to the door and opened it without allowing another memory to ambush him along the way. His mother lay across the bed, fully dressed, her body turned away from the door. He walked around the bed quietly, hoping to find her asleep. But her eyes were open, staring blankly at some fixed spot on the wall.

He came close and bent down. She didn't look at him. He touched her shoulder gently, and she looked at his eyes. "I know," she said. "I know John is gone."

"They announced that none of the six men had any family in New York," he said.

She sighed deeply. "I'm sorry for sending you. As soon as you left, I knew he couldn't be among so few in number."

John was surprised to find her so calm. "Are you . . . all right, Mother?"

She sat up. "For the moment. I have no more tears."

He looked at the china cup by her night table. "Can I get you some tea?"

"I suppose," she said.

"Something to eat?"

"I'm not hungry."

A few quiet moments passed. "I should probably go and tell Father, then Evelyn."

"You do that," she said. "I'll be here. I have nowhere to go."

He stood up. She reached for his hand and squeezed firmly. "Thank you, Joel."

He forced a smile, then turned and left quickly. Another moment and he would lose control completely. As he came to the front door, Beryl stood at the ready, as always, coat and hat in hand. "Beryl, be a good man," he said. "Make sure Mother doesn't see the newspaper for the next several days."

"I understand, sir."

"And could you have someone get her some tea?"

41

John awoke to a warm breeze blowing on his face. He still felt motion beneath him, but it was subtle and stable. He heard voices, in English and some other language. But perhaps the best thing was that he heard footsteps on wood.

"Wondered if you'd sleep right through lunch."

John lifted his head and looked into Robert's face. Behind him, big, white, beautiful sails flapped in the wind. He saw rigging and men going up and down on the shrouds. He smelled coffee.

"There's still some gruel left," Robert said. "It's been sitting a few hours, but when I ate it, I could have sworn it rivaled the finest omelet I ever tasted."

John smiled. *I'm going to see Laura again.*

It was the best possible thought. No other thought even mattered. He sat up. He wanted to shout in the worst way, to properly express his gratitude to God for life itself. He was safe. The sentence of death reprieved.

"Want me to get you a bowl?"

"That would be wonderful, Robert. What time is it?"

"Not sure, but well after eleven o'clock."

"Where is the ambassador?"

"Up by the bow, taking in the view. Be right back with your food. Care for some coffee?"

"Can you believe it, Robert? You're asking if I want coffee?"

Tears welled up in Robert's eyes. "I was sure seawater would be my final drink." He turned and walked away.

John stood up and headed for the rail. The sky was a royal blue with a few scattered clouds. The sea had a light chop, and the ship moved through it at a solid clip. He turned and surveyed the ship more closely. *Thank God, a ship.* It had three masts, square-rigged. No damage that he could see. Must have missed the hurricane altogether. He looked to the top of the mainmast, eyed the Dutch flag. That was the foreign language he'd heard.

Last night the captain had said his name and the ship's name, but John could remember neither. He looked back toward the wheel, saw a man on the quarterdeck with an air of authority standing beside it. John had seen the captain briefly last night, but it had been so dark. This man looked like him. John wanted to thank him, but Robert was coming back.

Robert held out a bowl and a tin cup with coffee. "Not a lot of food in there. The captain said he'd feed us better at lunch, and even better at dinner. Something to do with our stomachs having shrunk while we were adrift. I don't really care. I'm happy just having fresh water to drink. And this coffee."

"I can't believe we are rescued," John said. "That we're actually going home."

"I know," said Robert. "I'll see Mary and the children. I didn't think—" He choked back tears. "I have you to thank for that, John. I owe you a debt I can never repay."

"You don't owe me, Robert."

"I do, you saved my life. Several times. On the *Vandervere*, out on the raft. Even last night . . . the ambassador told me what you did, diving in after me when the raft overturned."

"Did he also tell you I almost drowned?"

"He did. I don't know what I would have done if you had survived a shipwreck and all that time on the raft, only to have drowned during our rescue."

John smiled. "I'll be relieved to get off the water. I'm wishing we didn't have to sail back to San Francisco, after we visit my family, that is." What an odd thing to say, he thought. He'd said it as if nothing in their plans had changed. He took a bite of food and swallowed, then looked down. "Laura must be having a terrible time right now. I can't believe the mess I've put her in."

"Because she thinks we didn't survive?"

"It's worse than that." John explained the situation more fully, the content of his note, the implications. Robert's changing expressions confirmed that it really was as bad as John feared. "I don't even know where she is right now," he said.

"The *Cutlass* must have already docked in New York," Robert said.

"But no one in my family even knows she's coming."

"She has the gold. She should be all right until you arrive."

"I suppose," said John. But the pain and loneliness she must be feeling right now. He ached to see her, to comfort her. "I wonder where we are now, how far till we reach New York."

"The captain gave a little speech, but you slept through it. He said we're less than a day from Norfolk, so that's where he's taking us. He's just come across the Atlantic and is low on provisions."

John was relieved to hear they were so close to land. He sipped his coffee again. It was a wonder in itself.

"I'm not sure," said Robert, "how I'll find my family once we arrive. Mary had planned to meet me in New York. Now she thinks I'm dead. I don't know if she's still there or has taken a train back to Boston."

John wondered the same. Where was Laura? What was she doing right now? How would they find each other once he came into town?

"But it will turn out all right," said Robert. "If God can appoint a bird to hit a sea captain in the head, cause that captain to change course, then steer him right through the middle of our group in the dark of night, then I suppose he can reunite us with our families."

"Whatever are you talking about, Robert?" John finished his last spoonful.

"That's right. You didn't hear Captain Houtman's story. It's the most amazing thing you've ever heard." Robert pulled up a barrel and sat. "It was a miracle, John, of biblical proportions."

42

Laura sat on a bench against a wall of lapboard siding, just a few yards down from the back door of the steamship office. The reporters still huddled about, but they'd shifted their focus from the steamship management to the passengers.

The ones who had family waiting.

They called out as the survivors passed by like shameless carnival hawkers. Some flashed cash, promising more for an exclusive story. A few of the women had been drawn in, but most wanted no part of it.

Laura just ignored them. She sat alone on the bench, waiting. For what, she wasn't sure. An idea that might break through the muddle in her mind. Perhaps a single thought that made any sense.

Twenty minutes ago, when she'd climbed down the gangway, she caught a glimpse of her reflection in a few panes of glass. It startled her. She hadn't bathed in almost a week. Her hair was ragged and matted. She looked like a washerwoman at the end of a long day. It had been easy to lose track of things on a ship filled with women who looked much the same. But seeing all the women in the waiting area, the way they looked at her . . . maybe it was a good thing John's family wasn't there to greet her.

"Laura?"

She looked up. It was Melissa.

"Are you waiting for John's family?"

How is it that she looked so beautiful? She hadn't bathed either. Was it the smile, the joy in her eyes? Laura shook her head no. She wasn't waiting for John's family.

"I want you to meet Tom."

That's right, *her Tom.*

Stepping out from behind Melissa, Laura looked up into the face of a tall, well-dressed young man with bright blue eyes. He removed his hat, revealing a full head of dark hair. He reached out his hand. "How do you do?"

She shook it gently. But she felt so embarrassed at her appearance. "Melissa has told me so much about you," she said politely.

"Then you must know what a coward I was to have ever let her go." He looked down at Melissa with adoring eyes and reached for her hand. "But that won't ever happen again."

How nice.

Stop it, she scolded herself. It was nice, for them. But she just wanted to be left alone. How could she get that message across?

Melissa sat beside her. "I don't understand. If you aren't waiting for John's family, then . . ."

"They aren't coming," Laura said, "because they don't know I exist."

"What?"

"They don't . . . they don't know—" Laura couldn't go on. She buried her face in her hands and cried.

"You poor dear," Melissa said, rubbing her back. "I'm so sorry."

After a few minutes, Laura regained her composure and told them about John's note.

"But surely they will want to meet you," Tom said. "Once they know."

"I'm not sure of that at all. John wasn't sure. That's why he hid this from me."

"But that was before he—" Tom stopped.

"Before he died." Laura finished his thought. "But it doesn't change anything. He wrote the note thinking he might. And still, he wondered if they'd reject me once we met. I've been piecing together other things he said. I think his family is very wealthy, in a much higher social class than me. If I met them now, and it doesn't go well . . . I can't bear any more pain. I just can't." She began to cry again.

"It's all right, Laura," said Melissa.

"I know of the Fosters," said Tom. "A little. And they are very wealthy, several rungs up the ladder from my family in Philadelphia. But I don't believe they'd turn you away. Especially now."

Laura looked up. "I can't do it."

"Here, I'm sorry," he said kindly, handing her his handkerchief. "I'm not trying to pressure you, really I'm not. But people like the Fosters, of all things, they care about perceptions. Some of their parties have even appeared in our society pages. Even if they didn't want to, they would still treat you well."

Melissa shot him a look that said: I can't believe you said that.

Tom's return look showed he had no idea what her look meant.

Laura said, "Thank you both for trying to help me. Honestly, I am grateful. But I think I'm just going to sit here awhile longer. I don't have the strength to face them. I don't want to bother John's family or make their lives difficult. I'm so tired. I just want to sit here awhile."

For a few moments, no one said a thing.

Melissa finally said, "Laura, I don't feel right just leaving you here. Tom's been staying in a fine hotel just down the street. We're going there now, then we'll head home in the morning."

"I've rented a carriage," Tom said. "We'd be happy to drive you."

"You could take a bath," Melissa said. "A hot one. Sleep in a nice bed."

Laura couldn't help it. A bath. It made her smile.

Melissa stood up. "Come, Laura. Let us take you there."

"It's the least we could do," Tom said.

Laura stood up. "It does sound nice. I think I'd like that."

"Get him out of there," said Captain Meade.

Ayden Maul decided not to resist as two crewmen dragged him from his bunk. What was the point? But every twist and turn stung like bee stings, every time his shirt made contact with the wounds from the lash. He squinted as they dragged him out to the main deck. He hadn't seen the sun in two days.

"Take him to the gangway," the captain said.

"Would you please untie me?" Maul said.

The captain stood less than a foot from his face. The two crewmen were on either side, holding his arms. "I have half a mind to deliver you over to the police. But with all these reporters hanging around, I don't want to take a chance they'll make you a part of their story and badger these poor women further. Untie him."

The crewmen obeyed.

"I want you off my ship and off this dock. Don't even think about trying to get a job sailing out of here. I plan to spread the word throughout the harbor. No one will hire a thief."

The crewmen walked him to the edge of the gangway and gave him a shove.

Maul hurried down and didn't look back. He was ready

to be free of this ship and its worthless crew. He looked up ahead toward the steamship office building.

He couldn't believe his eyes.

Walking away just now was that Foster woman, the lady who kept putting her nose in his business. She was the one got him caught, ruined all his plans. Stood up for that old slave rather than a member of her own race. Weren't for her, he'd be moseying off the ship with the rest of the crew when the captain gave liberty. With enough gold in his bag to set him up for life.

Now he had nothing. She had to pay.

He waited until she walked a little farther then crept up behind her, keeping his distance. He followed as she turned a corner around the office building, then hurried before he lost her in the street crowd. He stood just behind the corner and watched as a young couple escorted her to a carriage. He had to act fast, or he'd lose her for good.

On his left, three horses were tied up by the curb. He looked around for any sign of the owners, anyone looking his direction. He glanced back at the carriage; it started to pull away. He quickly tied his bag to the saddle and hopped on the middle horse.

It was a good horse, did what it was told. He backed it out and turned down South Street, keeping his eye on the carriage, now about a half block away. He waited for someone to shout, to cry out for the police to stop him. But no one did. His horse now.

He quickly closed the distance but stayed back a ways. Didn't want to take a chance that Foster lady would spot him when the carriage stopped.

But when it did stop, he'd be there.

She had to pay.

43

Micah had been cleaning up most the morning, still had lots more to do 'fore he was through. Crabby was movin' along right next to him all the while. She didn't do much, but make what he do not as hard somehow. She so happy, all the live long day. Like God put her on this earth for one purpose. To bring him joy.

He stopped picking things up a minute to look over the rail at the dock. Most the women be gone now. A sad thought kept knocking on his door, and he kept trying not to let it in. About Mrs. Foster. He thought they had become friends, felt quite sure it was so. But she was gone now, and she never come find him to say good-bye. He wanted to find her, but Cap'n had him cleanin' down below when all the ladies left the ship.

She must a' had her reasons, and he knew they must be good ones. 'Cause they was friends; he felt quite sure it was so.

He looked up the rail a few feet, right where he saw her last. The whole deck had been filled with a ruckus, people going this way and that. But not Mrs. Foster. She stood so still. He felt so bad for her, knowing the sadness she be feeling, all her dreams sinking four days ago with that ship. He said a prayer for her, but then he had to get below again.

Just now Crabby run to that spot, sniffing and pawing at a piece of paper. "What you got there, girl?" He walked over and picked it up. Right off, he was sure it was a letter of some kind. Had fancy writing all over it. He wished he could read it, know what it say. He saw two wet spots, like raindrops on the middle of the page. But he knew it wasn't rain.

This was right where Mrs. Foster had stood. He had a quick feeling, the kind he come to recognize might be the Holy Ghost. This letter be hers. She must have dropped it somehow. If she didn't want it, she'd have tossed it over the side. He knew she wouldn't just throw it on the deck for Micah to clean up. She not like that. And with them tears on the page, he had a strong feeling this note was very important.

"Cap'n will know what this is," he said to Crabby.

"I don't have time for this, Micah," Captain Meade said. "You see all what's going on here." He was in his cabin, sitting at his oak desk. "Got to finish my log, then get ready for a big meeting with these steamship people." He looked back at his work.

"I'm sorry, Cap'n. Don't mean to cause you no trouble. Can you just tell me if this belongs to Mrs. Foster? Don't gotta read the whole thing."

He ignored Micah a few moments. Micah decided he should stay put. Either Cap'n get more angry or give in.

"Bring it here." He turned in his chair, held the note up to the light coming in the window. He mumbled out loud as he read. A few lines later, his face got real serious; he even shook his head back and forth, let out this big sigh. "It's from her husband, guess his name is John."

"I thought so."

"Looks like he wrote it just before they parted."

"She so brokenhearted."

"They all were," the captain said.

"Yessuh, but Mrs. Foster somethin' special, the way she helped everyone."

"She was a nice lady."

"Weren't for her, Missuh Maul get everyone thinkin' I stole they gold."

"Now, Micah, I never would have believed that."

"Nice a' you to say, suh. But Cap'n, we got to get this to her."

"Micah, we can't do that. She's already left the ship."

"But these the last words her husband ever say."

"I understand, but she's gone, Micah. Nothing more can be done." He turned back toward the desk.

"Can I ask you somethin', Cap'n?"

"What?" He didn't look up.

"Just . . . can I go find her? Can I get this note to her?"

"Now, Micah, how you going to do that? You know where she went?"

"No suh, but—"

"But nothing. You need to just get back to work." He handed the note back to Micah. "I want this ship ready to sail. You know what needs doing before we can leave."

"Yessuh, I know." He started to walk away. "But Cap'n. If I work extra hard, get all that needs doin' done, then can I go? I feel real bad 'bout her not havin' this."

"I don't see how that's possible."

"But if I do, can I?"

"Now, Micah, you aren't thinking of running out on me, are you? I haven't ever whipped you, but if you ran off—"

"Cap'n. You got my word, I'll be back way before we set sail. I'll leave Crabby here, so you know I ain't lyin'."

Captain Meade thought a moment. "I suppose it's okay

then. But Micah, you better not skip out on any chores. There's a lot more needs doing with all these ladies and kids being onboard."

"No, suh, I promise I'll do it all."

"How you expect to find her? You never been in a city like this."

"Don't rightly know. Just pray, I guess. God want me to find her, I 'spect I will."

44

The carriage drove slowly down Broadway for well over a mile, providing Laura a nice diversion. At first, Melissa and Tom had tried to include her, but her short answers and long stares out the window eventually released them to what they more eagerly desired: to exchange smiles, adoring glances, and whispered compliments.

New York City, at least what she'd seen so far, put her in mind of the finest San Francisco had to offer. But it was much bigger and the buildings much taller. Most were three or four stories high, and several were over five stories. She couldn't imagine people living and working at such heights. Then there were the stores, the shops, the restaurants for block after block.

Back home with John, she'd only felt she belonged amidst such fineries after months of his persuasion. But now here, especially the way she looked, she was embarrassed to even ride in a carriage such as this.

"We're here," Tom announced. The carriage slowed to a stop. "The Metropolitan Hotel. Wait till you see it, Melissa."

As they stepped out of the carriage, Laura was overwhelmed

by the sheer size of the place, then the elegance. "I can't go in there," she said quietly to Melissa. "Look at me."

"Look at me," Melissa said. "I look just as bad."

But she didn't. She was younger, prettier. Her face clean. She was in love.

"We'll go in, get cleaned up a bit. Then buy some new clothes in one of these nice stores."

"There's eight stores on the first floor of the hotel alone," Tom said. "Plenty more on every street corner if you don't find what you want."

"Okay," said Laura. Shopping could only help her disposition.

Tom tipped the driver and whispered something. The man nodded and stepped away. "Shall we?" he said, leading them toward the lobby doors. They were large single panes of glass framed in brushed bronze. A doorman dressed like a colorful toy soldier opened the doors, smiled, and bowed as they walked through. Laura noticed he gave her a strange look then tried to correct it.

She stepped into the lobby. She had seen nothing in San Francisco to compare with this. The high ceilings with crystal chandeliers. The shiny brass and gold trim. The upholstered rosewood furniture. The rich carpets and tapestries. As they stepped up to the counter she noticed it was made of the same marble as the mantel over the grand fireplace. It was almost too much to take in.

"Can I help you, sir?" the hotel clerk asked.

"I believe I mentioned my fiancée would be arriving today."

"You did. We have her room all ready. Just two doors down from yours." The clerk reached back and pulled a key from a row of hooks. "Miss Anders, pleased to have you with us."

Laura noticed he gave Melissa a slight disapproving look. When Laura stepped up, he seemed almost startled, confused.

He feigned a polite smile and said, "How can I help you, Miss . . ."

"Mrs. Foster. I'll need a room for a few nights at least."

"Has the gentleman made you aware of our rates, Mrs. Foster?"

She untied her black pouch and set it on the counter. She opened it. "Oh no. Where's the note?" Maybe it had gotten caught in the folds of her dress. Then she looked on the floor. "It can't be gone."

"Is something wrong?" the clerk asked.

"What is it, Laura?" Melissa asked.

"John's note. It's gone." Tears instantly filled her eyes. "I must have dropped it on the ship."

"Then we'll find it," Tom said. "I'm quite sure the *Cutlass* won't be leaving the harbor today."

"Can we go back?"

"I'll go back," said Tom. "While you ladies get cleaned up and buy some new clothes."

"Thank you so much," said Laura. "You are very kind." She turned to the clerk. "I don't know what your rates are, sir, but I have plenty of gold." She opened the pouch wide and pushed it toward the clerk.

He looked inside. "I'm sorry, but this isn't the Wild West, ma'am. We can't take gold nuggets."

Tom stepped up. "Listen, my good man. Both these women are survivors from the SS *Vandervere*. Have you heard about it?"

"Why, yes. It's all anyone is talking about."

"Mrs. Foster here just lost her husband. My fiancée barely escaped with her life. Can you make an exception? I'll vouch for her until we can convert her gold into cash."

"No."

"Excuse me?"

"I mean you don't have to do that. I am so sorry, Mrs. Foster. I had no idea. My manager gave me instructions that if any *Vandervere* survivors came in, they were to be given our finest rooms at no charge."

"Really?"

"Yes. May I have your key back, Miss Anders? If you don't mind," he said, looking at Tom. "That goes for her too. I can offer her a room just one floor above yours."

"No," Melissa said. "Thank you, but no. I'd rather just keep the room closer to Tom."

"Very well," he said. He handed Laura a key from the fifth-floor row.

"Thank you very much," Laura said. "That's very kind."

"Do you have any trunks or bags?"

"We lost them all," said Melissa.

"I understand. If there's anything else we can do for you, anything at all, just let me know."

"We will," Melissa said as they stepped away from the counter.

"And ladies," the clerk said quietly, leaning forward. "If any members of the press interview you, you won't forget to mention our hotel?"

"We won't forget," said Melissa.

"Well, you two take your time," Tom said. "I'll ride back to the ship and see about that note."

"There's a wonderful old black man, a slave named Micah," said Laura. "He should be able to help you." Laura suddenly remembered.

"What?" said Melissa.

"I can't believe it. I forgot to say good-bye." Again, tears instantly filled her eyes. "He was so nice to me the entire time. How could I just leave without saying good-bye? He must think I'm awful."

"I will tell him of your great regret," said Tom. "Your care is obvious. It will be easy to convey. Oh, I almost forgot." He reached into his pocket and pulled out a brass money clip. He handed Melissa a large amount of cash. "I don't think any of these stores will take gold nuggets, either."

"I will pay you back," said Laura.

"I'm sure you will. Before you go up, Melissa, may I have a word?"

"All right." She turned to Laura. "I'll meet you over by that set of chairs in two hours? Is that enough time?"

"I hope so," said Laura. She waved and headed for the stairs.

Tom walked toward the lobby doors, and Melissa followed. "What is it, Tom?"

He looked to make sure Laura was far enough away. "I am going to the ship, but feel I must tell you. I am not at all comfortable with Mrs. Foster's decision not to tell her husband's family about her situation. They have a right to know their son was married, that she's their daughter-in-law."

"I was thinking the same thing. But what if she's right? What if they mistreat her? She's already suffered so much."

"Then I won't mention it to her until I know their reaction. If it's clear they don't want to see her, I'll tell them of her desire to keep her distance also and assure them of my discretion. But my sense of honor tells me I have to try."

"Whatever you say, Tom. I trust you. But since you are going, let me tell you what I know about John and Laura. It may help if you knew a bit of their story."

Ayden Maul set his beer down and sat straight up in his seat. The fancy-dressed man from the carriage, he was coming out of the hotel. Maul watched through the bar window, across the broad intersection. Seemed the man was alone. He walked to the edge of the curb and waved his hand. From somewhere down the street, the carriage they used to get here pulled up to let him in.

Maul glanced back to the hotel doors. Still no ladies coming out. The carriage pulled away.

He still hadn't figured out a plan, how to get at this Foster woman. He couldn't just walk into the hotel, looking like he did. He thought he might sneak in the back, steal a uniform, and find his way to her room somehow.

Or else he could just sit here drinking beers watching the door. Liked that idea better. She had to come out sometime. Best thing would be if she'd come out after dark. Nobody to see him follow her. She better come out tonight. Maul only had enough cash to either keep filling this mug or rent a cheap room for the night, not both.

A highfalutin couple walked by, lady twirling a parasol. Blocked his view for a moment. When they passed, he looked around at each intersection and up and down the sidewalks, far as he could see. That was it. Plenty of fancy-dressed folk roaming these streets. He could just wait till sundown, get enough cash from one of them to drink all he pleased, *and* get a nice hotel room. Probably wouldn't even have to pull out his knife. Just threaten to.

That'll work, he thought.

So he'd just stay put. Drink beers. Watch the doors.

She'd come out.

45

"Sorry, young fella, but Micah ain't here. You can insist all you want to see the captain, but he'll just say the same thing."

"There's this note," Tom said. "One of the women from the *Vandervere*, Mrs. Foster, she left it on the ship somewhere this morning. She is quite sure of it. My fiancée and I are just helping her. It's very important to her, apparently the last words her husband said."

"Sounds important. You could take a look around the deck if you want. Not a scrap of paper up here. Micah cleaned everything up. And I know for a fact he can't read, so he wouldn't have thought much of it. Hate to say it, but I'm afraid that note's in a rubbish box somewhere. Maybe you can talk to the steamship people, see where they put their rubbish."

"No, that won't be necessary. I had to try. Thank you for your time."

"You're welcome."

The young man turned and walked toward the main dock area and was soon out of sight. Maylor, Captain Meade's first mate, walked over to the hatch leading to the main hold. As he opened it, he heard someone moving below. He thought the entire crew had already gone. "Who's down there?" he said in a stern voice. Better not be that thief Maul.

"Somebody say something?"

"Micah, that you?"

"Missuh Maylor?"

"I'll be darned," said Maylor. "I thought you was gone. Captain said he let you go, to take care of something before we leave."

"He did, but Cap'n said fust I had to do all my chores, ever' last one."

"I just told this well-dressed young fella you'd done taken off."

Micah quickly climbed the stairs. "He still here? Say what his name was?" He hurried toward the bow.

Maylor followed right behind him. "He's gone now. Said something about looking for some note for that nice lady, Mrs. Foster."

"Must be this one." He pulled a wrinkled paper from his pocket. "It's a note from Missuh Foster, her husband. His last words."

"Yeah, he said something about that."

Micah ran to the bow. "I don't see any fancy-dressed gentleman."

"Told you, he's gone."

Micah looked up at the sky. "Only a few hours till the sun starts goin' down. Wished I knew how far I had to walk to find that Foster place."

"How much more work you got to do?"

"Just clean up the hold, that's it."

"C'mon. I'll give you a hand."

"You will?"

"Mrs. Foster really was a nice lady." He turned back toward the hold. "And you ain't so bad yourself."

"Thank you, suh."

"You're an ugly old coot, but you ain't so bad."

"Yessuh, Missuh Maylor."

46

"Mother's finally asleep," Allison said.

"Sally brought us some coffee," said Joel. Allison came in and joined him on the veranda. "I forget how you take it."

"As if you ever knew." She sat down, smiled briefly. "We better not let her sleep too long or it will throw her off completely tonight."

"I'll let you handle that one, dear," said Joel, taking his first sip. "This is really quite good." It was the first moment bordering on normal in two days. "I can't believe Father still hasn't come home."

"I'm not surprised," said Allison. "I wouldn't be surprised if he made up some excuse to stay there well into the evening."

"But I can't stay here all evening. Evelyn is expecting me home for dinncr."

"Does she know what's happened? About John?"

"She should. I sent her a note with the driver."

"Is she coming here?"

"I don't think she should. You know Mother barely tolerates her. Didn't want to add any more pressure to Mother's already fragile condition."

They both sipped their coffee a few moments. "Well," said Allison, "I've always liked Evelyn."

"Thank you," Joel said.

"Excuse me, Mr. Foster, Miss Allison." It was Beryl standing in the veranda doorway. "We have a guest, a young gentleman. He says his fiancée was a survivor from the *Vandervere*. He says he has news of great concern to the Foster family."

Joel stood up, then Allison. "See him to the library, Beryl. I'll meet him there."

"Very good, sir."

"May I come?" Allison asked. "Please, Joel."

"It could be difficult news to hear. It may be about John."

"I'm not a child, Joel. Please."

"All right." He took a final sip of coffee and left the veranda.

They walked quietly to the library. Beryl had wisely closed the door. Joel opened it, stood aside to allow Allison to enter. Standing between an upholstered chair and the bookshelves was a tall young man in his early twenties. He immediately turned and walked toward them, holding out his hand.

"Mr. Foster, my name is Tom Hayward."

"Pleased to meet you. This is my sister, Allison."

"Pleased to meet you."

"I understand you have some news for our family?"

"I do."

"Let's have a seat. Can we get you something to drink? A glass of water, some lemonade?"

"Water would be nice, thank you."

Joel nodded to Beryl. He walked out and closed the door.

"Did your fiancée know our brother John?" Allison asked.

Joel cast her a look that said: "Let me handle this."

"No, she didn't. And please, may I express my condolences

for your great loss. I was there on the dock this morning when they announced the news."

"As was I," said Joel. "So what news do you have for us?"

"I've been trying to think of different ways to say this, but there's just no easy way."

"Please, speak freely. It's been a trying day. If there is more we need to hear, I'd like to hear it now, not later."

"My fiancée—her name is Melissa—was onboard the *Vandervere* when it went through the hurricane. She was among the women and children rescued aboard the *Cutlass*. On the four-day voyage here, Melissa became good friends with a woman named Laura Foster. Do you know her? Have you ever heard of her?"

"No," said Joel. "She bears our family name, but I don't know anyone named Laura."

Allison shook her head no also, but Joel noticed her expression had changed, something close to joyful anticipation.

"I thought you might not," said Tom. "Then here is my news. Your brother John had married this woman, Laura. This was, in fact, their honeymoon voyage."

"What?" Joel said.

"How wonderful!" said Allison. "What's her name again?"

"Laura," Tom said. "I am told John had made you aware he was coming but had decided to keep this news a surprise."

"I'll say he did," said Joel. "He only sent one letter, about two months ago. The first we'd heard from him since he left two years ago."

"I don't know anything about that. I've never met John, and I've just met Laura today."

"What's she like?" asked Allison.

There was a knock on the door. "Come in, Beryl," Joel said. He walked in silently, handed Tom a tall glass of water, and left.

"Laura seems very nice," said Tom, "but of course, I'm meeting her under the most trying time in her life, I'm sure."

"When can we meet her?" Allison asked.

"Allison, please, let the man finish what he came to say." Joel could hardly comprehend what he'd already heard. He wondered if this news wouldn't send his mother tumbling over the edge.

"As of now, Laura has no plans to meet you. She doesn't even know I'm here."

"No, that . . . that can't be," Allison said. "She's family."

"Allison."

"She's all we have left of John. She can tell us all about him, what he was like in San Francisco."

Joel ignored her. "With respect, Tom . . . if Laura doesn't plan on meeting us and doesn't know you are here . . . why *are* you here?"

"Melissa and I both felt it was the right thing to do. Your family has a right to know this information. And we both felt Laura is too overwhelmed with grief and sorrow right now to make sound judgments."

"I appreciate your courage to do the right thing." It felt like the right thing to say. Though Joel wasn't completely convinced he believed it.

"But why would Laura not want to meet our family?" Allison asked.

"I feel very awkward telling you. It seems entirely inappropriate that I should even know this. And please understand, I've formed no judgments about your family."

"Please, go on."

"It would appear that John kept all of this hidden from Laura as well. She didn't find out until this morning that you didn't know she and John were married."

"How is that possible?" asked Allison. "I thought they parted four days ago."

"John had written her a note, which he gave her when they parted. But she didn't read the note until this morning when the *Cutlass* came into port."

"There was something in the note that caused her to decide not to meet us?" Joel asked.

"Apparently, but nothing explicit. He said something implying uncertainty as to whether your family would accept her. He sought to protect Laura from the hurt that might come, should your family react negatively to the news of his marriage."

"I can understand that," said Allison. "Perfectly."

"Allison, please. Do you have any suggestions as to how we should proceed?"

"Mr. Foster, I assure you, I wouldn't begin to advise you on matters of such importance. I don't want you to feel obligated to tell me any of your family's plans, either now or in the future. I simply wanted to leave this with you and trust you to do whatever you deem best. I will go back to our hotel, and Laura will know nothing of my visit here this afternoon. If you choose to contact her, you can find her at the Metropolitan Hotel."

"She's staying at the Metropolitan?" Joel said. "Please, how much do we owe you? It's the least we could do, to pay for her expenses."

"You owe me nothing," Tom said. "The hotel has offered to let any *Vandervere* survivors stay there for free."

"That's very kind of them," said Joel. "Do you know how long she plans to stay?"

"I don't. I believe I heard her say at least a few days, but I don't think she's had time to form any plans." Tom stood up.

Joel did as well. "Can I give you some money for clothes? I would imagine she would have lost her luggage when the ship sank."

"Mrs. Foster has no need of financial help, as far as I can see. I saw in her possession a bag of solid gold nuggets, worth well over a thousand dollars, maybe two."

"What?"

"Would you expect her to be in need?" Tom said. "No, I'm sorry. I shouldn't have asked that."

"As I said, my brother John only sent us the briefest note. I have no idea how he fared out West."

"Well, Melissa told me he had become a wealthy merchant. They had traveled the entire voyage in first class."

"Is that so?"

Allison looked at Joel, so excited by this news. "We must go at once to meet her, Joel. Please say we will."

Joel walked over and shook Tom's hand. "Thank you, Tom. You have served our family well. I shall not forget your kindness and discretion."

"My pleasure," he said and walked out the library door.

"Joel, we must visit Laura."

"I know how you feel, Allison. It's just all so much to take. I need a few minutes to think." He sat down in the chair again. "There's more to consider than just doing what you or I want to do."

But really, only one thought rose to the surface. That is, how to break all this to their mother.

47

Against Allison's wishes, Joel had waited two more hours before waking their mother. Of course, there was no sign of their father coming home, so the responsibility once again had fallen on him. He had absolutely no premonition of how she'd take it. But he was certain he stood the best chance if she was properly rested.

As he walked the main stairway, he thought about the part of the news that he found the most surprising, and unsettling: that John had somehow become a wealthy merchant. That he'd traveled here from San Francisco in first-class accommodations. That his wife carried with her a large bag of gold. There was nothing Joel had ever detected in John that would have led him to believe his brother could become a success. He seemed to have almost despised the family business and, at best, showed total indifference to business chatter between Joel and their father at the dinner table. He'd never once joined them in the library for brandy and cigars when the talk became too much for the ladies.

Joel reached the top of the stairs and turned left across the balcony leading to his mother's room. As he neared the doorway, he heard her snoring. No need to knock. He opened the door quietly and saw her lying on her back, the covers up to her chin, her nose pointed at the ceiling. He closed the door hard, hoping it would save him the task of waking her.

It did not.

"Mother," he said loudly. She didn't awaken. He felt sure the staff made terrible fun of her behind her back because of this, the ones who took turns waking her for breakfast each day.

He reached her bedside and shook her. "Mother, wake up. Mother, it's me, Joel." He used the same volume one would use calling down from the stairs. A few more times and finally her eyes opened.

"Joel . . . did I fall asleep? What are you doing here? What day is this?"

He sat on the empty spot beside her. "You've just had a nap, Mother. Remember?"

"Oh yes . . . John."

Her eyes were puffy. He almost didn't have the heart to go through with this. "How are you feeling?"

She inhaled deeply and sat up. "A little better, I think. I don't know. It all seems so unreal. Doesn't it seem that way to you?"

"Yes. And even more as the day unfolds."

"I'm sorry I'm so useless. I haven't even considered how you and Allison are doing. You've had the same shock as I."

"Don't worry about us, Mother. We seem to be doing fine. Allison is still downstairs. I think she's having dinner."

"I've slept through dinner?"

"No, there's still plenty. But I have some more news to tell you."

"News?"

"We've had a visitor this afternoon, while you slept."

"Who . . . who was it?"

"A young man whose fiancée was aboard the *Vandervere*. She was among the survivors who came ashore this morning on the *Cutlass*."

His mother sat up straight. "Truly? Did she know John, did she have any news about John?"

"Well, yes, in a manner of speaking."

"Tell me."

"It's . . . well, I'll just say it. She didn't know John, but on the rescue ship she became good friends with John's wife."

"What!" she yelled.

The volume startled him. But her expression was more like Allison's, something closer to happiness. "It appears John was planning to surprise us by bringing home a wife."

"Did she survive?"

"Yes, she's here in New York, staying at the Metropolitan Hotel."

"My goodness, how wonderful!" She got up out of bed. "This is the most wonderful news." She walked toward her vanity, sat down, and started brushing her hair. "What is her name?"

"Laura."

"Laura . . . a wonderful name."

Joel saw tears streaming down her face through the reflection in the mirror. Over the last day she had become a woman he had never known.

She turned to face him. "Part of my sorrow was never knowing what had become of him after he left. What his life was like out West, what kind of man he had become."

"Well, here's another surprise then. It appears John had become a wealthy merchant. I'm not sure doing what, but they traveled here in first class. The young man said John's wife carried a bag of gold worth a great deal of money."

"So he did well? I was so worried he'd come back to us like you said, like your father said."

"I am more surprised than you on this point."

"But why is she staying at the Metropolitan? Why didn't she come here?"

Joel walked over and stood behind her. "This part of the story might be harder to hear." He spoke softly but shared with her all that Tom had conveyed, about John's note, about the hesitation in John's heart of them returning, the concern that the family might reject him and his new bride.

"Oh, John," she said as he finished. She bent over and sobbed. "It's true. His fears were not unfounded. I'm such a horrible mother."

"No, you're not," he said. He leaned over and patted her on the shoulder.

"Yes . . . I am," she said, her head still in her lap.

"Do you want me to go and get her?"

"Yes, we must." She sat straight up. "Would you? You must bring her here. You must convince her she will be welcomed and accepted completely."

Joel stood up. "Then I will." But he wondered if he could properly convince John's wife. "I'll bring Allison with me."

"Yes, do. Allison will help her see. Can you ask her to come up here? I want to tell her myself. She needs to know how much I want this. It's not a time to be proper or guarded with our words."

Joel could hardly believe what he was hearing.

"Go, Joel. Get Allison. I won't be long with her. You get the driver ready to leave as soon as I am through."

"Very well," he said. He kissed her forehead and headed out the door. He called out over the balcony, "Allison."

"I'm here." She was sitting on the upholstered chair closest to the stairway.

"Mother needs to speak with you," he said. He was relieved his mother had handled this new development so well, but he was thoroughly confused.

48

John had seen many fine sunsets out on the water these past many weeks, but none to rival the one he saw now. It wasn't the dazzling array of colors that spread across the sky. Its most remarkable feature was the dark silhouettes that ran along the base of the scene.

Buildings and steeples, ship masts and trees, low rolling dunes.

It was Norfolk. He was seeing *land*.

Seeing it now brought fresh thoughts of glory and gratitude to God, for John had firmly concluded he would never see land again. But here it was, drawing nearer each moment. Within the hour they would dock.

He would step onshore, sharing the same body of land as Laura, separated only by hours and minutes of travel, not by the veil of eternity.

49

It felt so strange, walking the earth.

Micah had been on that ship so long, almost forgot what it felt like. For the first few blocks, he'd keep looking back, sure someone was coming after him. Till he finally realized what it was. This was the first time he been by hisself on land when he wasn't running away or being chased. But Cap'n said he could find Mrs. Foster, if he could get back before the ship sailed tomorrow.

And Micah would keep his word.

But he talked to the Lord each time the feeling come to break that word. It be strong. And it came many times already, 'fore he even got three blocks from the ship.

He didn't have a plan to find her. Just stop and ask the colored folk he met along the way, hoping somebody knew something. So far no one did. He came to this one street, called Broadway. Biggest street he ever saw. It was already getting dark, but this street had lampposts, all up and down. Bright little lights flickering behind glass.

He thought about Crabby and that sad look she give him as he left her tied up on deck. She got that look as if he never coming back. She all sad and whining. But he had to tie her up. All the men coming back and forth, no one paying her any mind. She'd take her first chance, come flying down that gangway, pick up his scent. She run out one of these roads, smack-dab into one of these carriages. Then where would he be?

Up ahead, he saw a shoeshine boy. That's what they called 'em, even though this boy looked as old as he was. He weren't shinin' no one's shoes presently. "'Scuse me, suh."

The man looked at him. "You call me sir? No one call me sir. The name's Obadiah. Sounds like you from down South."

"That's right, but mostly I'm out on a ship these days. The name's Micah."

Obadiah looked up and down the street. "Seems like everyone's shoes shiny enough for another day." He smiled real big when he said that, then sat down on his shoe-shining chair like he sitting on a throne.

"Can you help me?" Micah asked.

"I'm fixin' to call it a day."

"I don't mean for you to do my shoes, just need help findin' someone."

"They lost?"

"Not exactly. You heard about that big ship sunk a few days ago?"

"All my customers, that's all they talkin' about these last two days."

"Well, I'm from the ship that rescued them."

"You don't say. Now that's a wonderful thing."

"Thank you. See there was this lady, a fine Christian woman. And she left a note on board, the last words her husband wrote to her. I'm tryin' to get this note to her, but I don't know where she live. Well, where her family live."

"What's the name?"

"Foster. Her name is Laura Foster."

Obadiah thought a moment. "Ain't never heard of no Laura Foster, but a Mr. Foster's one of my best customers. Has some big company just down the road a ways. He get his shoes shined 'bout every other day."

"Really? You know where he live?"

"Not right where, but I can get you close. If it's the same one. I've heard Mr. Foster talk about a place called Gramercy Park. Never been to his home, mind you. But I been by that neighborhood a time or two. Big fancy homes, bigger'n you ever seen."

"Sounds about right. Had a feelin' they be plenty rich."

"The Fosters been good to our people too. He say his wife hiring runaway slaves to work at their house, get their rich friends to do the same. At church, we got people who can help. That is, if you lookin' to get away. You a slave, right?"

Micah nodded.

"I could get you to meet up with some folks who happy to help. Do it all the time."

"You a slave?" Micah asked.

"Me? No, sir, I'm a free man. I start the day when I want, and I end the day when I want. I get money for what I do, and I keeps all of it. Don't have to give any of it to no white man. You could be free if you want."

Oh Lord, Micah thought. He almost said out loud, "Get behind me, Satan," like one of them old preachers, but he knew it wouldn't make any sense. "Thank you, but I best be on my way. You know how I can get to this . . . Grammasee Park?"

"Just keep headin' the way you goin'. Got a long way to go from here, but with the sun goin' down, shouldn't be too hot. Gotta stay on this street here all the way till it come to this big square, call it Union Square. Just a few blocks away then. Ask any colored folk you see there. They probably know just where the Fosters live."

Micah smiled. God already helping him. Both finding Mrs. Foster and saying no to the devil.

The ride south on Broadway to the Metropolitan Hotel was two miles. Allison talked almost the entire time. Joel hardly said a thing. He wasn't lost in thought. For the first time in a long time, he had no thoughts at all. The logical, rational world that had been so large and so clear just one day ago had shrunk to the confines of this little box, the ornamental walls of this carriage.

Here there existed only the excited, nervous chatter of his sister. And the task of convincing this woman he had never met to come home and stay with a family that just one day ago would have renounced her outright before she'd opened her mouth to say hello.

"There it is, Joel. We're almost there. It's so beautiful at night."

Allison was sticking her head out the window like a child. Joel tapped on the little door to alert the driver.

"Yes, Mr. Foster."

"After you drop us off at the main entrance, there's a section for guest carriages around the corner. You can wait for us there. Honestly, I have no idea how long this will take, but I suspect no more than fifteen to twenty minutes."

"Very good, sir."

They pulled up and went inside. It wasn't a bad place at all, Joel thought. A bit overrated from what he'd read in the papers. He stepped up to the counter, Allison right behind him. "My good man, my name is Joel Foster. I believe we have a relation, one of the *Vandervere* survivors, a Mrs. Laura Foster, staying at your establishment. Would you be so kind to tell her that her brother-in-law and sister-in-law are here and wish to speak with her?"

"Is she expecting you, sir?"

"No, she is not. We've just learned she is here a few hours ago. We'd like to . . . to welcome her, see if there's anything we can do for her."

"Very good, Mr. Foster." He looked down at his register, then at the wall behind him. "We do have a Mrs. Laura Foster staying here, and I believe she is up in her room. We can send someone up with a message. Would you like to wait in one of our receiving rooms?" He pointed to the interior of the hotel. "See that large fireplace? There is a nice room just beyond it on the left. If you'd like, you could wait in there."

"That would be fine." Joel stepped back as the man began to write a note.

"Please, sir," said Allison, "tell her we can't wait to see her."

"Come, Allison," Joel said.

50

Laura was just about to change into her nightclothes but stood for a moment looking at herself in the mirror. She remembered on evenings she would see John, how nervous she'd get on her last look in the mirror. *Is this the right dress? Will he like it? Do the shoes match? What hat should I wear? Am I pretty enough?* Now she must return once again to dressing without any purpose or anticipation.

At least she felt clean. And she had a warm bed, a real bed to sleep in tonight.

A knock at the door. Who could it be? Had Melissa left something in her room? She looked around as she walked to the door. "Who is it?"

"A message for you, ma'am, from the front desk. I'll just slip it under the door. Sorry to bother you."

She reached down to pick it up.

Mrs. Foster,

Two relatives of yours are waiting downstairs to see you. Your brother-in-law and sister-in-law. They wish to welcome

*you and offer their assistance. I've directed
them to wait in the receiving room just
beyond the grand fireplace on the left as
you come down the stairs.*

Charles

The front desk

Her hands began to tremble. How was this possible? This had to be a mistake. She looked down at the note. It *was* addressed to her. But how could anyone in John's family be downstairs? She wasn't ready to see them; she didn't want to see anyone.

What if she just ignored the note? If she waited long enough they would go away. At first, they might think her rude, but then they would likely consider she must be tired from such a trying day and had already gone to sleep. No, that wouldn't work. They'd go to the front desk. The messenger would confirm that she spoke to him through the door.

She sat in an upholstered chair and sighed. She would have to go down. But she wasn't ready. What would she say? She didn't have the energy for polite pretenses.

John hadn't told them about her.

He was afraid to.

Why must she face this now? But she must.

She took another look at herself in the mirror, which didn't help. She picked up the new shawl she'd bought and wrapped it around her shoulders. She reached for the knob and took one more look at the note.

*They wish to welcome you and offer their
assistance.*

This was promising. They wanted to welcome her. And the second part . . . she could simply say, "No, thank you, I have everything I need," and make the visit short and polite.

She locked the door behind her and started the painful journey down the flight of stairs. On the way up she'd wondered why a hotel would put the nicest rooms up so high. It was more like a punishment than a luxury. She supposed it was because of the view. Little good it did her at night.

She finally made it down to the lobby and was surprised to still see so many people walking about. She looked up at a large clock on the far wall and realized it was only 8:00 p.m. Across the lobby was the big fireplace, beyond that . . . the room.

Go, she thought. Just walk right in and get it over with.

She turned the corner, and there they were, sitting on the edge of two matching rose-colored chairs. A finely dressed man instantly rose to his feet and looked at her. She was stunned at the resemblance. Clearly, John's brother. Her heart was immediately warmed by the visual reminder. He took a step toward her, but the young woman—must be Allison— leapt from her chair and rushed past him. She was blonde, pretty, full of smiles.

"Laura, you must be Laura." She seemed ready to embrace Laura, as though they were long-lost friends, but stopped short, as if held back by a sudden impression of etiquette. She held out her hand politely. "I am Allison, John's sister. I could not be happier to meet you."

Laura didn't see as much of a visual resemblance in her but felt John's warmth in her tone and countenance. "Allison, nice to meet you too. John has spoken of you often."

"He has?" Quickly tears formed in her eyes. "I'm sorry," she said as she pulled away and sat back in her seat.

"My name is Joel. I'm John's older brother." They shook

hands. "Not sure how much John spoke of me. I suppose the fewer words the better."

Laura simply smiled and said, "Nice to meet you, Joel."

He backed up to the chair. "Please . . . Laura, may I call you Laura?"

"Please do."

"You must be tired. Please have a seat." Across from the two rose-colored chairs were two additional chairs, similar but beige. Between them, a white oval table with a glass top. Joel sat in the rose chair after she sat in the beige one.

Laura looked over at Allison, the poor thing. She seemed to be regaining her composure. Joel looked at her, reached over, and patted her wrist. "My sister and I are here, really sent from our mother—"

"But we would have come eagerly on our own," Allison added.

"Yes. And we, well, we just learned about you a few hours ago."

"We didn't know John was married," Allison said.

"Please accept our apologies," said Joel. "Had we known, we would have welcomed you at the dock. I was actually there this morning, when the steamship company gave the news . . . well, that's not important."

"Please, it's all right," said Laura. "I understand. I'm not sure I was ready to meet anyone this morning. I had just read this note from John that said he hadn't told you about us." Laura fought back a rush of tears.

"We know about the note," said Allison.

"Well, we haven't read it," Joel said. "We were told something about it by a young man who came by our home. His name is Tom. I forget his last name."

Now it made sense, Laura thought. When Tom had returned this afternoon, he seemed rather nervous. Laura had just assumed it was because he had been unable to locate John's note.

Perhaps seeing her expression change, Joel said, "Please don't think ill of him. He was greatly conflicted about coming to see us. He even said he wouldn't mention it to you, in case . . . in case we decided not to respond."

"But as soon as our mother heard the news," said Allison, "she instantly asked us to come and meet you. You simply must come and stay with us. She desperately wants to meet you."

This was totally unexpected. "I . . . I don't know."

"Please say you'll come. We have so much to talk about."

Laura had no energy for conversation; all she wanted was to sleep.

"We won't talk tonight," Joel said. "But we would like to invite you to stay in our family home."

"When?" Laura asked.

"Tonight, if possible," said Joel.

Laura hesitated, and Allison leaned forward. "Say you'll come, Laura. If John loved you, then I want to know you."

Laura was relieved at the warmth of their words and the strength of their desire to see her, but she could hardly imagine finding the reserves to leave now, at this moment. "My things are upstairs," she said.

"I could get them for you," said Allison. "I'm sure you must be exhausted. But I don't mind going up the stairs. I've just been sitting around all day."

Laura loved listening to Allison talk. She reminded her so much of John, and she was so eager to please. Laura just didn't have the heart to tell her no. "Okay, then. I'll come."

"Thank you," Allison said, leaping out of her seat. She bent down and gave Laura a hug.

Laura stood up and handed her the key.

"Do you have any luggage?" Joel asked. "I could send a bellhop up to get them."

"No luggage," said Laura. Just then she remembered . . . all her wedding gifts. This was a moment she had so looked forward to: meeting Allison, showing her all the presents, spending time talking over each one. She could fight the tears no more. She sat back down, covering her face.

"I'm so sorry," Allison said, bending down beside her.

They cried together a few moments. Joel stood patiently, not saying a word.

After, she stood. "I'm sorry," she said to Joel.

"No apologies needed."

"As I said, I don't have any luggage. But there are two shopping bags on the bed." She leaned toward Allison and said quietly, "There is also a black pouch full of gold on the dresser by the mirror."

"Allison," Joel said, stepping closer, "please be discreet. Keep the pouch out of sight on your way back down. You never know who might be watching."

"I'll be careful," she said.

51

Micah was plum wore out with all this walking. He was feeling his age all up in his hips, his back, even down in his knees. Long time ago, he remembered walking this far for days on end, never had any trouble. But there it was, finally. The Foster mansion. Just like that shoe-shinin' fellow Obadiah said, someone at Union Square set him straight to it.

It was quite the place. Like someone took a plantation house down South and put it smack-dab in the middle of this big city.

Sure could use a glass of water.

As he got closer, he saw this fancy-dressed old fellow, older than he was anyway, peek his head out the front door. Then he walked down these fancy winding steps to the sidewalk. Held his hand over his eyes to block the light from a nearby lamppost as he looked down the street. He looked right at Micah but didn't see him. He turned around, did the same thing the other way.

"Excuse me, suh," said Micah. Man didn't seem to hear him, so he said it again a bit louder. Old man turned around, looked Micah over. Had a nice face but didn't smile.

"Can I help you?" he said.

"I hope so," said Micah. "This be the Foster place?"

"It is, but I'm quite sure the family has all the help it needs at the moment."

"I'm not here lookin' for work, suh. I actually come bringing somethin' for Mrs. Foster. I mean, Mrs. Laura Foster."

The old man's face lit up bright. "You do? What might that be, may I ask?"

"Is she here?" Micah asked.

"Not at the moment. I was just looking for the carriage she might be riding in just now. So what is it that you have for Mrs. Foster?"

"I have a note." Micah pulled it out of his pocket. He had worked it real hard, trying to smooth out all the wrinkles. "She leave it on the ship. That's where I come from. Thought it was mighty important, and the cap'n agreed she should have it. Even let me come all this way just to make sure she get it."

"May I see it?"

"Yessuh."

The man held it, then stepped back to see it better in the light. "My goodness," he said. "It's from John."

"Yessuh. Mrs. Foster's husband. Cap'n say it be the last words he say to her." Then Micah saw something strange. The man's eyes got all teary. Just then, the front door swung open.

"Beryl, are they here?"

Micah looked up and saw this woman in a fancy dress looking down at them both.

"Is the carriage here? Who is this?" she asked, looking right at him.

The man, Beryl, blinked his tears away. "No, Mrs. Foster. It's not here yet. But this man just walked up to me, said he was from the ship that brought John's wife here."

"What?" she said loudly.

"I'm holding in my hand," said Beryl, "a most remarkable

thing. A note written by John to his wife, Laura, just before they parted at sea. These are his last words."

Micah saw the tears come back to his eyes. The woman looked like she gonna fall straight down them steps.

Both men ran up to catch her. They helped her back inside. In a moment, she was standing again. Beryl helped her to a big chair nearby. Then he walked back and closed the door. Micah had never been inside such a place before. He couldn't keep his eyes from roaming all about.

"A note from John?" she asked.

It looked to Micah like all the wind was suddenly out of her sails. Beryl handed the note to her. Micah stood by just off to the side.

She looked right at Micah. "Thank you so much for bringing this. How did you get here?"

"I walked, ma'am."

"You must be exhausted. Beryl, would you please get him a large glass of water?"

"Right away, Mrs. Foster."

She held the note so she could read it better by the lamp. Micah wasn't sure what he should do. Felt like he should excuse himself, let her read in peace. But she wasn't paying attention to him.

She began talking out loud, as if John were in the room. "How hard this must have been for you!" Then Mrs. Foster pulled out a white handkerchief and dabbed her eyes. She turned to Micah and said, "Look how much he loved her."

Now Micah saw that white cloth catching lots of tears, and felt even more unsure of himself.

As she continued to read she said loudly, "Oh no. I'm so sorry. But you were right." She dropped the note then, and it fell to the rug. John's mother put her head down into her hands and cried all the more.

Beryl walked in, not seeming the least distressed. He handed Micah the water, walked over and picked up the note, set it on a little table beside her. Then stood back. He looked up at Micah as she cried. Micah saw all kinds of care in his eyes. He could tell this man was a servant, though not a slave. But he been here a long time, like he almost a part of the family.

Micah drank the whole glass down. It surely helped.

After she was through crying, or at least get to where she could talk, she looked up at Micah. "What is Laura like? Did you know her?"

Now Micah didn't know why, and he surely didn't see it coming. But tears rushed up from inside as he said, "She may be the finest woman I ever know."

No one said anything for a moment. Then Mrs. Foster said, "I am not at all surprised."

Micah felt he should say more. "She so brave. Care for others way more than herself. Treat me and . . . my dog better than we ever been treated."

Mrs. Foster looked up at Beryl. "I so hope Joel was able to persuade her."

Beryl nodded.

"Would you like another glass of water?" Mrs. Foster asked.

"Maybe just a little," Micah said. "Help me on my way back to the ship."

"You're going back tonight?"

"Well, Cap'n say we might be leavin' tomorrow. Gave him my word I be back before then."

"Beryl, could you give him something, some money? To thank him for all his trouble." Then she stood up, came right over, and shook Micah's hand. "Thank you, Mr. . . ."

"The name's Micah, ma'am." He didn't want to shake her hand, his hand being so dirty. But he did.

Beryl came back and handed Micah some gold coins. "No

need for this, Mrs. Foster. I'm happy to come, do anything I could for Mrs. Foster. Well, the other Mrs. Foster."

"I insist," she said. "Perhaps you could find yourself a hotel or at least a decent meal."

"Thank you kindly, ma'am. I guess I best be going." She looked like she wanted to give him a hug, but she just patted him on the shoulder. He nodded, put his hat back on, and headed for the door.

Beryl walked him out, all the way to the street. "Do you know your way back to the ship all right?"

"I 'spect so. Just head back to that Union Square, then follow that big wide street south."

"Very good," said Beryl. "You've got the idea. Thank you for taking the time to come, and bringing the note." He leaned forward. "Mrs. Foster has had a troubling day, but I could tell, she was very grateful."

"Thank you for sayin' so, suh. I best be on my way."

Well, things did work out all right, he thought, making his way down the steps. But he was sad he come all this way and didn't get to give Miz Laura the note himself or say a proper good-bye.

He thought surely she had been his friend. Felt quite sure it was so.

52

Ayden Maul could not believe what he saw through blurred eyes. It was that Foster woman, coming right out the front door of that uppity hotel across the street. He had just finished his last beer of the evening and was settling up his tab with the barkeep when he glanced out the front window. "Gotta go," he said. "Keep the change."

God or the devil, one had opened up a window of opportunity, and he was jumping through. He'd already figured the woman must have gone down for the night. He was just about to go out and refill his pockets with some dandy man's cash down some dark alley.

That would have to wait. He had another tab to pay.

He walked outside and stayed in the shadows until a carriage came around the corner and stopped by the front doors. It was different from the one that brought her here, bigger, much nicer. His horse was tied to a rail not twenty feet away. As soon as the lady and her two companions got in the carriage, he jumped on the horse.

It seemed late for a woman of her status to be venturing out. She didn't load any luggage, but he saw a few shopping bags. Maybe she was going out for a little while, maybe leaving for good. He didn't have a plan made up just yet. The main thing was not to lose her, to keep her in his sights.

He found opportunities had a way of presenting themselves if you just paid attention. He followed behind just enough to stay out of sight. The carriage headed north on Broadway. Wasn't hard to keep track of them now, streets were almost clear of traffic. All the stores were closed and most of the restaurants.

About fifteen minutes down the road, it was clear they had left the business district. He was starting to see more homes than shops and, he noticed, more trees.

More trees was good; it meant more shadows.

For Laura, the carriage ride was taxing. She barely had the energy to keep her eyes blinking, let alone discern and satisfy expectations Joel and Allison had of her, not to mention what awaited her at the Foster home. It was at least a relief to find they were not hostile as she'd feared. Allison continued to be warm and congenial. Under better circumstances, Laura felt sure she would even enjoy her company.

For the most part, Joel said nothing. Allison talked occasionally. Thankfully, she hadn't asked the kind of questions Laura was certain she'd wanted to, about John. Laura could tell they both sat upon a mountain of tears, ready to release with the littlest prodding.

Joel sat up and looked out the window. "We're just three blocks away now."

"Does this remind you at all of San Francisco?" Allison asked. "I've read so much about it."

"Hard for me to compare," said Laura. "I've only seen a fraction of this city before dark. Maybe tomorrow I could answer better. I will say . . . it's a much larger city, with much taller—"

The carriage stopped abruptly. Everyone fell forward in their seats.

"Did we hit something?" Joel said.

Lot nicer to walk in the cool of the night, thought Micah. Quiet too, now, almost no one out on the street. And Laura's kin treated him very kindly. Didn't know exactly what to do with the money she give him, never stayed in a hotel before nor ate a meal in a restaurant. He figured he best just keep walking all the way back to the ship.

But he figured, he saw someplace that sold food to colored folk, any kind of food, he could be talked into stopping a spell. No hurry to get back to eatin' what ole Smitty made. Barely right to call it food.

A big carriage came down the road just up ahead. Micah saw this young colored man dressed like a fancy dancer holding the reins. Now what kind of life he must have, they let him dress like that every day.

The carriage stopped suddenly. Micah looked around the wheels, like maybe something broke or it hit some animal. He looked up at the young man, who just staring at him like he seen a ghost.

"Daddy?" the young driver said.

Micah looked behind him, wondering who he was talking to.

"Daddy?" he said again, louder, tying up the reins on a hook. Still looking right at Micah.

"It's you, Lord Almighty. It is you," the driver said.

A man from inside the carriage spoke up. "What's going on, Eli? Why'd we stop?"

"Daddy," the driver said again, crying, coming down quick off that carriage.

Eli? Did he say . . . Eli?

Micah looked at the young man as he jumped to the street. "Eli? That you, son?" Tears falling down his face like rain, 'cause Micah knew it now.

His boy Eli.

Eli rushed on him, hugged him so hard his fancy hat tumbled off his head into the street. "Daddy, I thought I'd never see you again."

"Eli . . ." Micah couldn't talk, couldn't think. Joy was comin' out of him every which way. He held Eli so tight. They both crying so hard, neither one ever wanting to let go.

"Something strange is going on," said Joel. He opened the carriage door.

Laura looked out the window. She could see in the shadows the colored driver was holding another colored man in a strong embrace. Both men were crying. Joel stood by on the sidewalk.

"Let's go see," said Allison.

They both stepped out and carefully made their way to the sidewalk. A moment later, the two men, still holding each other at the shoulders, separated slightly.

"Look at you," the older man said. "You all growed up and dressed so fine."

Laura recognized the voice. It couldn't be.

"Micah!" she yelled. "Is that you?"

"Mrs. Foster?" he asked. "God be praised. How you be . . . you know my boy Eli?"

She looked at the young man, his face awash with tears and a smile wider than she'd ever seen. "Is this your son?"

Micah nodded.

But of course it was. Laura ran over and wrapped her arms

around Micah; she didn't care how improper it might look. She pulled back a little. "I thought I'd never see you again. I'm sorry I didn't say good-bye." She turned to Eli and held out her hand. "Your father has told me so many things about you. Mostly about how much he missed you."

"I missed him too, ma'am," he said. He looked back at his father, then hugged him again.

"How wonderful," Allison shouted. "So this just happened?"

"Eli, this is your father?" Joel asked.

Eli nodded. "Yes, sir, Mr. Foster. Sorry for stopping so suddenly. I couldn't believe my eyes. There he was, just walking down the street."

"Extraordinary," Joel said.

"How did you get here?" Laura asked.

"Walked all the way from the ship," Micah said. "Cap'n let me go to bring you that note, the one your husband give you."

"My note? John's note? You have it?" she asked.

"Just give it to Mrs. Foster . . . the other Mrs. Foster. The mother," he said.

"You've just come from our house?" Joel asked, sounding concerned.

"Yessuh, your man let me in. Said your mother want to read it."

"What did it say?"

"Don't know exactly. Can't read. But my son Eli can, right, Eli?" Eli nodded. "Whatever it say, she cried a good spell but then seemed real happy. Thanked me all kinds of ways."

"I can't believe you're here," said Eli. "You said you came from a ship?"

"That's right. Been on it the last three years."

"This is quite amazing," Joel said. "Thank you for taking the trouble to deliver the note all the way here, and on foot.

Is there anywhere we can take you? Eli can drop us off at the house then take you anywhere you need to go."

"And you can tell me all about what you've been doing, Daddy."

"Joel," said Allison. "You can't do that. They've just seen each other again after years of being apart. When do you have to be back to your ship, Mr. Micah?"

"Tomorrow."

"There, then it's settled," she said. "He can stay with Eli tonight, and Eli can bring him there in the morning, after a good breakfast."

"I suppose that would be fine," Joel said. "Well, then, shall we get back to the house?"

Eli walked to the front of the carriage. "You can sit up here with me, Daddy." He thought a moment, smiled, and said, "Got another surprise for you too. When we get back to the house."

"Don't think I can take too much more," said Micah.

Laura stood back by the carriage door. "This is so amazing," she said. For the moment, it had taken all her sadness away.

Ayden Maul hung back about thirty yards, in between two lampposts, under a large elm. He wasn't sure what all was happening with the carriage. But everyone was out, standing around on the sidewalk.

He might never get a better chance. The Foster woman was by herself, near the back of the carriage, in the shadows.

He silently got off his horse and pulled out his knife.

53

It all happened so quickly.

Laura first noticed Micah's face. Instantly it changed from elation to terror. He was looking at her. No, beyond her.

Joel, off to the side, turned toward Micah's gaze. His expression also changed, a look of confusion.

Thumping footsteps behind her. Running, coming closer.

"Hold on, now," Joel yelled.

Laura turned toward the footsteps, saw a dark shape rushing toward her from the shadows. A man's shape, his arm raised. A flash of metal in his hand. He was attacking her. He'd be on her in a moment. She lifted her hands to protect her face.

"What?" said Allison, turning. She screamed.

"Daddy," Eli yelled.

Laura closed her eyes, awaiting the blow. A prayer began to form in her head.

Loud footsteps now rushed in front of her, past her. A loud sound near her, behind her. Shouts and groans. Men colliding, falling to the street. She opened her eyes.

"No, Missuh Maul." Micah wrestled with someone on the street. They rolled over and back.

"You're a dead man!" the attacker shouted.

"Stop!" Allison said. "Make them stop."

One of the men cried out in pain. Another shape rushed past her and jumped into the fray. It was Eli.

Eli grabbed Maul, lifted him in one motion, spun him around, and punched him square on the jaw. He fell to the street, tripping over Micah's feet. Eli jumped on him, pounding him with his fist over and over. "You're the dead man," he shouted through clenched teeth.

The knife fell from Maul's hand.

"Stop, Eli, you'll kill him," said Joel, hurrying toward the two men.

Eli didn't stop.

"Son . . ." Micah said weakly, rolling to his side. "Eli, stop." He reached out and grabbed his son's arm.

Eli stopped. He was panting like a racehorse.

Laura couldn't stop trembling. Maul was trying to kill her.

Joel touched Eli on the shoulder. "Come on, son. You've knocked him cold. He's not going anywhere." He looked at Micah. "You're bleeding."

"Daddy," Eli said. He got off Maul and crawled to his father, cradling his head in his lap. "He cut you. Where are you hurt?"

"Got me in the shoulder, I think." He moved a little and winced in pain.

"He's bleeding a lot," said Eli. "I need something to stop it."

"Do something, Joel," said Allison.

Joel walked up to her and bent over.

"What are you doing?"

He ripped a part of her dress below the knees then walked over to Laura. "You need to take Eli's place. Hold this to Micah's wound."

Laura took the cloth and turned toward Micah. She stared at Maul lying unconscious on the ground. "What if he wakes?"

"That's why I need you to take care of Micah. Eli, you need to watch him. You obviously know what to do if he comes to."

"Yes, sir, Mr. Foster."

Allison looked at Joel. "What are you going to do?"

"I'm going to get help. A policeman usually patrols our neighborhood this time of night, sometimes two. I'm going to find him, have him take this scoundrel off our hands."

Laura bent down and exchanged places with Eli. "I'm going to press this on the wound, Micah. It may hurt."

"Press hard, ma'am. Need to, or it won't stop bleedin'."

"I'm so sorry," she said, pressing down.

He groaned. "It's all right, you doin' just fine."

She looked up at Eli, standing now with his foot resting on Maul's chest. Then down at Micah's face. "Micah . . . you saved my life."

He smiled, then grimaced in pain. "Yes'm. Guess I did."

"He was going to kill me."

"I 'spect he was."

"But why?"

"Saw the hate in his eyes on the ship, twice. The time you helped me after the whuppin' and when he stole all that gold. Cap'n threw him off the ship this morning. Guess he blamed you for all his trouble."

Laura sighed. She was still shaking.

"Don't you worry, Mrs. Foster," Eli said. "He won't try to hurt you again."

Joel was already gone. Allison walked closer. "Can I do anything?"

Eli bent over and picked up the knife. "Pray this man doesn't wake up," he said. "He does, and I'll kill him."

54

The *Angeline* had docked. John was on land. The absence of motion, an indescribably wonderful sensation.

Word spread quickly through Norfolk that another rescue ship bearing survivors of the *Vandervere* had arrived. A crowd had instantly gathered, rejoicing and cheering. Once on shore, John and the other men understood that the shipwreck story had run in all the newspapers. And every story said they had all perished.

The survivors were told the National Hotel in Norfolk had offered them rooms at no charge. Several restaurant owners and merchants offered food and new clothes. The mayor said that tomorrow they could begin the journey north to New York. A passenger train made a regular stop in Norfolk around 10:00 a.m.

Wagons were provided to drive them to the hotel. When they arrived, John had just one thing on his mind: to get back to Laura, or at least send her word that he was alive and well. As the men stood in line to register, John noticed amidst the crowd in the lobby one of the Norfolk men who'd spoken out earlier, a clothier John remembered, wearing a derby hat.

"Excuse me, Robert. I'll be right back."

"Where are you going?"

"I need to talk to someone." John found the man talking to another well-dressed older man sitting in a high-backed chair. When they saw John, they stopped and turned. "Sorry to bother you," John said.

"No bother at all," the man said. "Anything we can do for you men."

"Thank you. Would you know if the telegraph office is still open at this hour?"

"I'm sorry, my good man. It is not."

John sighed. He had imagined as much. There had to be something he could do. "Are there any trains heading north tonight?"

"I'm afraid not. The first passenger train stops here tomorrow, 10:00 a.m. I believe."

"I know about that. Any other trains? A freight train perhaps?"

"Come to think of it, there is one. I use it at my store sometimes." He looked at his timepiece. "Comes in about forty minutes, as a matter of fact. And it rides right up the eastern seaboard, through New York City . . . if I understand what you're aiming at."

"You do," said John. "How far is the station from here?"

The man smiled. "Much too far to walk. But I'll take you there in my carriage."

"Thank you. I have to get to New York as soon as possible."

"Happy to oblige, young man. But we need to leave now if we're to make it on time."

"Can I say good-bye to a friend?"

"By all means."

John hurried back to the line and found Robert.

"I heard you," said Robert. "I guess this is it, then." Tears welled up in his eyes.

John held out his hand, and Robert pulled him into an embrace. "I'll never forget you, John."

"Nor I you, Robert. You sure you won't come with me?"

"I'm too tired to travel anymore tonight, and I don't want to feel anything moving beneath me, if only for a while. Here," he said, handing John a slip of paper, a small advertisement from the hotel. "I borrowed a pen and wrote my address there in the margin. If you and your wife can spare a few days while you're still on the East Coast, I'd love for you to visit me in Boston, so my wife and children can meet the man who saved my life."

"I would love to. I'm sure we could arrange that." He looked up the line and saw the ambassador just now interacting with the clerk at the front desk. "I wish I had time to tell him good-bye properly," John said. "Please do it for me."

"I will."

"If you can get the ambassador's address, perhaps I could get it from you in Boston and write him."

"I know he'd like that."

They embraced again, and John hurried to join the man in the derby hat, standing by the door.

55

"Let's get Micah into the carriage," Joel said, redirecting everyone's focus to a more pressing matter. "He needs to see a doctor."

Two burly policemen had just dragged off Ayden Maul, tied and bound, into a police wagon. First, Joel had given them the details of the attack. Laura had explained who he was and what he had done on the ship. Maul had only partially regained consciousness. Laura was glad. She didn't want to ever hear his voice again.

She did her best to keep the cloth pressed to Micah's wounds until Eli and Joel slid him through the carriage door. Then she hopped in beside him and continued her aid until everyone was in and the carriage pulled away. He seemed much weaker, but his smile never dimmed.

For a few moments, no one said a word. Allison cried softly into her brother's shoulder. Laura felt numb inside, almost unable to absorb what just happened.

Someone had tried to kill her.

The momentum of the terror continued to pulse through her body. Thoughts and images continued without permission. This day had been filled with more highs and lows than a soul was meant to endure. She wished she could hide in Joel's other shoulder and release all this tension in a proper flood of tears.

But Micah needed her to stay in the moment.

She looked down at his face. His eyes were closed, but he was still breathing. Let him rest, she thought. Every day his life was harder than this day had been for her. She thought a moment about the highs and lows this day held for him.

She'd ridden a fine carriage away from the ship; he had just walked for miles. She had bathed in a luxurious hotel and bought new clothes; he'd worn the same clothes from when they'd first met. A rich and refined family had invited her to stay in their mansion tonight. Micah had been sent away from that mansion, back to the damp, dark quarters of a musty ship. A ruthless man had just tried to kill her. Micah had stopped that man, with no regard for his own safety.

But as she gazed at the look on his face, she realized . . . Micah was happy. He would end this night refusing to dwell on his many reasons for sorrow and despair. He would not care that as he strolled these stately streets, he was invisible to the wealthy inhabitants of the city. He cared only that God had allowed one man to notice him. And this one young man's gaze mattered more to him than if a dozen kings had invited him to a feast.

Lord, thank you for this kindness to my friend.

And for the first moment in this most harrowing of days, Laura knew true contentment and peace.

"It's just up ahead," Joel said. A few moments later, the carriage pulled over and stopped. Eli opened the door. Micah opened his eyes. "I'll take him," Joel said.

"Be careful," said Allison.

They carried Micah outside. Allison opened the iron gate. Laura stepped out and down onto the sidewalk. She noticed at once the beautiful curved stairway just beyond the gate that led to the front door. She looked up at this huge home and could immediately see that, even aided by the lamplight alone, it was far more impressive than the finest homes she'd admired atop Rincon Hill back home.

This was John's home.

Here he grew up as a child. Here he'd become a man. From here he had fled just a few years ago, so that they could meet and fall in love and—

The front door opened.

"Beryl, can you get Mother?" Joel was grunting as he and Eli reached the top step.

"I'm right here," a woman's voice said from within.

John's mother.

"Mother, it was so awful," said Allison on the steps behind the men. "We were attacked in the night. This poor man, he's Eli's father. It was like a miracle. They haven't seen each other in years. He saved Laura's life, but he was stabbed."

"Calm yourself, Allison," Joel said.

"Oh my goodness," their mother said as she backed out of the doorway. "This man was just here, not thirty minutes ago."

"I'll explain everything in a moment, Mother. We need to get him to the sofa."

"Beryl, quick," she said, "go get some linens and put them over the sofa."

"Yes, madam."

"And go get Sally. Ask her to heat some water, then warm some towels."

"Right away, madam."

Everyone moved from the doorway, through a massive foyer, into the biggest living room Laura had ever seen. She stood behind the group, glad the attention had shifted, if only for a few more moments. As they set Micah down on the sofa, Joel gave his mother a calmer, more lucid rendition of the attack. Micah listened to the entire story, but Laura noticed how distracted he was. She realized how strange this all must be for him. He wasn't accustomed to ever being the center of attention, let alone by a rich white family in the living room of their mansion.

Laura looked at Mrs. Foster. She was not how she'd imagined her at all. For some reason she'd pictured her as a short, heavy woman with severe dark eyes and even darker hair. But she was a very attractive woman for her age, slim and refined. An older version of Allison, though her hair was a mix of blonde and gray. Her eyes became more intense with each new aspect of Joel's tale. At the end of the story, Joel explained how Micah had saved Laura's life. Mrs. Foster yelled out her name, startling everyone.

She turned and looked at Laura. "My dear, we've forgotten all about you." Tears instantly filled her eyes and fell down her face. She rushed over and embraced Laura. As Laura returned the hug, they both cried. She heard Mrs. Foster mumble through her tears, "John loved you so much."

After a few moments, she pulled back and looked right into Laura's eyes. "Laura, please accept my apology for not being there to welcome you this morning." She stopped, shook her head once. "No, more than that. Being proper is all I know how to be, I'm afraid. What I mean is . . . forgive me for being the kind of mother to John that he'd have to wonder in his last moments if I would ever accept you at all."

Just the mere mention of his name, spoken aloud, and Laura fell into his mother's arms, sobbing. She felt his mother holding her tight, patting her back gently. After a few moments, she heard John's mother say, "Joel. You better send Eli to get Dr. Ames. His father needs more help than we can give him here."

"Agreed."

Laura pulled herself together, pulled out a handkerchief, and wiped her eyes. She saw Eli standing in the foyer at attention. Joel looked at him, signaling him to get the doctor. Eli nodded. He was just about to leave when Micah yelled out, "Lord have mercy!" startling everyone.

Everyone looked at him. Had his heart given way?

Sally had just come in from a side doorway, carrying a stack of white linens. She jumped when Micah yelled. She took one look at him lying on the sofa. The linens fell to the floor. She fell on top of them, fainting right there on the spot.

"That my Sally?" Micah cried.

"Told you I had another surprise for you, Daddy," said Eli from the foyer.

"Sally," Allison yelled, and ran to her.

Laura looked at Micah, who was sitting up now, his eyes wide and bright.

"Sally's my sister," Eli announced to everyone. "She's Daddy's girl."

56

The following morning, Joel sat alone in the family carriage as it rode away from the nice section of Gramercy Park, where he lived, to the extravagant, luxurious section where the Foster mansion stood. The sun shone brightly through the carriage windows, so bright, in fact, Joel had to sit far back in the seat to avoid its glare.

He had barely slept a wink.

Yesterday, from beginning to end, had been the most extraordinary day of his life. And what had happened at the very end fit right in. Joel wasn't thinking about the violent attack or the circumstances that followed in the living room. But the disturbing situation that had unfolded after that, when his father had finally come home.

Most of the excitement had already died down. Joel knew the moment his father walked in the door that he wasn't in any mood to deal with an upheaval. His mother had hurried to the foyer, greeted him warmly, then tried to explain the scene. She'd brokered pleasant introductions between he and Laura, and then with Micah—"the very remarkable gentleman," to use her words.

Joel knew instantly that his father had become stuck on the

point that an old black slave was lying on the couch, covered in bloody linens and bandages. He'd extended a polite hand to Laura, followed by a weak smile. He then excused himself, walked toward the library, and asked Joel to join him.

He'd closed the door, asked Joel to take a seat, and explained the cause of his preoccupation. What he conveyed to Joel was shocking. What was even more shocking to Joel was his own reaction to what his father had said.

Apparently, his father had known all about the wonders of this new line of steamships and had invested a significant percentage of the firm's profits in the venture, without telling Joel. The tragedy caused by the *Vandervere* sinking, he said, was that the amount of losses they'd have to pay out in insurance claims had—in a single day—eaten up the entirety of the company's profits for the year.

Joel thought but didn't say, *No, father, the tragedy caused by the* Vandervere *sinking is that your son, my brother John, is dead*. What he had said, and this surprised both him and his father, was this: "It's only money, Father." Then he'd walked out and closed the door.

Suddenly, the carriage stopped. The jolt forced Joel's mind to the present. He looked out the window; they were still a block away.

The little door slid over. "Mr. Foster, I'm sorry, sir," said Eli. "The boy selling papers over there, do you see the headline?"

Joel looked at the headline and couldn't believe his eyes.

53 MORE *VANDERVERE* SURVIVORS FOUND

"Shall I buy one?" Eli asked.

"Yes."

After Eli got down from the carriage, Joel handed him a few coins out the window. He gave Joel the paper, and they continued on. Joel read the story, finishing just as they pulled up to the house. It wasn't the newspaper delivered to the house each day, the one Joel had asked Beryl to intercept. But he was sure the same story would carry the front page of every New York paper.

The question was . . . should he say anything about it?

It was a fact that fifty-three men had been rescued, and all of them had come ashore last night in Norfolk, Virginia. But it was also a fact that more than four hundred men had not been rescued and were lost at sea.

Did he dare mention it, raising everyone's hopes, when the chances were eight to one that John was *not* among the survivors?

57

"Come, Laura. We're eating on the veranda."

It was the following morning. Laura followed Allison through the living room, walking quietly past Micah, who was still asleep on the sofa.

"Dr. Ames has already been by to check on him," said Allison. "Gave him something to ease the pain."

"What time is it?" Laura asked.

"We let you sleep a bit. Mother thought you might need it. It's just a little after nine o'clock."

They walked through a doorway, down a wide hallway with doors on either side. This led through a similar doorway and into a beautiful covered porch, with all manner of potted plants and garden boxes full of flowers and ferns. Out across a finely manicured backyard she saw a greenhouse made mostly of glass.

"Later, I'll take you out and show you my roses," John's mother said. "Come, sit."

Laura walked toward a white iron table. Beautiful china, white linens, matching teapot. She smiled as she sat down, then noticed John's mother's eyes were puffy. She had been crying again this morning. Laura thought her eyes must look much the same. "What a lovely place to eat breakfast," Laura said. "Sorry for sleeping so late."

"Nonsense. You needed it. I only rose thirty minutes ago myself."

Allison joined them.

"Did you sleep well?" John's mother asked.

"I actually did, the first time since . . . this ordeal began."

"I hope you didn't mind being put in John's old room."

At first Laura thought she would, terribly. But then, even before she fell asleep, she felt the closest to John she had since the rescue. "No, it was fine. And thank you again for taking me in."

"Please don't thank me," his mother said. "You are welcome to stay for as long as you want."

Quietly, Laura thanked God for whatever had brought about this change. John would have been so pleased by this, to know the very thing he feared had somehow been dissolved. Allison lifted the lid to a silver serving dish, revealing a delicious blend of scrambled eggs, bacon, and potatoes. Laura smiled, recalling her recent bowls of gruel.

"Micah's daughter, Sally, made this," Allison said. "She makes some of the most interesting dishes."

Laura took a spoonful; she was hungry enough to eat everything on the dish. "Do you mind if I inquire what the doctor said about Micah?"

"Not at all. I wasn't here, but Joel told me."

"Eli is taking Joel to Micah's ship right now," said Allison.

"Really?"

"Because of what Dr. Ames said."

John's mother gave Allison a look that suggested "please let me talk." "As you know, last night the doctor cleaned and stitched up all his wounds. This morning he said the wounds were closing nicely but felt that Micah cannot be moved, at least for a day or two."

"I was afraid of that," said Laura. "I overhead Captain Meade say he wanted to get underway this afternoon."

"Well, he'll just have to wait, or he'll have to sail off without Micah."

"He won't do that," Allison added. "Micah is his slave."

The carriage pulled up to the curb, just outside the US Mail Steamship building, as it had several times over the last few days. But what a different scene. There were no crowds, very little noise. Beyond the dock area, Joel saw the masts of the *Cutlass*. She was still tied up in the same spot.

Eli opened the carriage door. "I think you can stay right here till I'm through, Eli. I shouldn't be long."

"Yes, sir."

Joel stepped down. He looked across the street and saw a small group of reporters loitering around the front office door. Likely waiting for an official comment on the reports coming out of Norfolk about the fifty-three survivors. Joel had decided not to tell the ladies about this.

The atmosphere in the house had so vastly improved with the news about Laura, compared to earlier yesterday, when there had been nothing but grief and despair. Even with the chaos after the attack, the most significant thing everyone had dwelt on was how her life had been spared and Micah's heroic deeds. Joel couldn't bear to insert this news into such progress, with such a slim chance for hope. He knew the women would latch onto it with a tenacious hold, only to plummet once more into despair when they learned John was not among the survivors.

He couldn't let that happen.

He was just about to walk through the huddle of reporters into the office when he thought better of it. His business was with the captain of the *Cutlass*, who was most likely aboard the ship. He walked around to the side, and the ship came into full view. Seeing it now without the distractions, he thought it looked so worn and beat up. A number of crewmen were busy onboard, some high in the rigging tending to the sails, some loading boxes and crates.

He walked to the left side, down a wooden walkway that ran alongside the ship. "Excuse me, my good man," he called up to one of the men. He didn't seem to hear or was ignoring him.

"Excuse me up there, may I have a word?"

The fellow looked down.

"May I speak with your captain, Meade, I believe it is."

"Captain Meade asked not to be disturbed," the man said.

"But I must speak with him—it's about his slave, Micah."

"Micah? You know where he is?"

"Yes, but I really must speak with your captain."

Another man walked up, older. The first man said, "Mr. Maylor, this fellow says he knows where Micah is."

"Well, he ain't really missing, now, is he?" Maylor said. "Cap'n gave him till we're ready to shove off." Maylor turned toward Joel. "Anything you can tell me, sir? I'm first mate."

"I really need to speak with the captain. Micah has been hurt, pretty badly." The look on both men's faces registered instant concern.

"He gonna be all right?" the younger one asked.

"Can I please come aboard?"

"Suppose so," said Maylor.

Joel walked up the gangway and was led across the deck through a darkened doorway. He ducked his head and stepped inside. A knock on the door.

"It's me, Captain," Maylor said through the door.

"Mr. Maylor, I told you I want to be left alone. I've got to sort all this out."

"Sorry, sir. There's a man out here, a proper gentleman. Says he's got word about Micah. Got hurt bad somehow."

Silence for a few moments, then footsteps. The door opened, and a large man stood in the doorway. "Want to talk in here or on deck?"

"Wherever you prefer, Captain. I won't take but a minute of your time."

"On deck then. Too hot in here, no breeze today."

The three men walked outside. "Let's talk up here," the captain said. "You come too," he said to Maylor.

They stood near the bow. "You said Micah got hurt?"

"Pretty badly, in fact."

"What happened?"

Joel began to tell them about Maul's attack. The more he spoke, the greater their rage. Halfway through, he had to stop and reassure them how the story ended. Both men were ready to leave that moment and go after Maul.

"So where's Micah now?" Captain Meade asked.

"In my parents' home. But the thing is, the doctor said he can't be moved, his wounds are too severe."

"Where's he hurt?"

"Right here." Joel drew a line across his shoulder. "The doctor stitched him up last night and said he will eventually heal. But I'm told you're planning to leave this afternoon."

"Can't now," Meade said. "I need to leave as soon as we can, but . . ." He looked toward the steamship office building. "Those men in there. God'll judge them, I know that much."

Joel didn't know what he meant.

"After all I've done to rescue these women and children, bring them all the way up here."

"Are you saying they won't reimburse you?" asked Joel. It seemed hard to fathom, but he knew a bit about corporate greed.

"Paid me for the supplies but nothing for all my lost days and nothing to repair my ship. Look at it."

Joel followed his eyes but knew nothing about sailing ships.

"They said they're not responsible for all this damage, the storm is. What kind of attitude is that, after all we did for them?"

Joel thought he understood the steamship company's point of view. The storm damage wasn't their responsibility. They could have taken the high road and offered to help the poor man, but they had just lost a major ship. Not to mention a hull full of gold. Then there certainly would be an investigation, claims to be paid out to the officers' families, and—stop it! What was he thinking? He sounded just like his father.

"Gonna cost me at least a thousand dollars," the captain said, "get her seaworthy again."

"When do you think you'll be ready to leave?" Joel asked.

"Probably take me a day or two to drum up enough business to fill my hold, pay all these expenses. Wanted just to get the money, fix 'er up, and shove off, get down South where we belong."

"Hopefully, Micah will be healed sufficiently to leave then."

"No hope involved, sir. Fact is, I need Micah. I'll give him time off his chores to heal up, but he'll be healing up on this ship. When we're ready to leave, Micah's coming with us."

58

Joel had returned and briefed the family about his visit to the *Cutlass*, except what Captain Meade had said at the end. The news was a relief, at least for now. Immediately, John's mother had said Micah could stay on the sofa, if needed, until the ship set sail. Laura observed the surprised look on Joel's and Allison's faces and concluded an offering like this was completely out of character.

Sally sat on a stool next to Micah, holding her father's hand. She hadn't said much. Laura wondered if she was naturally shy or just overwhelmed at being allowed to mingle with her masters. Then Laura remembered, Eli had said that neither he nor Sally were slaves. They were servants who got paid for their labors.

"So kind a' you, Mrs. Foster," Micah said. "Seem like God knew what was gonna happen to me, keeping the *Cutlass* here couple more days. I'm sure I be ready then."

"Maybe so," said John's mother. "But don't worry about a thing. I told Sally she could look after you. And Sally?"

"Yes'm?"

"In between your chores for the next two days, you can sit

right there. I'm sure you and your father have some catching up to do."

Sally's face lit up like she wanted to shout for joy, but she pulled back and simply said, "Thank you, Mrs. Foster. Thank you."

"Joel, why don't you go and tell Eli that in his spare time he can do the same."

"I will, Mother. Very kind of you. I'm going to leave for about thirty minutes, go home and tell Evelyn all the news. I'll stop by after that, before I head down to the office." He walked over and hugged his mother, then extended his hand to Laura. "It's been a pleasure, Laura. I hope to see more of you in the days to come. I know my wife would love to meet you."

"Thank you," Laura said. "I look forward to it." She actually did. Joel turned and left.

"Come, Laura, come see my roses."

"Can I come?" Allison asked.

"Of course."

Laura followed them both through the house, through the veranda, and across a narrow walk that ran through the backyard, bordered by dwarf mondo grass.

She continued on and stepped inside the greenhouse; except for a few rows of brick, it was made entirely of glass panes. It was a square building, about the size of a large bedroom. The smell, rich and delightful. Laura inhaled deeply. Opposite the doorway she saw a workbench with stacks of small pots of various sizes. Hand tools hung neatly in rows on a wooden wall connected to the bench.

"Would you be a dear, Allison, and straighten up the bench a bit?"

"Yes, Mother."

"They are a little past their peak colors, but aren't they beautiful?"

Laura turned to see three rows overflowing with roses and ferns, a narrow stone walk between each. Red roses of every shape and size occupied the first two rows. But the third was a mix of yellow, pink, white . . . even orange roses. "I've never seen so many roses in one place." She followed John's mother down the first row. She stopped at every plant and spoke affectionately over each, as if they were children. Clearly, the work in this place was not delegated to servants.

At the end of the first row a small opening allowed them to cross over to the next. They walked up the second row toward the front. About halfway there, John's mother changed subjects.

"I hope after a few days," she said, "well, I don't mean to pressure you in any way . . ."

"What is it?" Laura said.

"I was hoping at some point, you and I might talk, when you are up for it . . ."

"You mean about John?"

"Yes. I so want to hear all about his time out West. How you met, how he spent his time, what your life together was like."

"How about if Laura and I tell you all about it together?"

That voice.

Is it possible?

Laura looked to the doorway. John was standing there. He was solid, not a mist or vapor.

Allison screamed.

John's mother, standing in front of Laura, muttered, "John," and fainted on the spot. All three—Allison, Laura, and John—rushed to catch her and set her down gently. Laura and John stood and looked in each other's eyes.

Allison held her mother's head in her lap. John took two steps back. Laura stepped over his mother. Then she leapt into his arms. For a few moments, neither spoke as they released a passion pent up over four days, and a lifetime. Both were crying.

Laura pulled her head back just enough to see his face. She was trembling all over. Through her tears, she said, "I thought you were dead. But you're here. How are you here? I don't understand. I was so afraid. Everyone said you were dead. I was alone again. I even read your letter. I thought—"

John pulled her close again. He began to sob, heavily. A few moments later, his head still buried in her hair, he said, "All I thought of was you. This moment, right here." Then he said, "I thought I'd never see you again."

She stroked his face. He was a mess. Unshaved. Oily hair. His face full of smudges. He didn't smell nice. And he was so thin. But he was the most handsome sight she'd ever seen. She crushed him again in a hug. "You're here. I can't believe you're here." They held each other a full minute, quietly. Laura felt a calm come over her. She instantly knew . . . she didn't have to be strong anymore. Or pretend she could make it on her own.

John was here.

They both turned to see Allison gently patting their mother's cheek. "Mother, are you okay?"

Her eyes fluttered and she came to. She looked up at John hugging Laura. Her eyes widened. Laura was afraid she might faint again.

"He's really here. John's really here," Allison said. She helped her mother up.

She stood there a moment, looking at John's face. Tears streamed down her face. "I welcomed her, John. I didn't turn her away."

"Thank you," John said. Still holding Laura, he opened his left arm wide to make room. His mother put her arm around his waist, and he held her close.

After she stopped crying, she said, "You are so thin. Are you hungry?"

John looked at Laura again and then answered. "I am very hungry."

"Then we'll fix you something to eat." She pulled away and took a step toward the door.

Immediately Allison ran toward John, filling the spot left by her mother. She didn't speak. She just cried, burying her head into his chest.

John rubbed her back gently and stroked her hair. "My baby sister. I've missed you so much."

A few moments later, their mother turned around. "You can cry some more, Allison, in the house. Your brother needs to eat."

She followed her mother through the door, John and Laura, arm in arm, right behind them.

"I don't understand, John. Everyone said you were dead. Even the newspapers."

"I'll tell you all about it back in the house." Halfway across the backyard, he whispered, "There's a colored man sleeping on the living room sofa."

"I know. That's Micah," Laura said. "After you tell us your story, I'll tell you mine." They walked the rest of the way without words, looking at each other every few seconds. Laura couldn't believe it. John was home, safe and well.

Her John.

59

While Sally prepared lunch, John was able to go upstairs and clean up. As he finished dressing in some of his old clothes, there was a knock on the door.

"You look very handsome," Laura said, smiling. She hugged him again. Her eyes were as bright as their wedding day. "We can go shopping later. Get you something . . . not so musty. I've already found some wonderful stores."

"I would love to take you shopping, my dear. Do we have any money?"

She walked over and opened the top drawer of his old dresser. There was the black pouch of gold. She set it on the dresser and opened it. He walked over. "Gold," he said, resting his chin on her shoulder. "We're rich."

She laughed. "They don't take gold here, my love. The clerk at the hotel said, 'This isn't the Wild West, ma'am.'"

"What hotel?"

"When I first got here yesterday, that's where I stayed . . . where I *thought* I'd be staying."

"Why? Did something happen with my family?"

"Don't you remember?" She pulled the note out of the

pouch and unfolded it. "Your family didn't know we were married, because someone decided not to tell them."

She said it playfully, but it still stung. He stood straight and put his hands on her shoulders. "I'm sorry, Laura, so sorry."

She turned and faced him. "It doesn't matter," she said. "You were trying to protect me. I know that. And you need to know, as soon as they found out about me, Joel and Allison came right to my hotel."

"So you stayed here last night?"

"Right over there in that bed."

John smiled and kissed her.

"I loved the note, by the way. And I can read it differently now that you're here." She held it up and read the last part aloud: "I will think of your face, your smile, the love I have cherished in your eyes, our precious conversations. If it must be so, that I am to sink into the deepest waters below, you are and will always remain my only love." She looked up at him. "When we get home, you need to write me more of these."

He smiled and hugged her again. "I remember writing every line. It seems a lifetime ago."

"When I read it yesterday, the wonderful things about it slipped by me. I was just overwhelmed that you were gone. But God brought you back to me." Tears welled up in her eyes. "I'm going to save it forever." She carefully put it back in the pouch.

"So what's next?"

"I was sent up here to get you. Lunch is ready, but I wanted to talk to you about something first." She touched the black pouch. "If we're to go shopping later, we'll have to convert these nuggets to cash."

"That's not a problem, any bank could handle that. I know of several nearby."

"How much do you think is there?"

"I don't know." He looked inside. "I'd say between fifteen hundred and two thousand dollars, depending on the going rate."

Laura smiled. "That's a lot of money."

"Well, we were going on our honeymoon. And I didn't know how much we'd need to spend on hotels and restaurants if . . . things didn't go well here."

"So we don't need most of this for the rest of our trip?"

"I suppose not. Haven't seen my father yet, but I don't see him doing anything that would cut our visit short. It was my mother I was mostly worried about. Her and possibly Joel."

"Joel? He seems so nice. Not like you nice, but . . . nice."

"Joel . . . seems nice?"

"Yes. But we'll have to finish this later. Everyone's waiting for us downstairs."

They walked down the hall toward the stairway, holding hands. "So . . . why the questions about the money back there?" he asked. "Something you're wanting to buy?"

"Something like that," she said. "I'll tell you about it when we're alone after lunch."

When they were halfway down the stairs, the doorbell rang. Beryl came out of nowhere to answer it. Beryl, John thought. What a sweet old friend. He had almost fainted dead away, like his mother had, when John rang that same bell thirty minutes ago. John had to steady him as he walked through the door. Then Beryl did something he hadn't done since John was a child. He hugged him, tightly. Beryl had always been so proper. When he straightened up, he had tears in his eyes.

"Mr. Foster," he'd said. "You have no idea how good it is to see you."

"And you," John had said.

As they reached the base of the stairs, John's brother Joel

walked through the foyer. When he saw John, he froze. An astonished look on his face. "John?"

"It's me."

"But how . . ."

John walked toward him, holding out his hand. It was the least he could do, though they had never gotten along.

Joel took his hand and pulled him into an embrace. "I thought you were lost to us, brother."

John couldn't believe it. Joel had tears in his eyes. He returned the hug and found himself suddenly overcome with emotion. Was it possible that they might, at long last, be brothers? "I *was* almost lost."

Joel pulled back, resting one hand on John's shoulder. With the other, he pulled out a handkerchief and wiped his eyes.

Allison walked in from the dining room. "Isn't it wonderful, Joel? Can you believe it?"

"It is. Were you rescued with the others in Norfolk?" Joel asked.

John nodded.

"Norfolk?" Laura asked.

"I'll tell you about it over lunch. Can you join us, Joel?"

"I can." He walked over to the sofa. Micah had just now awakened. "Have you met Mr. Micah?"

"I haven't."

"Micah, this is John, Laura's husband."

Micah's eyes opened very wide. "Missuh Foster . . . you alive?"

"I guess I am."

"John, Micah was injured last night," said Joel. "Some fellow from the ship came after Laura with a knife, and Micah stopped him."

"What?" John looked at Laura.

"I'm okay."

"Who attacked you?"

"He's in jail," Laura said. "Let's go eat. We can talk in there." She pointed toward the dining room then looked at Micah. "Have an appetite yet?"

"Startin' to."

Laura walked over to Micah. "Sally made a plate for you, and she'll bring it in whenever you're ready."

Micah smiled.

John walked over to the sofa and knelt down. "Mr. Micah, I hope to spend more time making your acquaintance. But for now . . . how can I ever thank you? Laura is my life."

"Happy to help, suh. Your wife the finest lady I ever meet. Treat me and Crabby better than anyone ever has."

They shook hands and John stood up.

"We'll see you in a bit," said Laura.

John walked with Laura a few steps toward the dining room, then whispered, "Crabby?"

60

It was midafternoon. They had talked around the table nonstop for almost two hours. Everyone had been amazed to hear John's rescue story, especially the part about the bird. At that point, John had looked at Laura and said, "I will only ever accept one explanation for that . . . God wanted us together." John had been just as astounded to learn of Micah and Eli's reunion on the street last night, equally remarkable. And so grateful for both men's quick action when Ayden Maul had sprung his attack.

At the moment, Eli was driving John and Laura through the streets of New York back toward the *Cutlass*. They told the rest of the family they were shopping for clothes. Later, they might actually do that. They had made just one stop along the way, to a bank, to convert the gold nuggets into cash. It had come to just over eighteen hundred dollars.

The carriage made a left turn, pulled over, and came to a stop. "We're here, Mr. Foster."

John opened the door and stepped out, then turned to reach for Laura's hand. Eli stood next to him, confused. "I'm supposed to open the door for you, sir."

"Thanks, Eli, for wanting to. But I can do that." John reached into his pocket and pulled out a few dollars in coins.

He handed them to Eli. "Is there any place you can go for a drink? We should only be about ten or fifteen minutes."

"To be honest, sir, I have no idea. I'd have to find a place that took coloreds. Think that might take too much time. You go, take care of what you need to. I'll be right here."

"Thanks."

John and Laura walked together, around the side of the office building toward the dock. "John, thank you so much for doing this."

"It's the least I could do, after what Micah did."

"But I want you to know, it's more than what he did last night when Maul attacked me. It's for everything he did for me on the ship too. He saved me from a very dark despair. He kept me from giving up hope. Next to you, I think Micah is the most remarkable man I have ever met."

"Then it makes what we're about to do all the more satisfying," John said. They walked along the side of the ship toward the gangway.

"Mrs. Foster."

She looked up. "It's Mr. Maylor, the captain's first mate. Mr. Maylor, is the captain on board?"

"He is, ma'am. But he ain't too happy right about now."

"Can we come aboard?" John said. "Maybe we can change that."

"Sure, anything for Mrs. Foster."

When they came aboard, John panned the deck slowly. This is where Laura had lived while he was on the raft.

"Mr. Maylor, meet John Foster, my husband."

"Your husband? No foolin'?" He reached out his hand. "I thought you were dead."

"I'm hearing that a lot today."

"Another ship rescued him and fifty-two other men," Laura said.

"That's wonderful, Mrs. Foster. Real happy for you." He led them toward the captain's cabin. He knocked on the oak door. "Cap'n? Mrs. Foster here to see you, with her husband."

"Her husband?" John heard through the door. "Well, I'll be."

The door swung open. "Glad to hear somebody's getting some good news." He held out his hand. "C'mon in, folks, have a seat. I was just reading about the Norfolk survivors. So happy one of them was yours, ma'am."

They shook hands. "Sorry to hear about what that Maul fellow did, Mrs. Foster. I knew he was no good."

"Well, he's where he belongs now."

"Captain Meade," said John, "I believe you met my brother Joel yesterday."

"I suppose I did, came and told me what happened and what Micah did." He laughed. "That Micah, he's full of surprises."

"Yes," said John. Get ready for another, he thought. "Joel said you felt the steamship company failed to reimburse you properly."

"They did. It's going to cost me a thousand dollars to make repairs. So far I haven't had any luck closing any deals. I really need to get out of here and get back to my customers down South."

"I'd like to make that possible. In fact, I *can* make it possible."

"What do you mean? How?"

John thought a demonstration was in order. He pulled his bankroll of cash from his inner coat pocket. He'd already separated out the amount he had in mind. He laid the cash on the table between them. The captain's eyes widened. "Here's a thousand dollars. It's yours. Laura and I would like to take Micah off your hands."

"You want to *buy* Micah? My slave?"

"I've done some checking. It's a fair amount, considering his age. Especially now with his injuries."

"It's more than fair," Meade said. "But I thought you didn't believe in slavery, Mrs. Foster."

"We don't," she said.

"Oh, I see. You're going to set him free. I'm not so sure that's a good idea. Micah's never been free. I don't think he'll know what to do with himself."

"We'll worry about that," she said.

"Do we have a deal?"

"I don't even need to think about it, sir." He held out his hand. They shook and he stood up. "Let me get the paperwork out of my box. We'll take care of that, and you got yourself a slave."

"No, we've got ourselves a friend," John said.

"Up to you."

After the transaction was complete, they shook hands again and walked out on deck.

"One more thing, Captain Meade," Laura said. "I don't see Crabby."

"She's down in the crew quarters. After Micah left yesterday, she just laid there where she last saw him, all day and night. Wouldn't eat, wouldn't drink. Had to bring her down there when she started howling."

"Can we have her?"

"What?"

"I know you care about her."

"She's just a dumb dog."

"Then can we have her? It would break Micah's heart to lose her."

John watched as Meade struggled to pretend he didn't care. "All right, she clearly wants to be with him."

"Thank you, Captain," Laura said and gave him a hug. "And thank you again for saving our lives."

"Happy to do that, ma'am. You take care now. Maylor, go get Crabby. These folks are going to take her."

"Really? 'Bout time."

He went down into the hold, then came back with Crabby. As soon as she saw Laura, she started barking and straining at the rope. "Hi, Crabby, it's me, girl." She broke free and ran to Laura, jumping and barking and licking her all over. "Let's go home, girl. Go see Micah."

The dog recognized his name and began wagging her tail even harder. They walked her toward the carriage. Eli looked surprised to see them, especially the dog. "This is Crabby," Laura said. "Your father's dog."

"My father's dog? What's she doing here?" Eli said.

"She's ours now, and so is your father," John said.

"I don't understand."

"We bought Micah's freedom from Captain Meade. And the captain gave us his dog."

"Your father loves this dog," said Laura.

"You freed my dad?" Eli said. "He's really free? He can stay with us in New York?"

"I don't see why not. We'll have to talk things over with John's parents, but he's not going back on that ship."

"I don't know what to say." His eyes filled with tears.

"Would you mind, John, if we headed back to the house?"

"Not at all. We can shop later."

As they opened the carriage door to get in, Laura stopped. "John, Crabby's so dirty. What will your mother say if she gets fleas in the carriage, or paw prints."

"Hop in, Laura." John was smiling.

She did, and Crabby jumped right in behind her.

"After what I've seen today, I think this family can actually handle a few fleas and paw prints." Eli closed the door, and the carriage got underway.

Laura snuggled up close to John. Crabby instantly jumped up on the seat across from them and stuck her head out the window. Laura reached over and patted her on the shoulder. John realized something then: the San Francisco Fosters were very likely going to have their own dog someday.

Laura said, "I can't wait to get home and surprise Micah with the news."

61

Four Weeks Later

Tomorrow they would begin the long trip home to San Francisco. Laura had already finished packing the trunks. Both dreaded the thought of taking a long sea voyage . . . anywhere. Joel had done some research for them and learned these terrible hurricane storms rarely made an appearance in late October. Still, Laura would only agree to the trip after John had promised they'd take a train as far south as Savannah.

John did have a store to run back home. They had written Laura's brother the day after John had come home, knowing letters often took weeks to reach the West Coast. They realized he'd have heard about the ship sinking, and they wanted him to know they were both safe and well. A week later, when their plans were more settled, John had written again, asking him to please mind the store for another month. They hadn't heard back from him yet, but both assumed he would be sympathetic.

John and Laura had spent the first week with his family, becoming reacquainted. John's father was the only one who seemed a little put off by everything. But he warmed up to them after a few days. His mood improved dramatically when he'd learned that the firm's losses weren't nearly as bad as he had imagined that first day. The *Vandervere*'s sinking did send a temporary panic through Wall Street. Some had feared it would even set off a depression. Now the papers predicted a mild recession, and the Foster Insurance Firm was predicting it could still end the year in the black.

John and Laura spent the next two weeks making short trips together, mostly by train. They'd visited Washington DC and were able to tour the White House and the Smithsonian Museum and see the new dome being constructed on the Capitol Building. From there they went to Baltimore. Laura had wanted to see Fort McHenry, the place that inspired Francis Scott Key to write "The Star-Spangled Banner." There they ate the most fabulous crab dishes either had ever tasted. Laura could just imagine Crabby running down the deck with one in her mouth.

Next they had traveled to Philadelphia to see Independence Square and the Liberty Bell. And finally, at the end of last week, they'd visited Boston, to meet Robert and his family. Robert took them on a tour of all the historical sites around Boston. It was a marvelous reunion, and both men had said things that convinced Laura they would likely remain friends for life.

John and Laura had spent the last few days reconnecting with his family in New York.

But of course, the biggest and most satisfying experience for Laura—a moment she would never forget—happened in those first few days after they purchased Micah from Captain Meade. It was the day they'd handed Micah the documents that certified he was a free man. Micah had cried tears of joy and shouted, "Praise the Lord!" and "Glory be to his name!" The whole family was present in the living room, except John's father, but including Eli and Sally. Everyone clapped and hugged him.

The biggest shock to all present was that John's mother allowed Crabby to come in the house. "Just for a little while," she'd said. "Then she goes right back out."

They retreated to the dining room, where Sally had prepared a very fine sheet cake, chocolate with white icing. She'd said, "I made this black and white, to celebrate what you white folks done for us." She had said this through tears of joy, and there wasn't a dry eye in the room when she began cutting that cake.

Micah had gotten the first and biggest piece. "I never ate cake before," he had said. His eyes lit up like a child's with the very first bite.

At one point, Laura saw something bordering on hilarious. She had observed the refined and proper Mrs. Foster sneak a small piece of cake under the table. Crabby had eaten it up in two bites.

Presently, John and Laura were walking on the sidewalk under a row of shady trees down Lexington Avenue. They had just said a tearful farewell to Micah. It was hard for Laura to let him go.

They walked the first five minutes in silence. Finally John said, "Are you going to be all right?"

"I will be," she said. "I've only known him such a short while, but he's almost become like a grandfather to me. But I do feel so much better leaving, seeing how happy he is and how well he's doing. Did you see how excited he was showing us his living quarters? 'Best place I ever had,' he said."

"Seems to get along well with the Harrisons," John said.

The Harrisons were another well-to-do family in Gramercy Park, just two blocks from his parents' home. They had hired Micah to care for all their horses.

"Micah gets along well with everyone." She thought a moment and remembered why. "We were having this conversation shortly after I came aboard the ship. I don't remember what I said, but I remember what he said. He was quoting the verse where Jesus says, 'If the Son maketh you free, you shall be free indeed.' Then he told me something he'd learned from it. He said, 'No man is free when his heart isn't free. They may be free the way man sees it, but not the way Jesus sees it. Because they aren't free in here.' Then he pointed at his heart."

"That's . . . that's quite profound," John said.

"Isn't it?"

Micah, she thought, now you really are free indeed. Not just the way God sees it, but even in the eyes of man.

A Note from the Author

The Deepest Waters is most definitely a work of fiction. But historical fiction tales are often based on things that actually happened. Sometimes you'll see the phrase "Based on a True Story" on a book cover. That means *most* of what you'll read actually happened, though some details have been changed (for any number of reasons).

Then there's the phrase "*Inspired* by a True Story," which better describes this book. It means a true story inspired the work of fiction, but the book likely contains more fiction than fact. Just how much, I guess, is up to the author.

While all my characters are fictitious, as are most of the plot points, many things in *The Deepest Waters* really did happen. In fact, some of the most amazing aspects of the story are true. I had been watching a documentary about the SS *Central America*, a paddle-wheel steamship that sank in the waters off North Carolina in September of 1857. I couldn't believe some of the things I saw. It captivated my attention. I was *inspired*. I soon ordered a number of books about the shipwreck to find out more, and then I began to write this novel.

I won't take time to mention all the true things in my story, but here are some I found the most fascinating:

A steamship filled with tons of gold really did sail straight into a hurricane, spring a serious leak, and sink (before it did, the men aboard tried to bail her out in a bucket brigade).

A newlywed couple really did board that steamship for a honeymoon cruise back East, and the wife really brought all her wedding gifts along.

The steamship passengers had given up all hope of rescue when an old sailing ship appeared on the horizon. But it wasn't big enough to rescue everyone, and over four hundred men were left behind. The newlywed couple was separated then, and the wife sailed away, firmly convinced her new husband had perished.

When the steamship sank, most of the men aboard drowned; many right away, others as they grew weary, floating in the ocean clinging to debris.

The rescue ship, carrying all the women and children, really did run out of food but was saved by another ship that appeared. The captain of the second ship was a Christian and gave the rescue ship all the food and water they needed to finish their journey. He wouldn't take a dime in repayment.

Perhaps this is the most amazing of all . . . a large bird really flew out of nowhere and careened into the head of a captain sailing another ship over one hundred miles out at sea. It caused him to immediately change course. That night, his ship sailed right through the remaining fifty-three survivors from the steamship and rescued them.

The newlywed husband was among those fifty-three survivors, and he really did help save the lives of several men adrift with him at sea.

As you can imagine, a few days later, the newlywed couple enjoyed a most remarkable reunion.

As I studied this amazing story, I was reminded of a passage in the Old Testament:

> Those who go down to the sea in ships, who do business on great waters, they see the works of the LORD, and His wonders in the deep.

Psalm 107:23–24

One of the most enjoyable aspects of writing historical novels for me is the research. I always learn such amazing things. Take the part where Micah's children, Sally and Eli, find each other and work as servants in the same New York mansion. When you consider the fascinating true story of the Underground Railroad, it's not hard to believe something like this could have happened (I'd encourage you to read more about this on the internet). Now, the part where Eli and his father, Micah, meet that one magical night . . . I hope you'll agree, if God can appoint a bird to smack into a sea captain's head and get him to alter his course so that he rides right through the middle of a floating band of shipwreck survivors on a moonless night . . . it's not a stretch to believe he could accomplish anything I imagined as I wrote this book.

One final thing: as much as I loved writing and researching this book, I am grateful that the few sea voyages I've taken with my wife have all been aboard very large ships with marvelous buffets and unlimited servings of soft-serve ice cream and iced tea.

Acknowledgments

This is now my third novel, written with the help of essentially the same team as my first two. I could simply ask these precious friends to reread what I wrote about them in my first novel and say "ditto" for their help with *The Deepest Waters*.

But I won't.

Because they've helped me so much more with this book, and my appreciation for them and their help has grown so much more since then. Starting with my wife, Cindi. Many authors take the time to thank their spouses for their love and support and their willingness to sacrifice the needed time apart, so that the novel could be completed. I understand those sentiments and do thank Cindi for them as well. She is the love of my life and my greatest friend. But I must add my thanks for how much better this book is because of her input and suggestions. It's almost as if I have the help of two gifted editors, not one.

Speaking of gifted editors . . . my thanks to Andrea Doering, my editor at Revell. You helped me with my first two books. You *really* helped me with *The Deepest Waters*. My readers now have, by far, a much better story than the one I originally sent you, because of your input and advice.

And thanks to Michele Misiak, Claudia Marsh, Donna Hausler, and the whole marketing/publicity team at Revell. What a joy it is to work with you behind the scenes. Thanks for all you do to get my books on the shelves and into readers' hands. I want to thank Kristin Kornoelje for helping keep me on track and for all the wonderful little things you catch that nobody else sees.

A special thanks to Twila Bennett, Cheryl Van Andel, and the team responsible for the cover of this book. I loved my first two covers, but with this one . . . what can I say? You hit it out of the park! I'd love to hang it as a painting on my wall.

And finally, my thanks to Karen Solem, my literary agent and friend. I am in your debt and able to just relax and write because I'm always in such capable and caring hands. You're simply the best.

Dan Walsh is the award-winning author of *The Unfinished Gift*, *The Homecoming*, and *The Deepest Waters*. A member of American Christian Fiction Writers, Dan served as a pastor for twenty-five years. He lives with his family in the Daytona Beach area, where he's busy researching and writing his next novel.

A YOUNG BOY'S PRAYERS, a shoebox full of love letters, and an old wooden soldier make a memory that will not be forgotten. Can a gift from the past mend a broken heart?